SAY I DO

SOUTHERN HEARTS: BOOK 2

JANICE MAYNARD

1

Even minus the requisite white wedding dress, the woman fleeing down the front steps of a large, imposing church in downtown Orlando had a definite *runaway bride* vibe thing going on. Morgan Webber was minding his own business as he strolled along the sidewalk when she literally slammed into his shoulder, threatening to send them both crashing to the pavement.

Only his bulk and her quick footwork saved them. She tossed out a muttered apology, evaded his grasp, and darted out into the street. He watched aghast, wincing at the cacophony of blaring horns and screeching brakes, as she danced between the vehicles.

When she made it safely to the opposite curb, he actually glanced over his shoulder expecting to see a distraught groom in hot pursuit. But at the top of the steps, the sturdy oak doors, both decorated with large white ribbons, remained firmly closed.

Two things kept him from going on about his business. The first was simple curiosity. He sensed a drama in the making. But the second reason was even more compelling.

The brief physical encounter smacked him square in the chest with a powerful sexual attraction.

His mystery lady was tall and slender and had masses of wavy brown hair that bounced and tumbled on her shoulders. Even when she wasn't in a dead run, he suspected that her extravagant hair would seem alive with the current of energy she exuded.

While he watched, bemused, she unlocked a fuchsia Kia, rummaged in the glove compartment, and backed out of the car to do a reverse dash, once again ignoring the irate motorists who tried to keep from killing her.

As she retraced her route, he jogged up the church steps close on her heels, compelled by an urgency that was probably only a reflection of hers. But he ran anyway, unwilling to miss the next act in this unfolding mystery.

By the time he stepped into the cool, dimly lit church, his fleet-footed, graceful gazelle was kneeling beside a tiny, gray-headed, supine female, opening the woman's mouth and tucking a small pill beneath her tongue. A minister and a rail-thin, octogenarian groom hovered helplessly nearby along with a bald, middle-aged fellow who was apparently the best man.

Morgan held his breath unconsciously until the old lady's eyes fluttered and opened. She looked up at her rescuer. "Stupid angina. Damn it, Hannah, my girl. What took you so long?"

In the flurry of nervous laughter that followed, Morgan allowed himself a closer inspection of the female who seemed to be in entire control of the situation.

Hannah grinned down at the small, elderly bride. "Sorry, Miss Beverly. Next time let's leave those pills in your pocket."

Beverly snorted as she allowed herself to be lifted to her

feet. "No next time about it. This is my last trip down the aisle."

Morgan lingered in the back of the church while the abruptly aborted wedding service continued. Shafts of sunlight filtered through massive stained-glass windows, painting Hannah with a rainbow of soft colors. Her generous lips curved in a smile as she watched the older couple repeat their vows.

If she knew Morgan watched her, she made no sign. But surely she must have sensed his intense absorption. He felt almost dizzy from the force of his heart pounding in his chest. He told himself it was the leftover adrenaline from thinking she would be hit by a car at any second.

But the truth was, he'd been the one to be metaphorically knocked on his ass. And he was in imminent danger of appearing to be a stalker and a wedding crasher at that. So he slipped into a pew at the rear of the sanctuary and sat quietly until the ceremony reached its conclusion.

There was no recessional, merely lots of hugs and congratulations and then finally a deep, resonant silence when the bride and groom, minister, and best man disappeared through a hallway at the side of the chancel area.

Now, only his Julia Roberts look-alike remained. She turned as if on cue and their eyes met. She was smiling, but it was a mocking smile. Whether she directed it at herself or at him, he couldn't tell. He rose to his feet and walked toward her. After a split second, she moved as well.

They met in the middle of the church. She cocked her head, her sultry lips and wide-lashed eyes, brown he saw now, making him sweat beneath his dress shirt. He'd had a meeting with the suits at the bank earlier, hence his unusual attire in the middle of a workday. He much preferred the shorts and boots he wore on the job.

Though he topped six feet by a couple of inches, the woman was tall, and their lips were in touching distance. That odd thought shook him even more. He swallowed against a dry throat.

Her ivory slip dress clung to her fit body and begged for a man's touch. Finally she took pity on his mute state. "Do I know you?"

Her husky alto took what was left of the starch in his knees. He shook his head, trying to clear it. "No, But seeing a woman nearly run over... twice... tends to grab a man's attention."

She lifted a hand to his chin. Her long, slim fingers brushed his jaw in a brief caress that made note of the slight stubble she found. He'd been up at five a.m. to shave and dress, and it was now mid-afternoon.

When her hand fell away slowly, he forced himself not to grab for it. She lifted one perfectly shaped eyebrow. "Your name?"

He forced the words past the lump in his throat. "Morgan Webber."

She observed him like an exhibit in a museum, as if by analyzing his form she could come to some conclusions about his identity or his motives or even his moral character. Then her eyes lit with a combination of mischief and outrageous bravado. "Can I do anything for you?" she drawled, the words dripping with sexual overtones.

He studied her mouth with rapt fascination. "You could marry me," he said, only half joking.

She lifted an eyebrow. "I'm afraid I don't think much of that venerable institution."

He frowned. "And yet here you are."

She shrugged, the epitome of haughty sophistication. "I

don't impose my views on others." Then her smile returned. "I'm assuming you have no desire to kiss the real bride, so perhaps I'll do as a substitute." She wrapped her slim arms around his neck, found his mouth with hers, and proceeded, like some ancient sorceress, to steal his heart away.

He sucked in a startled breath and managed to get with the program in a split second. She tasted like whipped cream and coffee, and her body in his arms was all curves, slippery silk, and sensuous woman.

Though his boner was perhaps a foregone conclusion, he would have liked to disguise its importunate presence. But his stunning playmate was having none of that. She nudged her hips against his, making both of them tremble. Her tongue fluttered on his.

He was breathing fast, too fast. His hands went to her hips, gripping her ass in an effort to get closer. He was pretty sure he was breaking at least nine of the commandments and maybe a few lesser ones he wasn't aware of.

But he couldn't stop kissing her. It was like a dream, a surreal but impossibly sweet image conjured up by the palette of muted, prism-spread hues that cloaked them like an intangible blessing.

He knotted his fist in her hair, testing its thickness, its softness. He'd waited his whole life for a woman like this.

He wondered if she knew how close she came to having him make love to her in front of God and a host of dead saints. But before their incendiary embrace reached its inevitable conclusion, the modest wedding party reappeared.

His mystery woman sighed and pulled back, her attention already lured away from him. She touched his face one more time, gently, as though fascinated by the feel of his skin. "You're a great kisser, Morgan Webber," she whispered.

And then his lovely, unexpected gift of a woman abandoned him without a backward glance.

He started after her, stopped, and glanced down at his watch with a curse. He had a very important meeting in exactly forty-five minutes. One he couldn't miss.

Damn it. He took one more step, then halted with a groan. He had people depending on him. This incident was far from over. But the conclusion would have to wait. Even if he didn't know her name.

∽

It took him six months to translate that breathtaking moment into an honest to God, real proposal.

"Hey, boss. Julio says that load of block is screwed. Some accident out on the interstate. We're going to have to wait until tomorrow."

Morgan cursed beneath his breath and jerked his mind back to the present. He wiped his face with the back of his arm and squinted into the blinding sun. Orlando in August was a bitch. Even though he'd lived here his entire life with the exception of the six years he'd spent at Georgia Tech, getting his undergrad and then earning a master's degree in civil engineering, he was as miserable as the next guy when the mercury topped ninety-five and the humidity was a numerical match.

He tried to concentrate on the expanse of rough, graded soil and filler that expanded in neat sections as far as the eye could see. The undertaking he faced required his utmost attention, and he'd do well to remember it.

He might be the project manager, but the big bosses

were always breathing down his neck, and he'd never yet failed to bring a job in under budget and on time.

They were in the midst of reclaiming acres of spongy land south of the airport in preparation for the construction of a massive theme park that would provide competition for Disney and Universal. *Time Travelers* would eventually boast opportunities for visitors to experience medieval jousts, piratical adventures on the high seas, dragon slaying contests, caveman battles, and a host of other improbable but entertaining activities.

Morgan was thankful that his work would be finished long before the first gangly teenage fans appeared on site, because his responsibilities were far more practical than whimsical. His task was to make sure that the acres of pavement to come were well drained. So he had to build an underground detention system, among other things, to catch, control, and regulate runoff from heavy rainfall.

They'd had to wait almost a year for the state to approve the Storm Water Pollution Prevention Plan, and now all systems were go. His geotech guys had designed the foundations and were now preparing to inspect the footings. So far, everything was falling into place. It gave him a deep sense of satisfaction to wrestle an unappealing swath of land into a usable, even attractive, piece of property.

The unique Florida soil presented some problems that other parts of the country rarely had to deal with, but it helped that he was a native and knew what he was facing. He'd never yet met a project he couldn't tackle with success.

Which wasn't to say that his personal life was as easy or as smooth. After that first day in the church, he'd had a hell of a time locating the elusive Hannah. Fortunately the minister was amenable to swapping some non-sensitive info for Morgan's sizeable donation. Hannah worked as a personal shopper for the residents of a trio of retirement communities, and as it turned out, she had a neat condo not far from Morgan's apartment.

The spark he'd experienced during their initial, emotionally fraught wedding encounter was still there when he showed up on her doorstep a couple of weeks later and asked her out. They flirted, they dated, they kissed... they ended up in bed. Repeatedly. And the sex was phenomenal, even from the beginning.

But Hannah was not easily won over, at least not when it came to things like commitment and permanence.

When Morgan first hinted at marriage, she dragged him to six weeks of counseling with a priest who had to be pushing a hundred. The old guy kept nodding off in the midst of their sessions. And although Morgan was fairly certain that Hannah was a nominal Catholic at best, she gave every semblance of being an earnest, well-intentioned bride-to-be. Which she wasn't. At least not then. Because she refused to actually talk about marriage in any but the most ephemeral of contexts.

It was understandable in a way. Her parents had married only long enough to make Hannah's birth legitimate. Hannah's mom was a new-age version of a hippie love child, and from what Morgan had gleaned, flitted happily from one partner to the next. She didn't believe in marriage, but at least she had spared a thought for her daughter's situation and had tried to make things somewhat conventional.

Hannah's father had never been in the picture after that, though he was apparently still alive and kicking somewhere not far away. Pulling personal information from the reticent Hannah was as difficult as finding an unbroken seashell on the crowded beaches. Despite her outgoing personality and the flashing smile that lit up a room, she had a deep vein of reserve that she wore like a protective cloak.

Morgan was no stranger to challenges. He'd been confident in his ability to win her trust. Finally, as of last night, Hannah Quarles wore his engagement ring, a large, square-cut diamond that seemed to weigh down her slender finger.

He should be feeling on top of the world. He should be crowing about snagging a woman who was everything he had ever wanted and more. He should be happy. Ecstatic. Justifiably proud.

Even for a man unaccustomed to spending much time on self-reflection, he was damn sure that something as simple as happiness was not even in the ballpark of what he was feeling at the moment.

The fact that he was having trouble concentrating at work was a red flag. His guts were twisted in a knot, and he felt like a jittery adolescent. He might have put a ring on Hannah's finger, but he'd be a fool if he thought the race was won. In a sick little corner of his psyche, a place he almost refused to acknowledge even existed, he was afraid that she had accepted his proposal because she was too softhearted to say no.

And that made him feel like shit. If it was simply her aversion to the whole marriage thing, he could be patient. But it made him flinch inwardly to think that he might be head over heels in love with a woman whose emotions were not nearly as involved.

With one last oath that expressed a wide range of frustrations both professional and personal, he jerked his cell phone out of his pocket and proceeded to raise hell with the cinder block supplier. He needed to strip a layer off of somebody, and that poor sap had just been nominated.

Hannah held her hand up to the light and admired the way the brilliant stone, nestled in a platinum band, sparkled and danced. It was the most beautiful piece of jewelry she had ever seen, much less owned. Unfortunately, she knew she had accepted it under false pretenses. She wasn't ready to get married.

But Morgan's dear face had been so boyishly jubilant when he popped open that damn velvet box, she hadn't been able to do more than smile weakly and allow him to slide the costly bauble onto the appropriate finger of her left hand.

She studied the ring carefully and curled her fingers into a fist. Now that it was on her hand, it was hard to think about giving it up. Surely it couldn't hurt to wear it for a bit. She might not be as naive or as idealistic as some women, but even so, she had dreams.

And Morgan was definitely the man to play the hero. She loved him passionately, though she was always careful to curb her adoration when they were together. He deserved someone far less screwed up than she was, and even though she might indulge herself in the short term... pretending they had a future... she knew the truth.

He was hers only temporarily.

But good Lord, it was hard to say no to that man. He was a steamroller, an affectionate, handsome, rugged steamroller. Everything about him from the dark wavy hair he kept cut short to the breadth of his powerful shoulders and the predatory gleam in his gray eyes, made her knees weak.

And in bed. She swallowed hard and her thighs tightened involuntarily. Just mentally reliving the first time they made love was enough to make her skin damp and to hitch her breath in a jerky gasp of remembrance. He was the most focused man she had ever met.

Whether that meant bullying his crew and the elements into submission or wooing a woman so sweetly she thought she might actually melt from longing, he made things happen. His way. On his terms. The results were so satisfying, she couldn't find it in her heart to protest.

Her phone rang suddenly, and she snatched it up with a guilty look at the clock. She'd been dithering in front of her closet. Now she was about to be late. She spoke briefly to the caller on the other end, hung up, and dressed rapidly

Engagement ring or no engagement ring, life went on.

Thirty minutes later, she pulled into her customary parking place at the grocery store and headed inside armed with seven different shopping lists. Mr. Potter wanted salt substitute and dried apricots. Mrs. Petersen had listed and underscored a bottle of chain-brand cologne. Two others wanted beer and cigarettes.

All of her clients had access to the cafeterias on site where they lived, but even so, they liked knowing they could have the little odds and ends they had enjoyed before their infirmities made them dependent on others. It made Hannah feel good to know that she provided a service.

Several years ago, she had dropped by the various retirement centers on a volunteer basis. At the time she'd been working in a real estate office, later earning her license. But after completing only a handful of deals, she realized that she wasn't cut out for the hard sell. She wanted to spend more time with the feisty, garrulous, oftentimes stubborn men and women who reminded her so vividly of her beloved Grammy and Papaw.

Both of her maternal grandparents were gone now, one to heart disease and the other to cancer. She missed them daily, and it eased the pain to be close to others of their generation. She fell into the habit of helping out by shopping for clothing, gifts, food, or any other items that weren't readily available to those with limited mobility or simply the disinclination to brave the roads.

After a while, several of her elderly friends urged her to make her service a legitimate business. Between them they found her enough tasks to keep her gainfully employed from week to week. The center administrators realized how valuable her assistance was and rounded up some grants to supplement the small percentages her patrons were offering as payment.

After several years, her situation was now permanent, and it made her happy and energized to know she was doing something meaningful with her life. Grammy and Papaw had been her touchstones. In her mother's absence, she had made her home with them, and she had never felt any lack of love and caring. They were her family

Now she had adopted a wider, extended family in their stead. A family whose idiosyncrasies might be frustrating at times, but a family who loved her unconditionally and who would do anything for her, as she would for them.

She pulled her little green Prius to a halt inside the front gate of the Fluffy Palms and got out. Hoisting two bags from the trunk, she made her way down the walk to the eighth apartment on the left, now a most familiar address.

When her knock yielded no results, she used her key and let herself in. "Elda... where are you, darlin'? I've brought you some things to try on."

A short, heavyset woman with improbably orange hair appeared around the corner, her gaze guilty as she rubbed what looked like brownie crumbs from her chin. "You're early," she mumbled, wiping her hands on her ample, polyester-covered hips.

Hannah dropped the bags on the table and rolled her eyes. "You were on the phone badgering me thirty minutes ago... remember?"

Hannah slid past her hostess to peer into the small kitchenette area. The incriminating evidence sat on the counter, a steaming square pan of goodies still warm from the oven.

She frowned slightly. "Elda, you know what the doctor said. Your blood sugar can't take this. It's important, love, that you stay on your diet."

Elda harrumphed and headed for the sofa. Her favorite soap opera played quietly as she gazed at the television screen mutinously. "Might as well be dead if I can't eat," she sulked.

Hannah leaned over the back of the cushion and pressed a kiss to her wrinkled cheek. "Quit pouting. Your handsome suitor may have ideas about that. Come on into the bedroom and try on this stuff. I bought you a dress that will knock his socks off."

Elda snickered, following her down the hall. "What if I want him to stay completely dressed?"

When Elda disappeared into the bathroom, Hannah plopped on the bed. "You know it's okay to fall in love again. Right? It's been a year and a half. You aren't betraying your husband's memory."

Elda poked her head around the corner. "Have you been watching too much *Dr. Phil*?"

Hannah grinned after her. "You were married sixty-four years. It's bound to be difficult to get back in the dating pool."

Elda's voice was muffled. "We're not dating. People our age don't date."

"Do, too." Arnie, for all his smarminess, got part of the credit for bringing Elda out of her grief-laden funk. He'd moved to Fluffy Palms right after Christmas, and his over-the-top gallant attentions to the sturdy old woman had perked her right up.

Elda stepped into the bedroom wearing an emerald-green dress that flattered her coloring and made her look taller and thinner. "It's a good dress," she said grudgingly. "You've got an eye. But where would I wear it?"

"Did you ever hear of *dinner and a movie*?"

Elda studied her reflection in the mirror. "He's probably thinking bingo and sex."

"Elda!" Hannah was shocked in spite of herself. She didn't want to think about her surrogate grandmother having intimate relations with anyone, much less Arnie. Hannah had her doubts about whether or not the amiable Arnie was on the up-and-up, but Elda trusted him, so that was that. Elda outweighed him by at least fifty pounds and could probably keep him in line under the worst of circumstances, so Hannah decided her own worries were probably unfounded.

By the time Hannah left thirty minutes later, Elda was already making plans for a night out on the town.

After that visit, Hannah spent the next three hours dropping off prescriptions, picking up dry cleaning, and showing Mrs. Lederman how to send an e-mail to her granddaughter on her new computer. By the time Hannah's stomach started to growl, she realized with a panicked glance at her watch that Morgan would be at her house in less than two hours, and she had done nothing at all to prepare for their celebratory dinner.

He'd taken her to a swanky restaurant the night before, and she wanted to return the favor by fixing him his favorite meal of fried chicken and mashed potatoes. His culinary tastes were uncomplicated. The genuine appreciation he showed when she cooked for him made her want to do it more. He spoiled her constantly. She enjoyed pampering him when he allowed it.

As she dashed back home and ducked into the shower, she pondered the implications of wearing his ring even in the short-term. It was bound to complicate things, and she had a feeling that with his symbol of claiming on her hand, he might renew his arguments about living together.

He cited things like saving money and spending more time together, but in his eyes she saw the real truth. She saw the hunger that mirrored hers. He wanted her in bed with him night after night. Their bodies tucked together in the aftermath of slow, sweet lovemaking. And God knows, she wanted it, too. But she didn't dare. Letting him down gently was going to be hard enough as it was. If he were entrenched in her apartment or she in his, it would be far worse.

By the time she slipped into white Capri pants and a skinny pink T-shirt, the chicken breasts were nicely browned, the potatoes were creamy, and the crisp salad waited for a final dusting of Parmesan cheese. When Morgan rang her doorbell at seven on the dot, her pulse actually fluttered. He was a disciplined man. Punctual, tidy, and a caretaker at heart. A woman would be a fool to let him get away.

She opened the door and squeaked when he scooped her into his arms and held her firmly against his hard chest, her toes dangling inches above the floor. He had showered recently, and his skin smelled fresh and masculine from the plain soap he preferred.

He captured her lips and ate at them lazily, taking his time, savoring the appetizer. When he finally set her back on her feet, she was breathless. He tucked a strand of her hair behind her ear. "How's my beautiful fiancée?"

The note of satisfied possessiveness in his deep voice amused her and at the same time filled her with a warm glow of happiness. She pushed her doubts to the background, where they could stay for the moment. She smiled at him, for once not trying to hide what she felt. "Pretty damn good, Mr. Webber. Pretty damn good."

2

Morgan blinked, almost taken aback by what he saw in her eyes. He was so accustomed to the way she guarded her emotions, it was a shock to witness her open affection and happiness. He sensed that for once he had gained the upper hand. Hannah's cheeks were flushed, and her big brown eyes were dreamy and drowsy with passion. She wasn't wearing a bra beneath that little nothing of a T-shirt. Her nipples thrust against the soft fabric, giving him a clear indication of her state of mind.

He picked up her left hand and kissed her knuckle just below the ring. "I love seeing this on your finger," he said quietly. Perhaps he shouldn't make himself so vulnerable, but he couldn't help it. His heart was bursting with pride and an entirely un-PC sense of masculine victory.

Her fingers curled around his and her lashes dropped, shielding her expression. She didn't answer his statement, though perhaps it didn't require one. He wanted to ask if she had showed off her new piece of jewelry today, but he stopped just shy of letting the words leave his mouth. He wasn't sure he wanted to know the answer.

Instead, he followed her inside and closed the door, sniffing appreciatively. "Smells wonderful, Hannah. I'm starving."

While he poured the wine he'd brought over, he watched her unobtrusively. She chattered as usual as she served their plates and set them on the table. Her movements were quick and graceful. He never tired of watching her. She was a sensual woman, though he guessed she'd never describe herself that way.

Her apartment was a comfortable amalgam of style and sentimentality Her cognac leather sofa was modern, but she'd graced it with a handmade afghan. Her dishes were vaguely European in design, white stylistic squares, but the glasses she liked to use were a set of Care Bear tumblers she'd found at an antique fair... similar to the ones she said her Grammy used to have when Hannah was a child.

He loved her contradictions and her unique approach to life. His apartment was nothing more than a bachelor's set of rooms with a big-screen TV and a king-size bed. It was a location to store his junk and to sleep. But Hannah's place was a home.

Every time he walked through the door, he felt the impact of her personality and her simple enjoyment of life. He'd give up his lease in a heartbeat if she would let him move in, but that was an argument he'd not yet won.

He'd told himself he would cultivate patience, but over dessert, he blurted out the thought that had been on his mind all day "So when do we set a date?"

Her hands stilled. She'd been cutting a bite of store-bought cheesecake, and now she put down her fork and fiddled with her napkin. "Plenty of time for that," she said lightly, not meeting his gaze.

The delicious meal he'd recently consumed suddenly felt like lead in his stomach. He inhaled sharply and told himself the pain in his chest was indigestion. "Churches and reception halls have to be booked months in advance," he said quietly, keeping his voice even with effort.

She reached for his hand, and it pained him to see that her teeth mutilated her lower lip. "Let's enjoy the moment," she pleaded. "I've never been engaged before. And besides, you know you're swamped at work... literally." She giggled at her own joke. "There's no way we could go on a honeymoon until that job is done... right?"

He knew he was sulking and couldn't seem to help it. "Fine," he muttered. "But I still want you to meet my parents. Soon. And I'd like to meet yours."

She grimaced. "Trust me, you don't. My mom will drive you nuts in no time, and my dad is not in the picture. So I'd just as soon forget a cozy reunion, if you don't mind."

He played with the ring he'd put on her finger. "I'm seeing the bigger picture. They were responsible for bringing you into this world, Hannah, my love. So they'll always have my undying respect."

She grinned at him, looking happier now that they'd dodged the date subject. "You say the sweetest things. And it makes me want to jump your bones."

He leaned back in his chair, refusing to be daunted by possible problems. "I like the sound of that." Then he sobered. "Hannah, I..."

She cocked her head. "What? You what?"

He sighed. "Not all marriages are bad." He said it bluntly, no longer willing to dance around the issue.

She flushed and the defensive flash of stubbornness that crossed her face made him groan inwardly. She lifted her chin. "I haven't seen much proof that marriage works in this day and age."

He ground his teeth together, refusing to lose his cool. "My parents have been married thirty-eight wonderful years. All it takes is hard work and commitment, both of which you and I are willing to do... right?"

She gathered up their plates and stalked to the sink. "Maybe in the olden days that was the formula," she said. "But it's a lot harder now. Monogamy isn't admired. Faithfulness is sneered at. Marriage itself is seen as a joke by many people. You can't deny it."

He followed her, staying out of the way as she rinsed dishes and shoved them in the dishwasher with jerky motions. "You're talking about the world at large, Hannah. I'm talking about us. We're different."

She whirled to face him, her expression belligerent. "What makes you think so?"

His jaw gaped. She'd cut the ground right out from under him. His neck muscles were so tight, he already felt the beginnings of a tension headache, and this fledgling engagement was barely twenty-four hours old.

He scooped her into his arms, ignoring the clatter of dropped silverware. "This makes me think so," he growled. He decided he couldn't make it as far as the bedroom. He tumbled them both to the sofa just around the corner and ripped up the hem of her T-shirt. He brushed her nipples with his fingertips. Then he caught the nearest one between his teeth and bit gently.

Hannah went wild in his arms. Her hands jerked at his belt buckle. He stripped her pants to her ankles. Both of them were clumsy and uncoordinated, but they got the job done. He positioned his aching erection between her legs and pushed hard. Every time he entered her tight body, he marveled that anything could feel so damned incredible.

She panted and cried out his name. He could feel the butterfly squeezes on his prick that signaled her imminent climax. He slid out slowly and teased her with a long, lazy stroke. When she called him a bad name, he bared his teeth in a tight grin. "Is there a problem?" He could hear the hoarseness in his own voice.

She wrapped her legs around his waist in a vice, threatening his backbone. "Please, Morgan. Don't make me beg."

He pumped once more and stopped. "I like begging. Especially from you."

She opened one eyelid and glared at him. "You're a sadistic, egotistical—" She gasped when he shoved deeper. Her brown irises were dark as molten chocolate.

He bent his head and found her mouth. "I love you, Hannah."

~

The sudden switch from eroticism to tenderness caught her off guard and plunged her over the edge. As she shuddered and gasped, she held him tightly, tears stinging her eyes. Her body shivered with pleasure.

Somehow he always managed to undermine her habitual defenses, and no matter how carefully she tried to guard her heart and her emotions, he refused to be shut out. In the beginning his utter focus on worming his way into her life had sometimes scared her. Now it provided a security she relied on more and more each day

And if that was weakness on her part, she couldn't find it in her heart to care.

As their ragged breathing slowed, the silence in the room grew louder. Darkness had fallen beyond the partially open drapes. The room was dim save for the light spilling in from the kitchen.

She ran her fingers through the damp hair at the nape of his neck. It was a strong neck, strong like the rest of him. But even so, her touch made him groan and nuzzle into her embrace. He'd kept most of his weight balanced on one arm so he wouldn't crush her, but his hips pressed her into the sofa. She had never once been afraid of his size or his physical power. Morgan was the kind of man who cherished those weaker than he was. But she feared his ability to make her want things that were not real. Things that could lead only to disappointment and hurt.

She felt she owed him something significant in exchange for the beautiful ring... something to acknowledge the pleasure it gave her to wear it. But what could she do or say that wouldn't send them farther down a path she wasn't prepared to explore?

Her lips trembled as she formed the words. "You could leave a toothbrush here, if you want," she mumbled, feeling self-conscious. She felt the sudden stillness that invaded his body. They were plastered so closely together she couldn't miss it.

The muscles in his throat worked. "You're sure?"

She nodded.

"And maybe a change of clothes?"

A bubble of laughter escaped her. "It's never enough with you, is it, Webber?"

He disengaged their bodies and rolled suddenly, settling her on top of him with a talented maneuver. She looked down at him, seeing the naughty twinkle in his eyes. His big hands cupped her bare ass. "It will never be enough, my love. Never."

He got up to leave soon after, and she couldn't decide if she was sad or relieved. It was getting harder and harder to put on the brakes. She wanted to throw caution to the wind and give him everything he wanted.

He paused at the door and reached into the paper grocery sack that had held the bottle of wine he'd brought. Slowly he pulled out a thick, plastic-wrapped rectangle and handed it to her.

She stared at it blankly, feeling the weight of his expectations. It was one of those impossibly heavy, glossy-paged bridal magazines. She held it by the edges, aghast that such a subversive piece of literature had found its way into her home.

He kissed her cheek and ruffled her hair, grinning widely. "Give it a chance, Hannah. You might learn something."

∽

The following morning, Hannah looked forward to the consuming pace of her job. She needed her comfortable routines to make up for the completely out-of-control feelings she had experienced the night before. But before she left the house, she couldn't resist examining Morgan's latest gift. A bridal magazine? Good Lord...what was he thinking? She'd sooner read a treatise on Middle Eastern foreign policy. At least the latter would have some redeeming value. The thick volume was nothing more than an overpriced homage to the unrealistic dreams of girls and their mommies.

She ripped away the shrink-wrap and thumbed through

the shiny, fragrant pages. Sleek, stylish wedding dresses stared at her from every angle. And all the women wearing them looked smug and perfect.

Hannah wrinkled her nose. Articles about invitations and the perfect reception merited no more than a glance. But suddenly, she quit flipping and stared at the heading on a page near the center of the magazine. *Explore Your Sexuality As a Couple.*

Despite herself, she started to read. A team of family therapists in California had come up with a novel approach to premarital counseling. Instead of focusing on the traditional topics like finances and communication, this new setup was designed to make sure couples understood their relationship in the bedroom. Role-playing was set up in the doctor's office. Unobserved, but later evaluated. Intense, unscripted, sexual encounters.

Hannah dropped the heavy magazine and ran a hand across the back of her neck. Wow. Imagining Morgan and her doing something like that made her heart race.

She laughed nervously and reminded herself she didn't believe in marriage or some goofy periodical celebrating the official, though not-likely-to-last, union of unsuspecting men and women.

Which didn't explain why she took the tome with her as she left the house. Perhaps she would give it to Elda. Elda and Arnie might be headed for orange blossoms and gold rings. They could put it to good use.

After a busy morning of errands that included all three of the properties where she found her clients, Hannah was hot and sweaty and more than ready to stop off for a late lunch at Elda's. The two women had a standing meal date at least twice a week. Elda was more than a client. She was the only person Hannah considered family... maybe not by blood, but in every way that counted.

Hannah let herself in and found Elda in the kitchen putting together chicken salad sandwiches. A pitcher of iced tea sat on the counter.

Hannah frowned. "You didn't put any sugar in that, did you?"

Elda shook her head in disgust. "Geez, you're as bad as my crabby-assed, dried-up old doctor. No sugar. I swear. Eat your lunch and try not to nag for a change."

Hannah laughed and bit into the soft wheat slice. Elda had a bread maker and liked to keep herself and her friends supplied with homemade loaves of cinnamon and whole wheat and other varieties. Even without her wry sarcasm and big heart, she would have won many friends with her baking.

The two women were halfway through their meal when Elda choked and leaned across the table. "Sweet Jesus. Where in the heck did you get that rock?"

Hannah felt her face turn red. She'd left the ring at home yesterday, but this morning she felt too guilty to take it off. Not when Morgan was so proud of it. She'd kept her hand hidden as much as possible during the course of the day, but relaxing in Elda's homey kitchen made her forget to be secretive.

Or maybe it was a Freudian slip. Maybe she wanted Elda to know. Self-analysis was a tricky business.

She smiled weakly. "Morgan gave it to me night before last."

Elda's eyebrows went to her hairline. "And you didn't tell me yesterday?"

At the unmistakable hint of hurt on her older friend's

face, Hannah hastened to explain. "I was conflicted. I needed some time to think it over. You're the first one who knows—I promise."

Elda took her hand and twisted it from side to side. "Ho-lee-shit. That boy's got damned good taste." She grabbed the phone. "This calls for a celebration."

A half hour later, Hannah stood in a crush of well-wishers, drinking champagne someone had procured from who knows where and fielding a barrage of pointed questions. She answered them patiently. "No, we haven't set a date. I don't know where we'll get married. No, I won't quit my job." The babble of excited voices rose and fell around her.

Every face in the room beamed. She felt like a sham, but she didn't know how else to handle the situation. You'd have thought she was a movie star the way they were carrying on. Finally, as the hands on the clock drew toward five, they all realized it was time to head to dinner, and they exited en masse.

When it was just her and Elda, Hannah sighed. "What a fuss. They're all so sweet."

Elda nudged her aside, heading for the kitchenette with a handful of wilting paper cups. "We'll want to plan something more formal really soon. Do it up big. We can use the community room, and Agnes knows how to make bells and doves out of white crepe paper. Beverly's niece will play the piano, I'll bet, and—"

"I wish you wouldn't." Hannah wrung her hands, feeling ungrateful and selfish.

Elda turned to face her, her dark eyes bright even bracketed in folds of wrinkled skin. "What's going on, kid? Spill it. You can tell me anything."

Hannah perched on the arm of the sofa, swinging her leg. "I'm not ready to make a big deal of this, Elda. It's barely just happened. There's plenty of time down the road..." She trailed off into an awkward silence, not able to articulate her misgivings.

Elda eased down beside her with a groan of arthritic proportions. "For heaven's sake, Hannah. This isn't like pregnancy, where you have to wait until the first trimester is past to kick up your heels. You're getting married."

"Maybe."

Elda scowled. "Come again?"

Hannah shrugged uneasily. "It's early, that's all. I don't know where this is going."

"But you took his ring anyway."

Hannah's cheeks reddened at the not-so-subtle rebuke. She lowered her chin. "He's a very hard man to say no to, Elda. And if you could have seen his face..."

Elda snorted. "Pity is a hell of a reason to get engaged."

Hannah jumped to her feet, pacing restlessly. "I don't *pity* him. He's a wonderful man."

"But you're not in love with him."

"I—" The words stuck in her throat. She couldn't say them. Not at all. Three little words. She sighed. "Elda, you know how I feel about marriage. I've told you about my parents. You watch the news. Why would anyone put themselves through that?"

Elda leaned back into the floral cushions, her expression sober. Hannah felt completely naked, as though all her insecurities and fears were laid out for public consumption. The old woman shook her head. "People do it every day, child. Some more than once. It's called hope."

"I'd rather face the truth. Marriage isn't what it once was. My Grammy and Papaw had an ideal marriage. As I'm sure you and Mr. Beale did. People of your generation knew how to make it last. But marriage is disposable now. And I don't see the point in pretending otherwise."

Elda shook her head, looking at Hannah the way a teacher looks at a prize student who has just turned in her first F paper. "Good Lord, Hannah. You couldn't be more wrong. If you think your grandparents had a perfect marriage, you're kidding yourself. I'm sure they had a good marriage, but the perfect marriage doesn't exist."

Hannah thrust out her chin. "It might have come close in the past... when life was simpler and relationships were easier."

"There's no such thing as the good old days. We girls married because that's what was expected of us. And a lot of women became no more than household drudges. We didn't have the luxury of outside jobs that made us feel important. The lucky ones had men who treated us well, but for every one of those husbands there were a dozen others who took the cooking and cleaning for granted. We didn't divorce because it wasn't easy or socially acceptable."

"But you were married for over sixty years. You made it work."

"I was married, yes. And most of those years were good ones. But there were days when I would have walked out the door without a backward glance if I'd had the opportunity. And if your Grammy were here, I'd bet my last dime she'd tell you the same thing." Hannah slumped against the wall, her mind a blur. "So there really is no such thing as love that lasts a lifetime?" Saying it out loud made her feel sick.

Elda propped one swollen leg on the coffee table. "Of course there is. But love isn't some pretty, sterile, clean emotion, my girl. Love is messy. And it hurts. And sometimes it brings more grief than joy. But it's a hell of a lot better than the alternative."

"Which is?"

"Being alone."

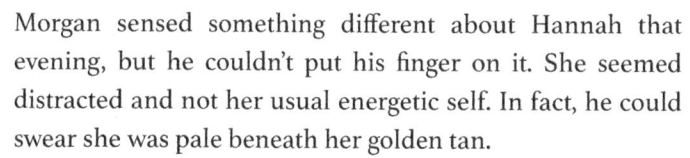

~

Morgan sensed something different about Hannah that evening, but he couldn't put his finger on it. She seemed distracted and not her usual energetic self. In fact, he could swear she was pale beneath her golden tan.

On reflection, he felt guilty about pushing her the night before. Setting a date could stay on the back burner for a bit. The important thing was that they were now an official couple. And he could wait on the rest... if he had to.

This was Hannah's late workday, so he picked up Chinese on the way over. They sat on the carpeted floor in front of her coffee table and watched the evening news while they ate. Hannah loved squabbling over politics and had even been known to switch sides in the middle of an argument just for the hell of it.

Her sheer contrariness amused him. He loved provoking her. If those heated discussions invariably led to something much less cerebral and more carnal... well, that was icing on the cake.

But something was definitely wrong tonight. He'd deliberately sided with her most hated talk show moron, and she hadn't even blinked an eye.

He scooted behind her and massaged her shoulders. Hannah turned off the TV and groaned, dropping her head forward like a broken flower.

He ruffled the curls at her nape. "Tough day at the office, dear?"

She arched her back and sighed. "Not especially. But

word got out about my ring, and suddenly I was the center of a paparazzi frenzy, minus the cameras."

He went still. "So your friends were excited for you?" He asked it carefully, still uncertain of her odd mood.

She groaned when his thumbs pressed deep into her neck. "You'd have thought none of them had ever seen an engagement ring before. We even had champagne."

He was glad she couldn't see his grin. "That's nice."

She grunted. "Sure. If you're good at playing twenty questions."

"And you're not?"

"I didn't know what to say."

"I told you we should have picked a date." But he said it teasingly so she would know he was kidding. Mostly. Maybe if he mentioned it enough, she would finally give in.

She turned to face him, linking her arms around his neck and draping her legs over his lap with a sly grin. Now the devilment he had come to expect from her was back. He had a funny feeling he wasn't going to like what was coming.

∼

Hannah studied his tanned, wind-burned face, trying to gauge his receptiveness to what she was going to say. His steel-gray eyes were wary. She knew her reluctance to set a date frustrated him, but he was moving too fast. Besides, he'd actually given her the perfect opportunity to drag her feet in the meantime. And it might even resolve some of her reservations about the *'til death do us part* thing.

She kissed his chin. "I read some of that magazine you gave me. I was going to palm it off on Elda, but I broke down and opened it. Some of the articles were interesting."

His brows lifted. "No kidding. That was my idea of a joke, Hannah. You're about the last woman I can see poring over a girly bridal magazine."

She pouted theatrically. "You don't think I'm girly?" She thrust out her boobs just for the fun of seeing his eyes glaze over.

He dragged his gaze from her chest and cleared his throat. "Of course you're girly. You're soft and you smell good and you have all the fun girl parts..."

"But?" She got such a kick out of teasing him. Especially when he was being a bit too serious.

He shifted restlessly on the carpet before gripping her ankles firmly. "You know what I mean, brat. You don't obsess about makeup and clothes and all that stuff."

"So you think I should fix myself up more."

He raised his face to the ceiling and audibly counted to ten. Then he slid his hands into her hair and dragged her close for a hot kiss. "I will not be provoked," he said firmly. "Now tell me what you read."

She unbuttoned his shirt and ran her hands over his chest. His abs were rock hard and he didn't even go to a gym. She loved that about him. She traced the fine line of hair that descended toward his belt buckle and grinned inwardly when he caught his breath.

Then she leaned into him, cuddling close, feeling the rise and fall of his rib cage as he breathed. "I came across an article that might help me feel better about actually setting a date. Something that's really new and cutting-edge. Something all prospective brides and grooms should consider before even attempting marriage."

He was frozen now, clearly not ready for whatever bombshell she was about to drop. And she fully expected him to pooh-pooh her idea. So she wasn't really playing fair.

Did she want him to say yes? Did she want to be persuaded?

He sighed. "And this was in the magazine I gave you?"

"Yep."

He dropped his head, beating his forehead gently against hers. "Why do I have a bad feeling? Go ahead. Tell me about this oh-so-very-important whatever it is."

She leaned backward, smiling widely. "Premarital sexual counseling."

3

Morgan wasn't sure what he had expected, but it wasn't this. He felt his face redden, and the incredulous note of defensiveness in his voice was beyond his control. "You think we have problems in the bedroom?" His poor dick wilted despite the fact that it had been raring to go just moments before.

Hannah tapped his chin with a chiding finger. "Don't be goofy. Of course not. But that's the point." Her eyes were wide, her expression earnest. "Lots of men and women get caught up in their hormones and confuse lust with love. Then after the ceremony with Aunt Ethel and the string quartet and the gold rings, he starts belching and drinking gin in his underwear and she turns out to be a whiny shrew. The marriage tanks."

"God, Hannah. You paint a lovely picture."

She wriggled to her feet and started stretching in a yoga position. "You know I'm right."

He leaned back on his hands, his legs outstretched. "So you think that when we burn ourselves out in the bedroom we'll have nothing left?"

She peered at him from between her legs, her red face upside down. "Well, I hope not. But that's the point. If we've worked through some other stuff, we won't be blinded by hot sex and thus be unable to see the pitfalls."

He rolled his neck, feeling the noose tighten. What had possessed him to give her that stupid magazine? "Exactly what would this counseling entail? I sure as hell am not going to lie on a couch and talk about my sex life."

She bounced to her feet and stretched toward the ceiling. "Not even if I'm the one pretending to be the doctor?"

He paused a moment to imagine Hannah wearing a white lab coat and nothing else. Not a bad image. In fact, it made him damned hot. With an effort, he dragged his attention back to the present. "And forget about two-way mirrors. I'm not a sexual lab rat, either."

She bent at the waist and placed her palms flat on the floor. "I'm sure it's nothing so weird. All the couples in the magazine said it transformed their relationships. They gushed, in fact."

He scowled. "I like our relationship just the way it is."

She finished her bouncing and stretching and plopped down on top of him, straddling his lap. She caught his face between her hands. "Okay. It was just an idea. Besides, I don't see us getting tired of each other anytime in the near future. We'll just keep on screwing like rabbits and hope for the best."

She punctuated that thought by nibbling his ear and then working her way down his neck. She hit a sensitive spot, and his erection bobbed and swelled. She was wearing a tiny pair of shorts. Feeling her long, bare legs hugging his hips made him the equivalent of a slobbering dog. How was he supposed to form a coherent thought when all he wanted to do was get inside her?

He took off her blouse and sighed in appreciation when her breasts, completely unfettered, snuggled into his palms. He thumbed the nipples, tugging them lightly and pinching until Hannah whimpered.

Then, taking her by surprise, he rolled her to her back, coming down on top of her and pinning her to the carpet. His shoulder caught the corner of the coffee table, but he barely registered the pain. She smiled at him, that wide flashing grin as familiar to him now as his own face in the mirror. He grabbed the thin nylon leg of her shorts and ripped it deliberately up to the waistband. Hannah's breath caught and her cheeks flushed. Her eyes went hazy. "Morgan..." She said his name on a long, groaned whisper that made the hair on the back of his neck stand up.

He freed his sex and settled between her thighs. "If this is only temporary," he muttered, "then we might as well enjoy it while it lasts."

∽

Three days later, he capitulated without a fight. Not that Hannah sulked or cajoled or any of those unfair feminine practices. She simply went about her business being... Hannah.

From the moment they met, it was always the same. Everywhere she went, she lit up a room. The sun shone brighter, the music played sweeter, the air was richer. Hannah's joie de vivre was contagious.

He'd made the mistake one afternoon of bringing her on site at the theme park property and then had to watch all the men on his crew fall over themselves to be introduced... to offer her rides on heavy machinery... to bring her drinks and chairs as they surveyed her with goofy grins.

Hannah was priceless.

So a man would have to be a fool to pass up an opportunity to seal the deal. Morgan was almost positive that she expected him to say no to the sexual counseling. She'd brought it up to point out in some weird way that they weren't ready to set a date.

But he wasn't willing to let that be the last word. If this sexual mumbo jumbo was seriously what she wanted, then he'd simply have to suck it up and be a man.

He bided his time, waiting for the right moment to outflank her. Over the weekend they had plans to take a group from Fluffy Palms to the beach. He figured the outing would be an ideal window. The senior set would nap beneath their umbrellas at some point, thus giving Morgan the perfect opportunity to talk to Hannah and not let her distract him with sex.

Not that he didn't appreciate that ploy in all its many delightful variations, but this was important.

Sunday afternoon on the hot sands of the eastern shore, he chatted with Elda while they watched Hannah and Arnie wrestle a deck chair into submission. Despite his advanced years, Arnie was getting an appreciative eyeful of Hannah's lithe form in her fairly modest black bikini.

Morgan recognized the urge to strangle the old coot for looking, but in all fairness, he couldn't blame him. A guy would have to be dead not to sit up and take notice of Hannah Quarles in a swimsuit. It was way better than watching a sunrise over the ocean, and that was saying a lot in the land of beautiful postcard mornings.

Elda nudged Morgan's ribs with a sharp elbow. "You're going to have to give her time, you know."

He nodded soberly, shielding his eyes from the glaring

sun and looking out toward the horizon. "Has she said anything to you?"

Elda shrugged. "She's skittish. But you knew that, I guess."

His jaw clenched. "Yeah." He'd have preferred head-over-heels enthusiasm for his proposal, but then she wouldn't have been his complicated Hannah. He sighed. "I told her I wanted to meet her parents."

Elda unfolded the beach towel beneath her arm and spread it out. "Not sure that's a good idea."

"Why not?"

"Don't know about the dad. He's never been around. I've met her mother only once, and she's a piece of work. Made Hannah cry."

His stomach tightened. He'd never seen Hannah shed a tear over anything. "How?"

"I don't really know. Me and Hannah were over at the mall one day looking for some support hose the doc said I needed. Suddenly this crazy, skinny woman with stick-straight gray hair down to her waist came up to us and started gushing. Hannah froze and got this weird look on her face. By the time I figured out who the chick was, she was gone. I didn't think much of it until a half hour or so later when I was in a dressing room trying on some slacks. I poked my head out of the curtain to ask for another size and there she was... my darlin' Hannah, crying these big silent tears. I'll be honest with you, boy. It tore my heart out."

He slung an arm around Elda's shoulders and kissed her leathery cheek. "Thank you for telling me," he said quietly. "You know she thinks the world of you."

Elda sniffed, her eyes overly bright. "My own son never had any kids. I reckon Hannah's like family, you know. I'd do anything for that girl."

After a rowdy picnic lunch, the elders in the group settled down in twos and fours to doze in the shade. The stiff sea winds were not as hot as they sometimes were, and the afternoon was pleasant.

When their charges were all comfortable, Morgan snagged Hannah's wrist. "How about a swim?" She had pulled her hair into a high ponytail on the back of her head, and her skin was smooth and pale gold in the harsh sunlight. He frowned slightly. "Do you need sunscreen?"

She shook her head. "I put some on at home. And besides, I never burn." She ran ahead of him toward the waves, leaving him to follow in a loping stride that caught up to her quickly.

He supported her waist as they trudged through the shallows. A narrow sandbar some yards out provided steadier footing, even though the water now reached up to Hannah's breasts. The only sounds surrounding them were the raucous cries of seagulls and the slurp and slap of tiny swells against their bodies as the ocean tried to drag them down.

He stared at her, regretting the necessary sunglasses that shielded her eyes from him and vice versa. "Too bad we have a dozen chaperones," he joked, trying for a lightheartedness he didn't feel.

She leaned into him, her breast brushing his arm. "Thank you for coming. This means so much to them. Sometimes I think they feel like prisoners."

He kissed her forehead. "You're their angel, you know. They love you."

She grinned wryly. "It's mutual."

They stood quietly for long minutes. He felt the wide embrace of the endless horizon and welcomed it. Even when he turned her in his arms and kissed her hungrily, they were so far out that no one onshore could really see anything. Like when he slid his fingers beneath the edge of her bikini bottoms and squeezed her ass.

She licked his nipple, making him jump. "I would love to spread my legs right here for you," she said, her voice dreamy.

His breath caught in his throat, and his legs trembled. For a split second he pondered the logistics and the potential for discovery. He was hard and aching. The urge to mate with her was almost inescapable.

He released her butt and gripped her shoulders, staring back at shore. The people on the beach were tiny blurs of color. He moved his hand slowly once again, this time sliding between her legs and slipping between the wet, slick folds of her sex.

Hannah shivered and pressed her hips toward him. He found her nub and played with it gently. Her lips parted. She murmured something inarticulate.

He slid his free hand down the back of her suit. Now he had her trapped in his arms. His fingers met between her legs. With one hand, he entered her. With the other he rubbed slowly, lazily.

She gripped his wrist, her nails biting into his skin. He'd never made her come standing up, but he sensed she was close. He kissed the tender skin beneath her ear and sucked gently at the damp spot his lips created.

Carefully, he thrust into her with three fingers as he probed the tiny sensitive spot that was swollen and hot.

Hannah cried out and staggered as he probed the inner walls of her sex. He felt the ripples of climax as they gripped her body.

He released her and caught her to his chest, kissing her with ragged murmurs. "I've got you, love. I've got you."

∼

Hannah was stunned. The afternoon sun beat down mercilessly on her bare head. She was dizzy and her mouth was dry. Good Lord, What had come over her? She'd pulled some outrageous stunts in her time, but letting a man give her a staggering orgasm in view of God and a slew of sun-worshipping Florida tourists was a new low.

Or maybe a high, if she was honest. Her limbs still shook, and her body hummed with pleasure. Morgan was supporting her weight, which was a good thing, because she wasn't sure she could stand alone at the moment.

She inhaled and let out a long, slow breath. "I suppose this gives a whole new meaning to riding the waves."

A corner of Morgan's beautiful, masculine mouth kicked up in a smug grin. "I live to please you, Hannah, my girl."

She staggered as a larger than normal wave washed against them. "I wonder if we could ..."

He shook his head firmly. "Don't even think it. I'm not sure there's a position known to man that could disguise what we were doing, even from this far away"

She reached beneath the water. "Then I'll have to take matters into my own hands."

She watched him as she gripped the cool, rigid column of flesh beneath his swim trunks. A sharp hiss whistled through his teeth. His entire body seemed to clench. She stroked him gently, enjoying the novel feel of touching him underwater. He was so hard, she wondered if his erection was actually painful.

She couldn't take him into her mouth. At least not

without some serious breathing practice. So she caressed him firmly, steadily, sliding her fingers from the base to the head of his shaft over and over.

They were facing each other now. His hands gripped the tops of her arms... almost bruising the flesh. His broad chest rose and fell with the force of his breathing. She teased the tiny eye, ran her fingers around the crest, and then reached down and cupped his balls gently before giving him one last, hard stroke.

He groaned and his whole body pressed against hers as he climaxed for what seemed like endless seconds. She wrapped her arms around his back, cradling him, absorbing his wild thrusts as she braced her feet in the shifting sand.

When it was over, he wrapped a fist in her ponytail and dragged her head back for a rough, penetrating kiss. "Are you trying to kill me?" he asked, breathless with what appeared to be only mild curiosity.

She laughed softly, loving the pretense of isolation, relishing the wicked force of the sun on her head. She felt vital and alive, as though she were somehow drawing life force from the sea.

She put her feet on top of his, linking her arms around his neck and swaying with the water. "I suppose we'd better get back to our charges. They'll be wanting an afternoon snack and a drink."

Morgan looked down at her, and even though she couldn't see all of his face at the moment, she sensed his shift in mood. He brushed her forehead with his lips. "We'll go in a minute. But I have something I want to say."

She cocked her head. "Oh?"

He smoothed a droplet of water from her cheekbone. "I have a proposition for you."

She lifted her eyebrows. "Is it kinkier than what we just did?"

"Possibly."

That stopped her in her tracks. She was intrigued. And all ears. "I'm listening," she said primly. Which was a hard attitude to maintain given the enthusiasm of her recent carnal water aerobics.

"It concerns setting a date for our wedding."

"But I—"

He placed a finger over her lips. "Hear me out. I've been thinking about the whole sexual counseling thing. Men and women really do have a different take on sex, so what could it hurt to try and learn something about each other? To mine the unknown..."

She nibbled her lower lip. "My suggestion was more impulsive than anything else. I don't know if this would actually work for us. We do fine in the bedroom. It's just my stupid hang-ups that are getting in the way of marriage."

"Yeah. I do know. I got it. Believe me. But I've been thinking about this. We both know that you aren't one hundred percent sure about this engagement."

Her cheeks went hot, and not from the sun this time. "Morgan, I —" She felt small and petty and guilty.

He shook his head briefly "Don't try to deny it, honey. I'm not a fool. But I'm confident we'll get there... eventually."

She swallowed hard. Was he right? She wanted him to be right... didn't she?

He kept talking, ignoring her awkward silence. "I want you to research this counseling thing. See if they do it in Orlando. Find out the time commitment, the cost. Decide if it's something you really want us to do."

"Do *you* want to do it?" she asked quietly.

"I'd rather eat nails," he said bluntly. "But if there's a chance this will advance my case, I'm on board. We can't be the only couple who has ever had doubts. Maybe this approach has some merit. I'm willing to try."

"You have doubts, too?" Somehow that had never occurred to her.

"About marrying you? No. But I wonder if you can ever give me what I want."

She moved back from his steadying influence in the water, feeling close to tears suddenly. "What is it you want from me, Morgan?"

He shrugged, his mighty shoulders glistening in the sun, the curve of his mouth almost grim. "Everything."

She gulped inwardly. How could one word sound so sinister? She blinked up at him, despite her dark glasses. The bright sun was beginning to give her a headache, or maybe it was the tone of the conversation. "So that's your proposition? That we go to sexual counseling?"

"Oh no," he said, his mouth twisting in a wicked grin. "If we make it through this, you have to promise to set a firm date for our wedding... and keep it."

She gaped at him. "Isn't that blackmail? And besides, plans change. Things happen."

He took off his sunglasses and cupped her face in his big hands. His long lashes were spiky, the gray of his eyes tinted with blue. "And we'll deal with whatever comes our way, sweetheart. I promise."

He kissed her one more time. This one was as different from the way he'd taken her mouth earlier as night and day. Those kisses had been filled with urgency, passion, raw desire.

Now his lips worshipped. They played over hers lazily as though he could stand there in the middle of the ocean and kiss her all day. He slid one strong arm beneath her butt and lifted her against him, never breaking the connection of mouth to mouth. Beneath her breast she could feel the steady, measured thump of his heart.

He made it all seem so easy. As though all she had to do was take his hand and walk off into a rosy sunset where nothing bad ever happened. It was movie worthy, endlessly enticing.

But still her unease remained. Somewhere deep below reason and faith. In the nasty, dark corridors of her past. Morgan couldn't see those places. Didn't even know they existed. So how could she convince him that her fears were real?

He released her finally and held one of her hands in the air. "Your fingers are getting wrinkly," he teased. "We'd better go back."

They linked hands as they began moving toward the beach. When they stepped from the sandbar, Hannah was over her head for a moment. She shrieked and grabbed hold of Morgan's waist. He supported her easily until her feet were once again on firm sand. It took them perhaps a dozen minutes to get back to dry land. To reality. And responsibilities.

But the bubble of intimacy they created out in Neptune's playground remained.

Most of their little band of beachgoers still slept, their mouths slack and their snores carried away on the salty breeze. Only Elda watched them as they dried off. Only Elda saw Morgan carefully wrap a thin beach shirt around Hannah's shoulders. Only Elda smiled. She might have been almost three times their age, but she knew that look on a man's face.

She lifted a hand. "I was beginning to think you were trying to be shark bait."

Hannah winced. "Don't even say that. I do my best to ignore the possibility. I've been playing in the ocean since I was a child, and I can't bear to give it up over the remote possibility that some nasty predator might want a piece of me."

Elda grinned. "I have noticed that you seem to fly in the face of danger from time to time."

Hannah snorted, her hands busy digging out napkins and cookies. "I work with senior citizens. How dangerous can that be?"

"Did you tell our hunky Morgan about the time you tried skydiving for your thirtieth birthday, and we all went to watch?"

Elda saw Morgan actually go white. "I guess not," she muttered. "My bad."

Hannah shot her a dirty look. "You have a big mouth, old woman."

Elda sniffed. "Insults will get you nowhere."

Morgan sprawled in an empty chair beside Elda. Perhaps Arnie had gone to find the facilities. "What else do you know? Spill it, dear friend. I think my fiancée has been keeping things from me."

Elda pursed her lips. "Well, there was the time she test-drove a Harley by herself. And then the Thanksgiving afternoon she climbed up on the roof and tried to hang Christmas lights on all our units."

"Tried?"

"Her foot got caught. She ended up dangling two feet off the ground."

Morgan felt cold and sick. "Please tell me you're exaggerating."

"Oh no. Not at all. I'd say she's been on her best behavior since you've known her. Trying to polish her image. But our little Hannah is a daredevil. When *Real World* did auditions in Orlando, she bungeed off a bridge."

Hannah settled into Morgan's lap. "Don't listen to her. She's making it sound worse than it was."

Morgan flashed back suddenly to that first day at the church and Hannah's death-defying dash through traffic. He scowled at Elda. "Is there more?"

Elda was clearly enjoying herself now. "I've seen her trying to get honey from a beehive. Got stung twenty-three times. And last winter she went ice-skating at an indoor rink with that cute orderly over in the medical center... Sven somebody... tall, Nordic, maybe a Swede. She made him do one of those death spirals with her and took the skin right off her cheekbone."

He looked at his fiancée's face, expecting to see an expression of remorse or at the very least sheepishness. But she was laughing, her smile a flash of white in the shadow of the beach umbrella. He was certain she didn't regret a bit of it.

And *this* woman was afraid to get married?

He wrapped his arms around her waist, pulling her back into his chest. "I can see I've got my work cut out for me. It's a good thing my CPR credentials are up-to-date and that I've got a working knowledge of first aid. I believe I've been bamboozled into thinking this lovely creature is soft and sweet and feminine."

Elda laughed until she cried. When she could catch her breath, she chortled again. "Our Hannah just might redefine the whole concept of feminine. She'll have your balls in a knot if you let her."

"Elda!" Hannah's outraged squawk woke most of the others.

Morgan just grinned and shoved her to her feet. Cuddling Hannah in his lap was having a predictable effect on his male anatomy, and he had a feeling that any alone time was long past.

He adjusted his trunks beneath the damp beach towel and reached for a cooler. "Who wants the first beer?"

4

Hannah had lived with herself long enough to know she had a regrettable propensity for leaping headfirst without pondering the consequences. Sexual counseling? Great googly moogly. Surely this had to be one of her more stupid ideas. Sex was private between a man and a woman. Sex was something you *did,* not something you talked about... especially with a stranger.

But Morgan had outwitted her. He'd called her bluff, and now she had no choice.

She picked up the magazine and flipped to the pertinent article. Toward the end there was a website address cited as a source for further information. When she went online and looked it up, she found a listing of state-by-state directories, and wouldn't you know it— Orlando had two sets of doctors certified for the premarital sexual counseling program. Damn.

She picked a name at random and dialed the number.

Morgan glanced at his watch and did a quick mental estimate of how much longer it would take to get the final sector of pipe laid. Despite the fact that three of his crew were out sick with a nasty bug that had been going around, things were still on schedule: He liked staying ahead of the curve, so when unexpected snafus occurred, he could absorb the interruption without derailing his timetable. At the moment, he was in an ATV headed to the farthest sector of the job to make sure no corners were being cut. He didn't micromanage, but it never hurt to keep tabs on the work.

His nice air-conditioned trailer provided respite from the sun and the heat, but he spent little time there. He'd discovered early on that his men respected him more if he was a visible presence in the midst of the chaos that was the inevitable first stage of a project like this. The theme park was only his second major assignment as site manager, and at age thirty-four, an undertaking like this was a hell of a lot of responsibility.

So far things had been smooth sailing. There were always minor glitches, of course, with deliveries and state paperwork and accidents... things beyond his control. But he prided himself on rolling with the punches and still getting the job done.

At the end of the day, he headed up the interstate to his apartment, his mind already on the evening to come. Hannah had promised to check on the sexual counseling thing. He was curious to see what she had found out. Maybe curious was the wrong word. Dread might better describe his emotions at the moment.

If he were lucky, there would be nothing available closer than Tampa or Jacksonville. And that would get him off the hook.

She arrived just as he was getting out of the shower. The pizza box in her hands emanated an aroma that made his stomach growl audibly.

Hannah grinned. "I'll put everything on the table while you get dressed."

He whipped the towel from around his hips and popped her on the butt with it. "Maybe pizza can wait."

She studied his nudity with raised eyebrows and evaded him with a laugh. "Pizza can *never* wait."

Over thick, cheesy slices loaded with everything but anchovies, he grilled her. "So... what did you find out about the counseling?"

She went to the fridge for more Coke, her face hidden by the door. "You can quit sweating it. It's not going to work out."

A weird mix of emotions grabbed him. "So nobody around here offers it?"

Now she stood at the sink with her back to him, rinsing off her hands where the can of soft drink had spewed when she opened it. "Well, they offer it, but it's too much of a time commitment. Your hours will never work."

He swallowed a bite and stared at her, his eyes narrowed. Something fishy was going on.

"I *am* the boss," he said mildly. "I can juggle my schedule."

Finally, she rejoined him at the table. But her face was blank. As though she had purposely erased all emotion. She concentrated on her pizza. "Don't worry about it. It was a crazy idea to begin with."

He reached across the narrow table and snagged her wrist. "Did you even call?"

Her head snapped up, her expression indignant. "Of

course I called. But I told you. It's too time intensive. Especially when you're in the middle of the theme park project."

She tugged at her hand, but he held it tightly. "Why don't you let *me* worry about my work schedule? Give me the scoop, Hannah. Quit stalling."

She tugged again, and this time he let her go, watching as she slumped back into her chair and picked at a piece of pepperoni on her paper plate. She shrugged her shoulders. "Honestly, Morgan. It's way more than I thought. They want you to commit to one group session every two weeks. And in between we would have to do two appointments at the office each week, just you and me."

He pondered the logistics. "If we could do our individual appointments late in the day... say four thirty, I think I could swing it. And what about the group sessions? When would they be?"

She wanted to lie. He could see it in her eyes. But she didn't have it in her. "The group sessions are on Friday evenings from seven until eight thirty"

He grinned wryly. "So it will work."

She stared at him glumly, her expressive face sullen. "You're so pigheaded," she complained. He laughed. "You would know."

She flipped a piece of crust at him. "I can't believe you want to do this."

"I don't," he said bluntly. "But it might even be good for us. And in the end... I get what I want." He actually saw her wince. It hurt. A lot. If a guy had to badger a woman into marrying him, was it worth it? He clenched his jaw and tried to smile. "Besides, if this counseling thing actually works, just imagine what great sex we'll have."

She got up and started dumping stuff in the trash, her face resigned. "I can hardly wait."

The office suite for the Drs. Hurst and Hurst was located in a generic downtown high-rise. Friday evening, Hannah, with Morgan by her side, rode up in the elevator to the thirty-second floor. Given the state of her nerves, the silence in the small, confined space was deafening.

When they stepped out into the corridor, their shoes echoed on the highly polished faux-marble flooring. With most of the building's tenants closed for the weekend, no sounds disturbed the hushed hallway.

Hannah consulted the slip of paper in her hand and then the placard on the wall. "It's this way, I guess. Three doors down on the right." Morgan followed her silently. She knew it hadn't been a great week for either of them. After sharing the pizza for dinner on Monday evening, she'd made up some lame excuse to go home. She felt jittery and unsettled, and she sure as heck hadn't been in the mood to stay and have sex.

Tuesday and Wednesday Morgan worked late. She hadn't suggested he come over, and he hadn't brought it up, either. Last night, they'd been to dinner and a movie with some friends, but they met at the restaurant and thus both had cars.

When the other couple left, Hannah and Morgan had stood in the parking lot. For the first time in their relationship, she hadn't been able to read him. He was usually an open book, his amiable personality a pleasant change from some men she had dated... though she was fully aware that his gentle, easygoing demeanor hid a streak of stubborn determination.

After an awkward silence, he had kissed her good night and climbed into his car.

Even tonight when he picked her up, the strained atmosphere between them made her regret ever having broached the subject of sexual counseling. She could call it off right now, but Morgan might press her to pick a date, and *that* she was not prepared to do.

It was two minutes after seven when they entered the medium-size conference room. The other couples were already in place as was the husband/wife counseling team.

After a flurry of introductions, Hannah and Morgan sat down on a comfy, floral-patterned love seat. Three more pieces of furniture just like it but with contrasting upholstery were pulled into a fairly tight circle.

Hannah surveyed the group, her heart beating fast for some unknown reason. She'd never been bashful about meeting strangers, but this whole setup had her spooked.

The couple to her right couldn't have been more than twenty-one or twenty-two years old, maybe younger. They looked scared to death. They were holding hands, white knuckled, and they barely managed to make eye contact with their fellow counselees. They had been introduced as Timmy and Rachelle, no last names...

The couple on Morgan's left was much older. Hannah guessed them to be in their early to mid-forties at least. The woman was slim and attractive. She was dressed in an upscale pantsuit with gold jewelry. Her husband was really tall and lanky, with a dimple that flashed when he spoke. Their names were Danita and Shaun.

The two doctors wore simple white lab coats and insisted on being called by their first names as well, Sheila and Pat. They were almost androgynous, both slim and lean with close-cropped salt-and-pepper hair.

Hannah tucked her purse at her feet and tried to relax.

Morgan seemed comfortable beside her, but she couldn't really tell.

Dr. Sheila got things rolling. With a businesslike smile, she greeted them. "Let me explain one thing from the outset," she said crisply, "This is *not* a group about sexual dysfunction. We do have patients with those challenges, but this group assembled here tonight has nothing to do with that. All of you are strong, committed, healthy couples. You've sought out this venue to improve what are already good sexual relationships."

She paused and looked at her spouse. He picked up the verbal pass. "Sheila and I have been married for almost forty-two years. We've been in practice together twenty-five of those. Ordinarily, we do group sessions for premarital sexual counseling based on our inherent belief that a healthy relationship in the bedroom goes a long way toward ameliorating difficulties that crop up in other areas. Morgan and Hannah are here for that reason."

He smiled at the two of them benignly and continued. "But we thought it might be nice to try a bit of a different approach. Our other two couples are already married, and so this will be more of an intergenerational exploration of the role of sexuality in the context of marriage."

Dr. Sheila leaned forward, her professional smile perfectly manicured. "Danita and Shaun are in a long-term marriage of twenty years. Timmy and Rachelle have been married only a year and have a three-month-old baby girl at home. Before we get into the specifics of how your individual couple sessions will be handled, why don't we get to know each other a little better?"

Dr. Pat nodded. "Excellent way to start. Morgan... will you tell us something about yourself?"

Hannah felt Morgan stiffen. "Well, I'm a civil engineer, a native Floridian, and I recently proposed marriage to the woman sitting beside me." He half turned and smiled, leaving Hannah on the hot seat.

She gulped inwardly, but managed not to blush. "I work as a personal shopper for the elderly, among other things, and I..." She trailed off, not sure what to say next.

Dr. Sheila filled the gap. "And have you set a wedding date?"

Now Hannah's blush came in full force. "Not yet," she muttered.

At a nod from the doctors, Danita spoke up. "I was a stay-at-home mom for eighteen years. Then I got my real estate license, and I've been doing that ever since."

Shaun crossed one ankle over his knee and stretched an arm behind his wife along the back of the sofa. "I work at Cape Canaveral in software systems... and I'm a runner." He left it at that.

Poor Rachelle looked terrified when all eyes turned in her direction. But she was brave enough to speak even if she didn't quite manage eye contact. "I dropped out during my sophomore year in college when we found out we were having a baby. I don't have any real interests as far as getting a degree, but I want to be a good mom. My parents were really upset and insisted that me and Timmy come here for this counseling. They're afraid we might split up."

Timmy, still with youthful acne on his face, squeezed his wife's hand. "And that's just plain stupid," he said quietly. "Me and Rachelle love each other like crazy. I'm still in school over at the community college. But I work evenings and weekends at an auto-body shop. I'm good with cars."

Dr. Sheila smoothed a nonexistent wrinkle in her lab

coat. "Very interesting, ladies and gentlemen. Now who wants to talk about sex?"

The comfort level in the room imploded into a million pieces, and Dr. Pat chuckled. "Don't let her scare you. We're not going to do any touchy-feely stuff, I promise."

Hannah released the breath she had been holding. "Then what did you have in mind?" She'd never been bashful about speaking when she wanted or needed answers.

Dr. Sheila reached behind her into a briefcase and pulled out a binder. "We're going to play a sexually oriented version of the old dating game that we like to call *If We Met in a Bar, Would You Do Me*?"

∼

Morgan tried to sneak an unobtrusive look at his watch and failed. God, how much longer was it until eight thirty? Not that the game was really all that bad. No one had been put on the spot to answer any indiscreet or salacious questions. And part of it had even been cute.

But they had been talking about sex for an hour now, and it had been almost a week since he'd made love to Hannah. He was tired and horny and ready to bail on this *Love Boat* session. He cleared his throat and tried to look innocent and committed to the game.

Dr. Pat looked at *his* watch. "Well, ladies and gentlemen. We'd better wrap this up, because we still have to give you the information on how to proceed from here." He took the binder from his wife. "Why don't you tell them what comes next?"

Dr. Sheila actually looked animated. "Over the course of the weekend, Pat and I will discuss what we have learned about each of you tonight. Then we will prepare six individual questionnaires, which will be e-mailed to you no later than Sunday afternoon. I'll do the women's, and Pat will do the men's. We ask that you not share the questions or your answers with your partner. On Monday, please return the questionnaires to us either by e-mail, fax, or in person. At that time you will need to contact our receptionist and schedule your first visit." She nodded to her partner. "Pat..."

He stood up. "If at all possible, we'd like you to plan for two sessions this coming week and two the week after. Then two weeks from tonight, we'll meet back here in our group. At which point, you can decide if you wish to sign up for another rotation. If you can manage only one time each week, then so be it, but for the full benefit of the program, a total of four would be best."

Shaun, who had been really quiet, spoke up with a puzzled look on his face. "But I don't understand. Why the questionnaires? What will the individual couple sessions entail?"

Dr. Sheila smiled benevolently. "Pat was getting to that. Go ahead, my dear."

Dr. Pat resumed his monologue, his hands stuffed in the pockets of his coat. "Your questionnaires will be used for Sheila and me to set up a sexual role-play situation that will be unique to each couple. When you arrive for your appointment, the receptionist will direct you to a room. We ask that you enter and follow the directions inside. Please remain in the situation a minimum of one hour and participate fully. However, you will have the room for a total of two hours if you wish to stay that long."

Dr. Sheila picked up the instructions and elaborated. "Be assured that your session is entirely private. You won't even see Pat or me. Following that first session, you'll get another set of questionnaires, and the process will follow in the same manner until you have completed all four. The group session on the final Friday in two weeks will complete the first module."

Timmy seemed confused. "But what do we do when we're in the room?"

A muffled choke of what sounded like laughter seemed entirely unprofessional coming from the oh-so-correct Dr. Pat. His eyes twinkled. "You'll be having sex, my boy. Lots of it."

After a split second of silence, the whole room broke into a nervous chuckle.

Dr. Sheila, a slight frown on her face, perhaps at the unauthorized levity, brought her charges back on track. "For our final exercise before we dismiss, I'd like each of you to share with the group as honestly as possible one important thing you think you have learned about being in a loving relationship."

Danita frowned. "You mean something we've learned tonight?"

Dr. Sheila shook her head. "No, I want to know something you've learned in the past, something you feel is of value. Who wants to go first?"

After several seconds of long, uncomfortable silence, Morgan stretched his arms over his head, and then rubbed his palms on his thighs. "I'll go."

Both doctors nodded briskly and spoke almost in unison. "Excellent."

Morgan faced the group and not Hannah, so she had to turn sideways in her seat to see his expression. He was solemn, thoughtful. "I've learned that people and relationships are not governed by the same dynamics as my work. On the job, I'm the boss. I develop plans and carry them out.

I make things happen." He paused and gave Hannah a small smile. "But relationships are seldom that straightforward. They are delicate and even fragile at times. And they don't always follow the path you might expect."

He fell silent and Dr. Sheila nodded. "Very insightful, Morgan. Thank you." She glanced at Rachelle. "Will you be next?"

The girl nibbled her lip. "Can I talk about the baby?"

Sheila nodded. "Of course."

"Well..." There was a brief pause as she gathered her thoughts. "Having a baby is real hard on a relationship. I'm tired all the time, and I think Timmy sometimes feels jealous of the baby. He's a wonderful daddy. But now that there are three of us, it's like we don't know how to act."

Dr. Pat, still standing, smiled at her. "That's a very common scenario, my dear. You're a perceptive young woman, and the fact that you see what's happening is a good thing. It will help you address those issues."

Shaun jumped in without waiting to be asked. "I remember the baby days," he said, his deep voice sympathetic. "But I think what I've learned is that people change. It's inevitable. And if you don't allow your relationship to change as well, you're in trouble."

Danita put her hand on his knee. "I've learned that it's not fair to expect someone else to make you happy. We're all responsible for our own fulfillment in life." She and her husband exchanged a smile that seemed to hold a wealth of lessons learned.

Timmy's face was bright red, but he managed to speak up with a voice that was only slightly shaky. "I've learned that love means lots of things. When you're a horny guy, you just want the sex. But now I'm feeling and seeing new stuff every day about what it means to love your wife or your kid. It's awesome, man... really awesome."

The six older adults in the room stared at him, visibly moved by his simple statement. Hannah had to blink back tears. How was she supposed to follow that? And why did she end up going last?

All eyes were on her now with expectation. And she was drawing a big fat zero when it came to finding something profound to say.

She twisted her hands in her lap, feeing sweat bead on her forehead. "Well, I..."

Dr. Sheila smiled at her encouragingly. "Take your time."

Hannah groaned inwardly. Great. Now she felt like the not-so-bright student who had to be coaxed along by the teacher. What the hell. She sucked in a breath and let it out. "I've learned that loving people makes you vulnerable, and that you can get hurt in the process."

An awkward silence greeted her blunt words. She cursed inwardly. She hadn't meant to say that at all, but the words just seemed to burst from her mouth. Now they were all looking at Morgan as if he were some kind of jerk who made her life a misery.

She backpedaled rapidly. "That doesn't really have anything to do with my relationship to Morgan. I was going farther back, I think... for the life lessons I've learned in the past. Is that okay?"

Now both doctors eyed her like a particularly interesting case study. Dr. Pat actually came back to the circle and resumed his original seat. He leaned forward. "Would you say that this particular lesson governs your actions in the present?"

Before Hannah could answer, Rachelle frowned slightly

and spoke. "I guess I always thought that was true of everyone. The people who can really get to us or make us feel bad are the closest ones to us in our lives. Like when my mom said she was disappointed in me for getting pregnant. I waited until I married Timmy to have sex with him. It's not like I was an unwed mother. So it hurt me a lot when she said that."

Danita winced. "Moms make mistakes, honey. I'm sure she didn't really mean that. Not when she had time to think about it."

Dr. Pat leaned back now, his gaze filled with interest as he monitored the conversation. "Again, Rachelle, you've hit the nail on the head. So I'll repeat my question to Hannah. Do you think you allow that lesson you've learned to govern your actions in the present?"

Hannah was no closer now to having a profound answer than she was two minutes ago. "Well... I think it's possible that I do."

She was extremely aware of Morgan's presence at her side. What was he thinking?

Dr. Sheila joined the interrogation, "Would you say that your fear causes you any problems?"

It was Hannah's turn to frown. "I didn't call it a fear... did I?"

The other woman smiled faintly. "We're all afraid of getting hurt. It's a natural human emotion. But in some of us, it's closer to the surface, particularly if we've experienced hurt in the past."

Hannah turned her head, her gaze drifting from one member of the group to the next. "No," she said, her voice a bit louder than she intended. "I can't see that it causes me any problems."

Dr. Pat glanced at his watch again. "Thank you, Hannah,

and all of you for being so willing to participate in this first group session. Sheila and I have enjoyed getting to know you a bit better, and we look forward to working with you over the next two weeks. Don't forget to watch your e-mail Sunday afternoon for the questionnaires, and if you parked in the main garage next door, Sheila will validate your parking stubs. Have a nice weekend."

5
———

Morgan drove on autopilot, his brain whirling with a thousand thoughts and emotions. Tonight was more than he had expected, but in a good way. And the group dynamic helped take the pressure off him and Hannah.

Having the different ages and viewpoints was an inspired idea. The doctors weren't bad eggs, a little pretentious, but not bad. And they sure seemed to love their work.

He had no clue whether Hannah had enjoyed the evening or not. She'd barely uttered two words since they got in the car. Once they were in her driveway, he shut off the engine. He'd brought an overnight bag. It was their custom on the weekends. But he didn't want to crowd her. So he sat quietly, waiting for Hannah to make the next move.

She sighed and turned to open her door. Then stopped and faced him once again. "Dis I sound like a complete Idiot?" Her words were quiet, filled with wry self-deprecation.

He reached his arm across the back of her seat and

played with her hair. She'd worn it down tonight, thick and glossy and incredibly sexy. "Of course not."

She stared out the windshield, her profile lit by the streetlights. "I liked the other couples."

As he let his fingertips brush the nape of her neck, he saw her shiver, and he smiled. "I did, too."

"Timmy and Rachelle are awfully young to have a baby. I can't imagine having so much responsibility at that age. No wonder her parents are worried."

Morgan sensed an opening for the question he had wanted to ask her for a long time now. "Have you ever thought about having kids?" he asked softly, monitoring the expression on her face.

He saw her teeth nibble at her bottom lip, but she didn't seem freaked out by the idea. She shook her head. "Not really. I'm not sure I have what it takes."

He traced the top of her spine. "Of course you do. Seniors and children have some of the same needs… love, companionship, safety, laughter. You have a lot to give, Hannah."

She wrinkled her nose. "Maybe."

It disappointed him that she was so uninterested in the subject. A lot of women tended to get all mushy and dreamy eyed when they thought about babies. But Hannah was rarely sentimental about things like that, so he probably shouldn't have been surprised by her marked lack of enthusiasm for the idea.

He tugged at her earlobe. "I've missed you this week," he said softly. He pulled her toward him. It pleased him when she didn't resist.

As he scooted her across the gearshift and into his lap, she giggled. "I have a nice bed upstairs, Morgan."

He kissed her forehead, her nose, her chin. "I'm weak

from sexual deprivation," he muttered. "I don't think I have the strength to make it that far."

He palmed her breast and toyed with the nipple. Hannah was slender, but her curves were full and firm. Her head fell back against his shoulder, and her eyes closed. A tiny smile curved her mouth.

He slid his hand beneath her silky blouse and under the edge of her bra. Every time he touched her he marveled that skin could be so soft. He was so hard she had to feel him pressing urgently under her hip.

He bent over her and kissed her, slipping his tongue between her lips and stroking the inside of her mouth. She went rigid. The nipple beneath his fingertip swelled and hardened.

"Hannah, Hannah, Hannah..." He cursed himself suddenly for starting something they couldn't finish. Even if he wanted to challenge the logistics of sex in a small car, they were in full view of anyone strolling by on the sidewalk. Nevertheless... She was wearing a plain khaki skirt, and it took nothing at all for him to locate her skimpy panties and drag them down her legs.

Now he could touch her intimately. He dragged his fingers through the tiny fluff of curls at her sex. She was wet and warm, and the scent of her arousal permeated the confines of the car.

He looked out the window, gauging the degree of privacy they had at the moment. Across the street two preteens on bikes careened by. At the corner an old man waited for a bus.

Even as Morgan toyed with Hannah's most intimate secrets, a patrol car appeared at the end of the street, cruising slowly, checking out the neighborhood.

With a groan of sheer frustration, Morgan released her. "Get out of the car, Hannah. Before we get arrested."

She moved back to her own seat, but she stared at him with a look of mischief on her face. "Too bad you're such a model citizen, I was hoping to give you a blow job."

He ground his teeth. "Upstairs, please."

She pouted. "No. Now. If you really want it."

He glanced at the patrol car. He glanced at Hannah. Her lips were red and moist and the thought of them wrapped around his boner made him shudder.

He swallowed the gravel in his throat. "Okay. Fine. But hurry."

She waited until they saw the cop speak to the two young boys across the street. Then she bent and put her head in his lap. He helped her open his pants and free his sex. "This is stupidly insane," he muttered. But knowing it and stopping were two different things.

He kept his gaze on the police vehicle as Hannah took him in her hands and then pulled him deep into her mouth. His fingers clenched on the steering wheel. Sweet Jesus. She sucked him like a Popsicle, tugging at his shaft with a firm pressure until his balls drew up tight against his body and he gasped. "Wait. Stop. He's looking this way."

She ignored him completely. Morgan started to shake. Sweat dripped from his chin. The night air was muggy and humid, and they had the windows rolled up. He felt his climax bearing down and tried to will it back. What if the cop decided to get out of his car? What if he caught the two of them engaging in lewd sex acts on a public street and issued a citation. What if...?

He groaned and flexed his hips as he came violently, trying desperately not to move, attempting in vain to keep his gaze on the nearby car. But his body betrayed him. His eyes rolled back in his head, and he got lost in the intensity of his release.

When he finally returned to the present, Hannah sat demurely in her seat, smiling at him with a naughty grin. Thankfully, the law-enforcement vehicle had moved off down the street.

He took in a ragged lungful of air. "Now can we go to your bedroom? Please."

Hannah was ready for Morgan to take her hard and fast. Playing with him in the car had made her hot in more ways than one. They didn't waste time when they got in the house. He locked the door, she tossed her pocketbook on a chair, and then they raced up the steps like children, laughing and teasing each other until they landed breathlessly just inside her bedroom door.

She sprawled on the bed, assuming an entirely unladylike position that reminded him she wasn't wearing any panties. "Come and get me, big guy."

He folded his arms across his chest. "What's your hurry?" he asked, his voice bland.

She frowned. "Some of us are still waiting."

He lifted an eyebrow. "For what?"

"You *know* what."

He sniffed his armpit. "I need a shower. I'll be with you in a minute."

Her mouth fell open. "I don't care if you're all man smelly. I need to get laid. Now." Her body was humming with arousal. Making Morgan come had seriously revved her engine, not to mention having him toy with her so intimately before that.

He turned his back on her. "You could join me."

Sadly, her shower had been built for utility and not foreplay. One adult was a tight squeeze. Two was physically impossible. Morgan disappeared, and she heard him turn on the water.

There was more than one way to skin a cat, as her Grammy used to say. Hannah stripped off what clothing she had left and walked into the bathroom. The shower stall had a clear glass door, so Morgan saw her the moment she walked in. But she ignored him.

She pinned up her hair and went to the sink. Taking a washcloth, she wet it and rubbed it with soap. Slowly, she washed her arms from wrist to shoulder. Then she soaped her breasts one at a time. The coarse washcloth rasped her sensitive nipples. She shivered.

Still, the water in the shower continued to run. She leaned her butt against the counter and lifted one leg to rest her foot on the small vanity stool. Carefully, she washed each leg from ankle to thigh. Then she rubbed between her legs. The double stimulation of her own caress and the knowledge that Morgan was watching almost made her come.

She moved the rag back and forth, pausing to separate the folds of her sex and cleanse every crevice. Her breathing was jerky now, her hands unsteady.

At last, thank God, Morgan turned off the water and stepped out of the shower. His erection reared against his abdomen, thick and long, as though he hadn't come only minutes before.

He didn't bother with drying off. He crossed the small distance between them, put his hands on her waist, and lifted her onto his shaft. He turned them so that his ass was now braced on the counter. Then he thrust upward in one powerful stroke that pushed him as far as she could take him in this position. Despite the fact that she had been wet and ready, her body strained to accept his girth.

She put her hands on his shoulders, her voice lost. She rested her forehead on his collarbone as he pumped in slow, shallow movements that must have strained the muscles in his arms to the breaking point.

She wanted to say something. Maybe to beg... to cajole. But it was all she could do to stave off the coming tidal wave. She wanted to make it last. To savor the delicious sensation of being stretched and filled.

His hands were clenched on her ass, supporting her, moving her to suit his whims. Her hands were linked behind his neck, her breasts flattened on his chest. She squeezed his penis with a deliberate flexing of her vaginal muscles. Morgan groaned and staggered sideways.

Then with a muffled gasp, he hitched her up in his arms enough to get his balance and strode into the bedroom. He tumbled them both onto the mattress, never allowing their bodies to separate.

The force of him coming down of top of her drove him even deeper into her aching passage. She whimpered as splinters of fiery-hot pleasure spread from her womb throughout her abdomen in endless ripples of heat.

In the aftermath, she could hear her heart beating in her ears. She swallowed against a dry throat. "Nicely done, Mr. Webber."

He wheezed and coughed as he rolled to his back. His cheekbones were ruddy with color, and his hair stood up in little spiky clumps where she had grabbed handfuls of it at a critical moment. His broad chest rose and fell as he tried to get his breath. He turned his head to look at her, his blue eyes slumberous and dark. "I won't ever get tired of making love to you, Hannah. I've never experienced with anyone else what I feel when I'm with you."

She'd been expecting one of his smartass teasing

comments. She loved his wicked sense of humor and their sexual banter. But the solemn gravity of his words took her completely by surprise. And she hated being surprised. She didn't know what to say. How could she put into words what he made her feel? It would be like trying to describe the Grand Canyon to a blind person.

She curled into his side, her right hand resting over his heart. Surely he could understand how she felt. She was wearing his ring. That said something, didn't it?

The opportunity for a lighthearted reply on her part passed, and now they were left with an awkward silence. Finally he sighed and stroked her back. "It's not all that late. We could watch a movie if you want."

Suddenly she was exhausted from the emotional roller coaster of the evening. She yawned and wriggled sideways to pull the covers over them. "Do you mind if we just go to sleep?"

He flipped the comforter into place and wrapped one strong arm around her, cocooning her in the dual warmth of man and material. "Not at all," he said, his words already tinged with drowsiness. "It's been a long week."

~

Sunday afternoon Hannah hovered near the computer, checking and rechecking her in-box. Finally, the Hurst e-mail address popped up. She opened it and printed out her questionnaire. When she was done, Morgan switched to his mailbox and did the same.

They took chairs on opposite sides of the room and got down to business. Hannah was surprised, right off, by two things. One—the survey was about a million questions long. And two—the questionnaires weren't at all what she had expected. Or maybe she simply hadn't known *what* to expect.

Do you feel safe when you are in bed with your fiancé? Do you feel safe in general when you are with your fiancé? Do you think about marriage often? Do you feel pressured to do things you don't want to do? How old were you when you lost your virginity?

That question stopped her cold in her tracks and filled her with distress. She'd been fifteen. And she'd done it to get her mother's attention.

It had hurt. A lot. Her membrane had been fully intact, and there had been lots of blood. Even now the memory shamed her. She'd tried to keep it from Grammy, but the old woman had the instincts of a hunting dog. She'd found Hannah crying in the bathroom late at night, and with one sharp glance had pegged the situation.

To Hannah's utter mortification, Grammy had made her go see a gynecologist, both for a physical confirmation that she was okay and to make sure Hannah received a pointed lecture about the ramifications of sexual activity.

Grammy had called Hannah's mother and asked her to accompany them. Vivian had declined. Hannah had cried herself to sleep that night for a whole laundry list of reasons that were far more complicated than losing her virginity.

She didn't have sex again for six years.

The brief trip to the past made her stomach churn. Her hand hovered over the question. No one would ever know if she lied. She wrote the number twenty-one. Then she stared at it. No one would believe that. She erased it and wrote eighteen.

Then she glanced over at Morgan. His head was bent, his attention focused on the list of questions. Were his similar to hers? They had never talked about past lovers or boyfriends or girlfriends.

Grinding her teeth and feeling her face heat even though no one was watching, she erased the number eighteen and wrote in the accurate digits.

On Monday morning Hannah delivered the questionnaires in person. One of her elderly clients had a doctor's appointment in the same building as the Hursts, so after getting the frail woman settled in the waiting room, Hannah rode the elevator once again up to the now-familiar suite of offices.

The envelope in her hand was sealed. She had wanted badly to rip it open and see Morgan's questions and answers, but she didn't follow through on the childish impulse. If this sexual counseling was to work, she had to follow the rules.

It was difficult to look the receptionist in the eye. Hannah felt her face flush and knew she must look comically guilty. Which was stupid, because the woman clearly dealt with this kind of stuff on a daily basis.

The lady flipped open her appointment calendar and asked Hannah to suggest some dates and times. Fortunately, there were no glitches. Hannah was able to schedule Tuesday and Thursday at four thirty both this week and the next. The second group appointment was already on the books.

The middle-aged woman smiled. "When you come tomorrow afternoon, I'll simply give you the appropriate key and you'll take it from there." Her eyes were kind. "Do you have any further questions?"

Hannah managed not to stutter. "No. I'm fine. We're fine. We'll be here. Thanks."

She escaped into the hallway and leaned against the wall, her heart pounding in her chest and her legs trembling. Something about that office scared the crap out of her. She had weird worries about things like two-way mirrors, electroshock therapy, and masked strangers.

She'd always had an imagination that worked overtime, and in this situation, it was a definite curse.

By the time Mrs. Beckley's appointment was finally over and Hannah was able to deliver her safely back to the assisted-living facility where she belonged, it was going on one o'clock. Hannah's stomach was growling, so she popped into the mall and gobbled down an order of Szechuan chicken and fried rice. She should have gone for something healthier, but her stress level was through the roof, and she needed comfort food.

Afterward, she wandered down to Victoria's Secret and looked in the window. Did tomorrow afternoon's appointment merit new undies? The mannequin in the window was wearing a lovely set of champagne satin bra and panties trimmed in ecru and chocolate lace. The perfect colors for a dark-headed brunette.

Fifteen minutes later, Hannah was fifty dollars poorer and no closer to solving her itchy sensation of impending doom. She had hoped to stay super busy today, but a couple of her regular Monday clients who had standing appointments at the beauty shop had canceled on her, and now the afternoon and evening stretched like an endless boring landscape in front of her.

She wouldn't be seeing Morgan tonight. One of the big bosses was coming in from out of town, and Morgan would be tied up all evening taking the man around the job site and then wining and dining him.

It seemed ominous that the next time she would see her fiancé would be at the offices of the Drs. Hurst and Hurst. What would be in the private room when Hannah and

Morgan opened the door? Silly stuff like edible underwear and porn videos? Or something even worse?

She couldn't get a clear mental picture of what *even worse* might be, but she was sure it would be scary. Or uncomfortable. Or difficult to endure. Why in the name of all that's holy had she ever teased Morgan about the sexual counseling? And when he had turned the tables on her and pretended to be interested in doing it, why hadn't she laughed him off and changed the subject?

By the time she got back to her apartment, she had worked herself into a complete mental tizzy. The message light on her phone was blinking, so she jabbed it eagerly, wanting to hear Morgan's voice.

Unfortunately, it was her mother. Asking for money. Hannah deleted the rambling message rapidly and put a hand to her mouth, feeling queasy. Would she end up having to tell Morgan about her flaky mother? God, she hoped not.

She went for a run to try and burn off her restless energy, but it seemed to hype her up more. Since she had eaten a big lunch, she decided to have microwave popcorn for dinner. While it was popping, she poured herself a glass of wine and downed half of it recklessly.

She rarely drank, because it made her sleepy. But tonight, oblivion sounded like a good thing. Then she wouldn't have to think about tomorrow.

At ten she showered and climbed into bed. She read for a little while, but the book, which was supposed to be a page-turner, couldn't hold her attention. Finally, she got up and rummaged in her closet until she found the hatbox at the rear. She pulled out the vibrator Morgan had never seen and then got back into bed.

Deliberately, she closed her eyes and summoned up an

image of Hugh Jackman. Nope. Not tonight. How about that country singer with the cute smile? Nothing.

Well, she could at least imagine herself in bed with her own yummy fiancé. If Morgan were here, he'd be under the covers already, with his head buried between her legs. Ah, that was it. She slowed her breathing, concentrating on the feel of the gentle ripples against her sensitive flesh. Would she and Morgan be doing weird things in that room tomorrow, or simply concentrating on good sex?

Honestly, she couldn't imagine much improvement in that area. Morgan was everything a woman could ask for when it came to the bedroom. He was inventive and funny and generous with his attention to her needs.

And his body... well, hot damn. The first time she had seen him naked, her heart had turned over in her chest. The physical nature of his job kept him fit and hard and tanned all over except for a strip of white at his hips.

His penis was above average, at least in her somewhat limited experience. After that one dismal youthful debacle, she'd been with only two other men before Morgan. And neither of them had been particularly exciting between the sheets. One had been unable to give her an orgasm, and the other one had been so quick off the mark every time, it had been embarrassing for them both.

She hadn't thought much of sex until Morgan had shown her how good things could be between a man and a woman. He'd coaxed her into being less reserved in the bedroom. Despite her reckless nature in other areas of her life, when it came to physical intimacy, she had definitely been the cautious type.

But no more.

Morgan made her have sex in the daytime. He had made her have sex with the lights on. He'd made her have sex in front of mirrors... or outside in the dark. Even once in his trailer after hours out at the work site.

And each time he had made her feel a bit more free, more confident, more comfortable as a woman. More aware of her femininity, her desirability.

She eased the vibrator a couple of inches into her throbbing sex, wishing fervently that Morgan were there to assuage the ache. She bit her bottom lip and increased the speed of the vibrations.

With her free hand, she toyed with the place that seemed on fire, rubbing it lightly, concentrating fiercely on the heat gathering deep in her womb. She imagined Morgan's fingers there, teasing her, playing with her until she begged for mercy. She moved the vibrator deeper, clamping down on it, her breath coming harshly now, her eyes squeezed shut.

She pictured his erection, glistening with moisture at the tip, waiting to take her. Shivers of arousal spread from her center into her stomach, her thighs, her breasts. She groaned and moved her hands more swiftly. The sudden jolt of heat dragged a shocked cry from her throat. She arched her back, dug her heels into the mattress, and came in wave after wave of clenching pleasure that left her drained and spent in her lonely bed.

The sudden ring of the telephone was a rude shock. She was still gasping for breath when she rolled over and picked up the handset. "Hello?"

There was a split second of silence and then Morgan's voice, laden with suspicion, came on the line. "What in the devil are you doing?"

She clenched her thighs together. "What do you mean?"

Something in her thick voice tipped him off. "My God. You just made yourself come."

She thought about denying it, but what was the point? "I miss you," she said softly, every ounce of yearning she felt in her voice.

She heard him curse long and low, a string of words that conveyed his utter frustration. Finally, he laughed, a hoarse chuckle that did nothing to mask his need for her. "Just wait until tomorrow, my love. Just you wait."

6

Tuesday morning Danita closed her eyes and leaned back in the big, comfortable massage chair. The nail technician at her feet was prepping Danita's toes for a pedicure. And not long before, Danita had recklessly paid for *and endured* a Brazilian wax job.

Shaun would have a cow.

But she was hoping his reaction would be the good kind of shocked. She was betting on the fact that seeing his wife with her private parts completely bare would turn him into a raging sex maniac.

She winced as she thought about yesterday's depressing session at the Hursts' offices. Danita had shown up there first thing Monday, desperate to schedule an appointment for Shaun and her as soon as possible. She had been almost sick with nerves, and she wanted to get the first visit over with quickly.

Fortunately, there was a cancellation at eleven. Shaun was his own boss at the accounting firm, so when she called him, he'd been able to get away without too much fuss.

They had met and entered that unknown chamber of sexual secrets, and then everything had gone wrong.

She had expected the Hursts to set up some romantic fantasy scenario. Instead, the room was furnished very simply—as an ordinary bedroom. The brief note on the bedside table had instructed them to make love as they would on a normal night at home.

Danita had been furious and trying hard not to let on. This was bullshit. She and Shaun needed help, not a replay of their dismal, lackluster sex life. They had been married for over twenty years for godsakes. Was it any wonder that their lovemaking had become mechanical?

She knew that Shaun was surely bored with seeing the same woman in his bed night after night. This business with the sexual counseling was supposed to spice things up.

She had been so upset by the bland bedroom scene that she'd been unable to climax. Shaun had given up, grim-faced and silent. Filling out the post encounter questionnaires before they left the premises had been frustrating in the extreme.

By seven o'clock last night, their new sets of questions had been e-mailed to them. She and Shaun printed out the numerous sheets and went to separate parts of the house to complete them. Danita had dropped the papers off this morning right before her spa appointment and had begged the Hursts' receptionist for a second appointment... today.

Perhaps Danita was a glutton for punishment, but she was desperate. Shaun had barely spoken to her last night, and the atmosphere in their lovely, comfortable home had been strained at best.

She knew the failure rested on her shoulders. Somehow she had lost her enthusiasm for sex, and the more she tried to force things, the more frozen she felt inside. At one point several months ago, Shaun had even asked her if she was having an affair.

Her blank look of shock must have reassured him, because he had exhaled gustily and then laughed. But there wasn't much amusement in his rough chuckle.

They had lost their way in the bedroom. Danita had been desperately counting on this sexual guidance to get them back on track. Deep down she was afraid Shaun might leave her if she didn't fix whatever was wrong.

She'd had three friends in the past year whose husbands traded in their longtime wives for younger models. Danita was afraid it was only a matter of time before her own spouse found a reason to do the same.

Shaun was an extremely appealing man. Unlike many of his peers, he'd kept himself fit and healthy. His waist was still trim, his belly flat. He was tall and strong, and when he smiled with that dimple in his cheek, her knees quivered every bit as much as they had on their wedding day when she was twenty-one.

Danita, on the other hand, was twenty pounds heavier than when they married. She had stretch marks from giving birth to their twin sons almost two decades ago. Her breasts were still firm, but perhaps not as perky as they had once been. And though her skin was good in general, the fine lines at the corners of her eyes gave away her age.

She winced suddenly when the manicurist got a little too enthusiastic with the cuticle nippers. Danita glanced at her watch. She had just an hour to grab a bite to eat and meet Shaun for their noon appointment. She could tell he wasn't enthused about going back. But he'd agreed.

Which sometimes pissed her off. Why did he always

defer to her plans? Why couldn't he express a simple damn opinion once in a while?

By the time she showed up at the doctors' office, she looked as good as she was ever going to get. She'd invested in a horribly overpriced thong that showed off her new wax job to perfection. And though she'd been too nervous to eat, she had downed two glasses of wine in hopes of relaxing herself and avoiding a repeat of yesterday's debacle.

Shaun was waiting for her and had already spoken to the receptionist. He smiled faintly at Danita as he fit the key in the lock of their assigned room. "You ready for this?"

She nodded jerkily and followed him into the room. During the first few moments after he shut the door, she thought she might cry. The room was exactly as it had been yesterday. She thought about the money this was costing. She thought about her inability to find satisfaction the day before.

She swallowed hard, trying desperately to get with the program. She forced a smile. "Well, what does the paper say?"

Shaun picked it up, and she saw him frown as he read it. Then his mouth twisted in a wry grin. He looked at her with one eyebrow raised. "It says we're supposed to spend a minimum of one hour having foreplay. But under no circumstances whatsoever are we to engage in sexual intercourse. And we're also not supposed to climax by any other means."

Even as she gaped at him in surprise, the knot in her stomach unfurled. "Really?"

He shrugged and tossed the paper aside. "That's what is says."

Danita wanted to laugh and cry all at once. A huge

weight she hadn't known she was carrying rolled off her shoulders. She *knew* how to do foreplay. She was a pro at it. And without having to worry whether or not she was going to have an orgasm, she might actually enjoy this.

She grinned at her husband. "I suppose we could handle that. What do *you* think?"

He kicked off his shoes and faced her in his sock feet. "I say bring it on."

Shaun saw the change in his wife the moment it happened. She was *relieved* they weren't supposed to have sex. Though her response stung his male pride, he was damn glad to see her smile. For the past couple of years she seemed so sad all the time. She probably thought he didn't notice, but he did. He knew her as well as he knew himself. And that meant she wasn't able to mask her emotions from him.

It started when their boys went off to college. Having twins made it worse, because they both left at once. Danita had been a lost soul for weeks.

But she was a strong woman, and she had picked herself up, found new interests, and carried on. The female problems she'd struggled with hadn't helped. He'd tried to be sensitive to her health issues, but he had missed their frequent lovemaking.

Things had improved in recent months, but he felt a reserve in his gentle wife that hadn't been there before. When she had suggested the sexual counseling, he had agreed quickly, eager for them to find their way back to intimacy and actually having fun with sex. As opposed to twice weekly quickies in the dark.

He slid his hands beneath her hair and cupped her neck. "I like the new dress," he murmured. The blue matched her eyes and complemented her blond hair. He kissed her, rejoicing inwardly when her lips seemed eager.

Just like that, he was hard, and though he sensed that he was in for some real frustration, he ignored the need and concentrated on his wife. Her skin was soft and fragrant, her lips lush and sweet. She had kicked off her sandals, and now the difference in their heights was magnified. She seemed infinitely small and precious to him.

His tongue dueled lazily with hers, causing them both to breathe more quickly. He found the zipper at the back of her dress and lowered it slowly, pausing to stroke the curve of her spine.

She stopped him when he had the zipper down to her waist. "Wait, Shaun. Let me undress you first. Please." Her eyes were filled with bashful entreaty.

He dropped his hands to his sides. "Be my guest." Danita rarely took the lead in their lovemaking, and though he was taken aback by her unusual assertiveness, he was pleased. Sometimes he felt like she tolerated his touch, no more. He'd approached her for sex less and less over the past few years, dreading the possibility that she was humoring him even more than he dreaded the possibility of rejection.

Her hands hovered over his chest and then settled in to unfasten the buttons on his shirt. He'd been at work when she called him. His first reaction had been to say no. Yesterday was hell on his ego and his general frame of mind. But he'd never been able to deny Danita anything, so he excused himself to his staff and made tracks across town, still wearing nothing more interesting than khaki slacks and a white cotton shirt.

Her head was bent as she went about undressing him. When she was done with the buttons, he shrugged out of the shirt. Danita still stood in front of him, head down. She put her hands on his chest, almost tentatively it seemed, and lightly stroked the dusting of hair that covered his pecs and arrowed down to his waist.

The feel of her warm hands on his skin was infinitely arousing. It had always been that way with Danita. Sometimes nothing more than one of her smiles made him hard. He'd known the first moment they met that he was a goner.

His heart began to thud beneath his ribs with jerky beats. He cupped her shoulders between his hands and tried to steady his breathing. This was a long-distance race —not a sprint—and he had to keep himself under control.

When her hands found his belt buckle, he wasn't sure he had the guts to do this. He felt like he had been hungry for her forever. It had been years since the days when the two of them had tumbled together in bed like playful puppies... eager and horny and completely unconcerned with the world outside their bedroom.

Life had gotten in the way. They had grown up. They had grown apart.

She had his zipper down now, her fingers brushing his throbbing erection with painful results. He sucked in a breath when she sank to her knees and untied the laces on his dress shoes. With her help, he stepped out of them and his socks. Even the touch of her fingers on the arches of his big, ugly feet made him squirm with lust.

She stood up again and slid her hands inside his pants and boxers, shucking them to his thighs and down to the floor. She stepped aside as he kicked out of the clothing. Now he was buck naked.

Her eyes were riveted on his penis. It bobbed as if it had a mind of its own. A bead of clear fluid oozed from the head.

He cursed when she closed her hands around him and gave him a most unorthodox massage.

He gritted his teeth, moaning softly beneath his breath. Her gentle touch sent a raging current of hunger zinging through his body from his sex to his spine and then sliding everywhere else along the way in electric connections from head to toe.

He panted helplessly as she cupped his balls and tested their weight. His knees trembled. After several long minutes, he caved. He shoved her away and backed up to the door, his bare ass hitting the cool wood. He held up a hand. "I can't take any more. We're not supposed to come. Remember?"

A succession of emotions flitted across her face as he escaped her grasp and retreated like a scared soldier. Hurt. Dismay. Sudden understanding. And then what was most assuredly smug satisfaction.

She grinned. "Men are so easy."

He snorted. "Just wait. Your turn will come. And I'll have you begging for mercy."

He was teasing her. Trying to get his own recalcitrant hormones under control. But his lighthearted words had an unusual effect on his wife.

Her pupils expanded as her lashes widened. Her hand went to her throat. Her mouth opened as though she wanted to say something, but she remained mute.

When he thought he could touch her without pushing her to the bed and mounting her in a frenzy of insanity, he walked toward her slowly, holding her gaze with his.

She wet her lips. "What are you doing?"

He grinned. "You have to ask, Danita? After all these years?"

He held her waist, keeping her at arms' length as he

kissed her lightly. It was sweet, chaste, slow, and lazy. And it wasn't enough. He peeled her dress halfway down, stopping to admire the hot-pink bra she wore. It was made of delicate, sheer lace in the front, and he could see her dark, pointy nipples.

He ran his thumb over one, then scraped it with his thumbnail. Danita trembled violently and closed her eyes. He bent his head and wet the lace with his tongue. He sucked the nipple and areola into his mouth and bit gently.

Now she whimpered, twisting restlessly in his embrace. He reached behind her and unfastened the bra, releasing the catch and tossing the delicate garment aside. He stared down at her tits. They were a guy's most incredible wet dream, full and bouncy and perfectly curved.

She was still covered from the waist down. He figured that was necessary if he was supposed to hold out for an entire hour. A man could only withstand so much temptation. He kissed her cheeks, her eyelids, the side of her throat. Danita's arms hung at her sides. Her eyes were closed now, and her chest rose and fell.

He deliberately took each nipple between his fingers and pinched. She gasped. He twisted and tugged them and then sank his teeth into the tender skin just above her collarbone. Danita went rigid. Her hips pressed restlessly toward his. The skirt of her dress brushed his erection.

He gripped her wrists and tucked them behind her back, bringing her body in full contact with his. He muttered in her ear, "You are so damn hot. I want to fuck you here. Right now." When Danita groaned and struggled, he licked the tiny set of teeth marks on her fair skin. "But I can't. We're not supposed to, right?"

Her eyes opened, blank with shock and hunger. "Why not?" she cried, clearly having forgotten their surroundings.

He bent her backward over his arm and sucked her nipples one at a time. She struggled to free her wrists, and he allowed it. Her hands clenched in his hair. He blew on the wet skin of her breasts. Danita made a keening cry.

He froze and thrust her away, holding on only long enough to make sure she had regained her balance.

She reached for him. "Please," she whispered, her cheeks flushed and her breathing ragged.

He held up his hands. "Foreplay only... remember? You were about to come."

Danita stared at him in shock. She glanced at the small, discreet clock on the bedside table. They had been in this little room for only twenty-five minutes. And she'd been on the brink of an orgasm already. What did that mean?

Her head reeled. There had been nights in the past year when Shaun had stroked her patiently—for hours it seemed —and she'd never been able to find release.

And now in no time at all, she was a seething cauldron of want and need, so close to an orgasm she could taste its shimmering allure just around the corner.

"They'll never know," she said wildly. "Please."

Shaun stared at her soberly. She knew he was as hungry as she was, the evidence impossible to hide. But he shook his head. "We're going to follow the rules, my love. Or why else have we come?"

She hated him for his self-control when she felt like shattering into a million ravenous pieces. How could he deny her when she needed it so much?

She frowned. "We still have at least a half hour." Then she took a deep breath. Torture went both ways.

Before he could protest, she went to him, knelt, and took him deep into her mouth. It was like sucking on stone wrapped in thin velvet. But the taste and smell of him made the experience come alive.

She'd been making love to the same man for many years. She knew the infinitesimal body signals that heralded his release. Before he could come, she squeezed hard at the base of his shaft and kept the pressure in place until his orgasm retreated. She'd never done that to him before, but she'd read about it in a magazine, and the alarming technique had stuck.

Shaun cursed and moaned and dropped to his haunches when she released him, his face red and his skin slicked with perspiration. "God Almighty," he muttered.

She kicked off her sandals and crawled onto the bed, still dressed from the waist down. With her back resting against the headboard, she spread her legs, keeping her skirt modestly in place. "I can hold out if you can," she taunted. For a split second she paused to wonder if she looked fat in this position, and then she pushed the self-defeating thought aside. She crooked her finger. "Let's see how far we can go without cracking."

Shaun stumbled to the bed, afraid to touch her, but unable to stay away. He put one knee on the bed, absently stroking his rigid shaft. God, he ached. Even the light touch of his own fingers was almost too much stimulation.

Danita watched him, her cheeks flushed, her eyes bright. Sitting there half clothed, she looked erotically lovely. Carnal. Available.

As he sprawled at the foot of the bed, he took the ankle nearest him and pulled it toward him, deliberately widening her legs. He bent and licked her anklebone. Then he used his tongue to trace a path upward to her knee.

He stopped there and sat up, making sure her eyes were locked on his. Without breaking their visual connection, he reached beneath her skirt and found her panties. It shocked him to feel how small they were.

Suddenly rabid with curiosity, he dragged them to her ankles. A thong. He held the scrap of dark pink silk in his fist and at that moment, something else registered. Something else was different.

He frowned. "Stand up, Danita."

She did as he asked, but he had to support her by holding her hand, because the mattress dipped and swayed. When she was steady, he finished lowering her zipper. Carefully, he pushed her dress to her ankles and helped her step out of it. When he raised his eyes, he actually gasped. Her mound was completely bare, the pale skin glistening and moist.

Sweet God in heaven. He looked up at her. Her expression was wary... uncertain.

He touched her with a single fingertip, marveling at the complete absence of hair. The slick skin was erotic, alien. His body tightened—everywhere, and his hunger grew. Without conscious thought, he lowered her to the bed on her back and bent to taste her.

His tongue probed gently at the crease where her leg and thigh met. Then he thrust into her navel with his tongue and used his fingers to explore the delicate, smoothly-waxed curves of her lower abdomen, all the way down to her raspberry-colored sex.

When he touched her there, she cried out. He traced the seam of her vulva with his fingertip and held up his finger. It was covered with her juices. He touched her mouth, forcing her lips gently apart. "Taste," he urged. "See how sweet you are."

She resisted momentarily, but he was insistent. Her mouth closed around his finger. He watched carefully. "Now you know why I love it so much," he murmured. "You taste like the most wonderful forbidden fruit." After that, he couldn't wait any longer. He moved between her thighs and held them firmly apart with his splayed fingers. He did a visual reconnaissance, drunk with the novel experience of seeing his wife's precious sex bare-ass naked. When he licked her the first time, her hips came off the mattress.

He nudged his tongue between her lush folds and probed her passage.

She cried out.

He buried his face in her succulent flesh and ate at her with sudden hunger, absorbing the scent and taste of her, licking and sucking wildly. Only at the last possible second did he remember their instructions. With superhuman effort, he withdrew and pulled her legs together.

She raged at him. She begged. She pleaded. Her fingernails left scratches on his shoulders as she tried to pull him back into his original position.

He gathered her in his arms and held her tightly. "Kiss me," he said roughly. "Just kiss me." He moved over her and possessed her mouth, taking it like he wanted to take her body—roughly, passionately.

They kissed for long minutes. His entire body ached with the need to be deep inside her. He rubbed his sex over her mound, tormenting them both. "Do you want me?" The question startled him. He hadn't meant to ask it.

She looked at him with hazy eyes. "Are you serious, Shaun?"

He shrugged, feeling oddly unsure of himself. "Sometimes I think I'm not what you need anymore."

All the while they were talking, he moved his erection against her center.

She squirmed, her face hot. "Of course I want you. I'm sick with wanting you."

The fervent note in her voice convinced him. He glanced at his watch. "Then let's get out of here."

⁓

He didn't let her put her panties on. Danita watched, grinning, as he stuffed them in the pocket of his trousers. He winced as he tucked himself inside his underwear and gently zipped his fly. She pulled out her compact and tried to smooth her hair. "Oh, hell," she said, struck suddenly by an unpleasant thought. "We have to fill out those damn questionnaires before we can leave."

They did them in record time, not making eye contact with the pleasant receptionist as they handed them over.

Once they were finally out in the hall, Shaun dragged her away from the elevators and toward the stairs. They made it down one flight before he pushed her against the wall and shoved his mouth over hers. His hand went under her skirt and toyed with her sex.

She wrapped her leg around his, wanting him to lift her and fill her with that wonderful, thick erection. He broke the embrace, panting and fumbling for his car keys.

She glanced around them wildly, noticing the dark corner beneath the stairwell. "Over there." She knew she couldn't make it to the parking lot. He followed without a word of complaint. She was lost to any concerns about being discovered. All she could think of was screwing her husband. There was no room to stand in the cramped space, and the none-too-clean floor was questionable enough that she was unwilling to stretch out on her back.

She went to her hands and knees. He was quick on the

uptake. He unzipped his slacks, flipped her skirt over her back, and entered her with a hard thrust. On the third stroke she came, her muffled cry strangled in her throat.

A split second later, his warm come flooded the mouth of her womb as he pumped wildly and buried his face in her back. She hung her head, breathing in great gulps, trying to get oxygen to her brain. Then she started to laugh and cry as the pain in her knees registered and she understood fully what she had done.

7

For Hannah, the hours of Tuesday crept by at about the same pace as some of her clients who were on walkers. After lunch, she gave up on looking at her watch. She was never going to make it until four thirty.

She went about her daily errands and chores on autopilot. Usually, she enjoyed chatting with her clients, and usually, she had infinite stores of patience. Some of the elders were cranky. Some of them were long-winded. Some of them were simply lonely and wanted a listening ear.

Hannah always tried to be caring and helpful. But today it wasn't easy. When old Mr. Evans spent forty minutes debating the merits of various shoe insoles, she wanted to drag him out of the drugstore by his thinning hair. But she didn't. She smiled and offered advice when asked, and pretended that today was the same as any other day.

At three thirty she dashed home, showered, changed clothes, and jumped back in her car for the twenty-minute drive downtown. She and Morgan were meeting at the Hursts' offices, since Morgan's job site was on the complete opposite side of the city.

When she pulled into the parking garage, her hands were clammy on the steering wheel. She still had deep reservations about what was about to happen, but it was too late to back out now. She lingered in the car park hoping to see her fiancé before they made the trek upstairs.

She wanted to kiss him and study his smiling face and reassure herself that nothing bizarre was going to happen. But Morgan never showed. She had found a spot near the entrance, and it was easy to monitor each vehicle that came in. Had she missed him?

Finally at ten 'til, she hissed in frustration, got out, and locked her car. When she entered the suite of offices on the thirty-second floor, Morgan was standing at the reception desk, his jaw tight.

She went up to him, wanting to pick a fight, but the handful of people in the waiting room curbed her impulse. She took Morgan's arm in a tight grip. "Where were you?" she hissed. "I was waiting in the parking garage so we could walk up together."

He frowned. "I was cutting it close on time. There was a spot on the street, so I snagged it and ran up here."

That took the wind out of her sails. "Oh." The adrenaline pumping through her veins began to subside. "Well, I'm sorry for all those things I was thinking."

He kissed her on the nose and grinned. "I don't even want to know." He held up a key. "We're all set. You ready?"

The lump in her throat refused to dissipate. "Of course," she croaked. "Let's do this."

The room they entered looked as if once upon a time it had been two exam rooms. A wall had been knocked out, and now the space was approximately twelve by sixteen. Not big, but not small, either.

She felt unaccountably bashful all of a sudden, and she

waited for Morgan to take the lead. He looked around with interest. She noticed for the first time that his hair was still damp. He must have cleaned up in the small shower in his trailer before coming to meet her.

Together they studied the ambience. The room had been set up to resemble a jungle hut. The floor was hidden with a rush mat, and the walls and ceiling were covered in burlap and palm fronds. A post in the center of the room might have been a support beam, or it might have been simply decorative. It was hard to tell.

A low, scarred wooden bench appeared to be the only furniture. The leather satchel resting on it looked like a prop from an Indiana Jones movie. Morgan picked up the sheet of paper beside it and began to read.

Hannah peered over his shoulder. "What does it say?" Maybe they were supposed to have sex on the floor and pretend they were jungle explorers. That might be fun.

Morgan had a funny look on his face. "I'm supposed to make you my prisoner and punish you. We're supposed to use all the accessories in the bag."

Hannah took a step back toward the door, and felt her knees quiver. It didn't take a genius to understand the genesis of this particular scenario. In the group session she had admitted to having trust issues. The Drs. Hurst were clearly testing her boundaries and her faith in her fiancé. She swallowed her instinctive misgivings. "Well, okay then. I'm game."

Morgan wasn't fooled. He dropped the sheet of paper on the bench and came to where she stood, plastered against her escape route. He brushed a strand of hair from her hot cheek. "Our time here is private, Hannah. We can do whatever we want."

She bit her lip. "I'm fine. We're in this together. We should follow the instructions."

His expression was troubled. "Are you sure?"

She nodded, beyond speech.

He stared at her for several long seconds, his eyes narrowed. Then he shrugged. "If that's what you want." He turned away, reaching for the satchel. "You'll need to get naked."

She had to force her feet to move. Her heart was pounding so loudly in her ears, she felt dizzy. She wasn't wearing much. It was summer in Florida. In a matter of seconds she had slipped out of her knit skirt, tank top, undies, and shoes.

Morgan's smoke-colored eyes widened when he turned to face her. She saw him swallow. His voice was low and ragged. "Come here." The blindfold in his hands looked sinister. But she obeyed.

As he slipped it over her head and smoothed her hair back into place, she shivered, blind and helpless. She'd never been a fan of the dark. Once, long before she went to live with Grammy and Papaw, her mother had made her hide in a closet while Vivian entertained a gentleman friend.

She had told Hannah that the man didn't like children, and Vivian didn't want him to know she had a daughter. The act was more careless than cruel. Vivian didn't have it in her to be deliberately mean. But she was extraordinarily self-centered, and her needs always came first.

The closet wasn't a terrible incarceration. The gap under the door was wide, and light filtered through enough to keep the small prison from being totally dark. Vivian gave Hannah a box of animal crackers and a sippy cup of milk. But beyond that, her young daughter had been on her own, terrified that if she made a noise, the man who didn't like children would do something to her.

As an adult, she had no idea how long she stayed in the closet. It seemed like days, but it was probably no more than two or three hours. Vivian's trysts usually lasted about that long. But eventually Hannah had to go to the bathroom, and as her discomfort grew, so did the depth of the scar on her emotions.

She hated her mother and loved her mother, and the terrible dichotomy ripped at the fragile fabric of her childhood.

Now Hannah stood immobile, assimilating the sensation of total darkness. The blindfold was leather, lined with some soft fabric that might have been silk. She smelled the pleasant odor of the tanned hide. Her eyelashes fluttered helplessly against the slippery fabric.

Morgan took her wrists and brought them together at her waist. She sucked in a startled breath when she felt him bind them tightly. Her skin crawled with unease. She forced herself to take deep breaths. This was Morgan. He would never hurt her.

Despite her mental discomfort, her body began to respond instinctively to the feel of her lover's touch against her naked flesh. As he manipulated her limbs, his hands brushed her skin gently, leaving little sparks of pleasure everywhere he passed.

He led her toward the center of the room and put her up against the pole, belly first. Then he lifted her hands and somehow immobilized them. Was there a hook? Her fingers fluttered futilely at the air, but she was secured at her wrists and the only thing her touch could verify was the pole itself.

She felt Morgan gather her hair and push it forward so

that it fell over her right breast. Then he kissed the nape of her neck. She sensed him move away and then heard rustling that was probably the sound of him undressing.

She shifted her feet on the rough mat. Had the directions said for him to remain silent? Or was he making that call on his own? She should have insisted on reading the sheet of paper from the start, but a part of her hadn't wanted to know.

She felt and heard him return to where she was standing. He put his hands on her shoulders. His palms were big, warm, slightly calloused.

He kissed the shell of her ear, tracing it with his tongue. "Are you ready?"

She nodded jerkily. "Will you tell me what you're going to do?" Her words came out in an embarrassing whisper. She felt totally vulnerable.

He rubbed her arms. "I'm supposed to whip you."

The guttural note in his voice sounded a lot like excitement.

Despite herself, her thighs tightened and her sex responded to his blunt assertion with a trickle of moisture. She cleared her throat. "And then?"

He pressed his large, hard frame to her back, bringing their bodies in contact from head to toe. His erection nestled between her ass cheeks, rubbing suggestively. "And then fuck you."

Her head drooped, her forehead resting against the pole. "Oh."

His arms slid around her, and he palmed her breasts. "I've looked at the whip, my love. It's made of thin strips of soft rubber. It will sting, but it's not meant to do any real damage."

"Oh, goody."

He chuckled at her surly tone. "We're supposed to play out this fantasy to the best of our ability. So that means you're not my fiancée. I'm not your sweetheart. Can you do that?"

She sniffed dismissively, but the arrogant expression lost something given her current position. "When I was nineteen I played the lead in a dinner theater production of *Oklahoma*. I'm a natural."

His chuckle sent a warm breath of air against the nape of her neck. "Okay, then. Duly noted." He tweaked her nipples and released her. "I'll finish getting ready, and then we'll get this show on the road."

Before she could protest, he slipped a gag between her teeth and knotted it firmly behind her head. She struggled instinctively, and this time he offered no comfort, verbal or otherwise.

As she gasped for breath, almost hyperventilating, she sensed his physical absence. Her heartbeat sped up as nervous energy and a completely understandable feeling of anxiety filtered into her bloodstream. Already her arms were tired, and her legs were shaky.

The first strike of the whip took her completely by surprise. She cried out, more from shock than actual pain. She braced herself and managed to remain mute for the next lashes. The thin strips stung, but she could tell they weren't breaking the skin.

Morgan's voice, slightly breathless, came out as a rough growl. "You deserve fifty lashes. You tease men and make them want you, but you refuse to let them have your body. So, you'll pay."

Blindfolded, bound and gagged, she had no choice but to submit. Encased in darkness, she reached for a port in the storm. She concentrated fiercely on Morgan. His scent. The sound of his labored breathing. The image of his tough, nude body.

Gradually her pulse slowed. She was safe. Morgan would protect her, even from himself. But no matter how many times she repeated the reassuring litany, her mind refused to settle. She hated feeling helpless. She'd spent her adult life making sure she was in control of every situation. Now that need to hold the reins was deeply ingrained.

As though Morgan sensed her distraction, his next blow landed with more force. She inhaled sharply and choked as dust and tiny cloth fibers clogged her throat. Tears stung her eyes. In the midst of her total capitulation, a sudden and completely unexpected arousal began to build. It was as if someone flipped a switch and her libido came alive, pushing aside all other concerns.

Was she insane? Getting turned on by this pseudo-domination? The longer the punishment went on, the more she wanted Morgan. Fantasies bloomed inside her head. In her mind, their roles were reversed. The thought of lashing Morgan with the whip—of having him completely at her mercy—made her wild with hunger.

She wanted to taunt him, to provoke him into prolonging her penalty. But she was helpless as a babe.

At long last, the final strike marked her butt. Her tormentor moved away. She waited for him to free her so she could pounce on him and ravage him with her sudden, urgent appetite for sex.

But her test was not over.

Morgan returned. His hands roved over her buttocks, smoothing, stroking, testing the irritated flesh. Then she felt him probe between her legs and separate her labia. She started to struggle in earnest. She tried to speak, but her words came out as nothing more than strangled, garbled syllables.

He ignored her. He pulled her backward so that she was awkwardly bent at the waist, and then he positioned his shaft and surged upward, possessing her with one firm stroke. She groaned in pleasure.

Her physical discomfort faded as her body zeroed in on the thick, firm flesh that was screwing her so forcefully and so well. Again she struggled for control, and again she was forced to accept her total helplessness.

He fucked her for what seemed like hours. Every time she thought he was about to come, he withdrew, reined himself in, and started all over again. It was as frustrating as it was wonderful. Her unnatural position and the ache in her arms, shoulders, and legs made it difficult to relax. That tension, coupled with the lack of direct contact where she craved it, made it impossible for her to come.

Her body strained for the peak, getting close time and again, only to fall short of the prize.

Time ceased to have meaning. Ordinarily she would have been checking her watch, cautioning Morgan about their need to finish without overstaying their appointment. But she was barely able to process a coherent thought.

She was hanging, literally in limbo, as the man she loved controlled her body thoroughly and masterfully.

His mighty thrusts shook her, smashing her breasts against the pole. His hands gripped her hips and lifted her into his strokes, so that her toes barely touched the floor. She was a puppet for his pleasure.

At last he shouted and went rigid as he finally let himself go, climaxing with an urgent pistoning of his hips that went on and on.

In the aftermath, the only sound was his labored breathing.

He left her then, and she slumped against her bonds, exhausted and unfulfilled. Images whirled in her brain. She had a good imagination. Despite the blindfold, she could see the two of them locked in a carnal embrace.

At long last he returned. She felt him lift her wrists and free them from the hook. But he left her bound, gagged, and blindfolded. He scooped her into his arms as if she weighed nothing at all and carried her a few steps. Then he lowered her onto her back.

She realized with dull awareness that he had laid her on the narrow wooden bench. Her feet rested awkwardly on the floor. Her hands curled on her belly.

And then she felt his hair brush the insides of her thighs as he kissed her poor, aching sex. The touch of his tongue on her swollen flesh sent lightning flashing through her abdomen. She gasped and tried to close her legs.

But he was determined and strong and of course, in control. He ran the tip of his tongue ever so gently across her nerve center. She screamed inside as liquid pleasure tightened her pelvis. He rubbed his thumbs over her hipbones, suckled at her opening, and buried his face in her sex as she climaxed with a muffled cry.

When it was over, she was boneless, exhausted, completely unable to function. Even when he untied her wrists and removed the blindfold and gag, she lay on the bench unmoving, waiting for her heart to stop running the Indy 500.

She licked her dry lips. Moments later she felt her head lifted as Morgan held a bottle of water to her mouth. She drank thirstily, letting him take care of her.

But sooner or later she had to look at him. When she

opened her eyes, the overhead lights were harsh and almost painful. He was crouched at her side, his eyes watchful. She sensed he was waiting for some response from her, but she had no clue what he wanted her to say or even if she had it in her to be coherent at the moment.

Finally, she managed a weak smile. "What time is it?" That wasn't what she had intended to say, but the words popped out.

He glanced at his watch, the only item that kept him from being completely nude. "Six ten." He touched her cheek. "Are you okay?"

She thought about it. "I think so."

"You want to get dressed?"

She struggled to sit up. "I'd say I don't have much choice. The receptionist leaves at six forty-five, and we still have to fill out our post session forms."

Morgan helped her to her feet. "Shit."

She nodded. "My feelings exactly."

They dressed in silence. She tried to analyze her feelings at the moment, and the one foremost emotion she came up with was embarrassment. What did *she* have to be embarrassed about? She'd been the helpless victim in all this.

When Morgan opened the door, it was all she could do to walk through it. They traversed the short hallway and entered the waiting room. Thankfully, it was empty, and the woman behind the counter was on the phone.

Two envelopes labeled with their names stood just inside the window. Morgan retrieved them and handed one to Hannah, along with a pencil. Then they retreated to opposite sides of the room and began their debriefing task.

Hannah stared at the first question blankly. *Did you enjoy this session with your fiancé?* There was a box to mark *yes* and one to mark *no*. Her pencil hovered over the choices. It should have been an easy answer.

She started to tick *no*, but then she remembered the climax that had racked her body with long minutes of frantic release. Maybe *yes*, then.

But what about the helplessness? The loss of control? What about the aching limbs, dry mouth, and shivering uncertainty? Okay, perhaps *no*.

She dithered for another thirty seconds and decided to skip that question for the moment. On to number two. *Did you feel safe with your fiancé?* That was easy. *Yes.*

Would you have enjoyed the situation if you and Morgan had been in opposite roles? Yes.

More or less? That was a stumper. Sure, she would have gotten a kick out of having her macho boyfriend at her mercy. But more than she enjoyed today? She picked the second answer. It was as honest as she knew how to be.

Which was more difficult to concede—physical or mental control? Skip that one, too.

At any time did you feel in danger of being hurt? No.

At any time were you angry with your partner? She winced. *Yes, but only briefly.* She wrote the explanation in the margin.

Did you feel dominated sexually? Yes.

Did you feel dominated mentally or emotionally? Yes.

Which was more difficult to endure? Again her pencil hovered. *The mental.*

Do you think your partner enjoyed today's session? She remembered the look on Morgan's face when she opened her eyes. *I don't know.*

Do you think men are capable of monogamy? The out-of-context question threw her. Where had that come from? And what did it have to do with today? She thought of

Morgan, dear, dependable, loving Morgan. The man who had proposed to her and given her a lovely ring. She bit her lip and wrote *I don't know.*

After that there was a series of questions about the room, its effect on her libido, how she felt during the act of intercourse, etc. Those were all easy questions.

Finally she was finished except for the two she had skipped near the top. She went back to them. *Did you enjoy this session with your fiancé?* She cheated. Instead of marking yes or no, she wrote in the margin *not entirely*.

And the last blank... *Which was more difficult to concede — physical or mental control?* She nibbled her eraser. The fact that she'd thought about the closet incident with her mother said volumes. She hated ceding physical control. But what about the feeling of utter helplessness, unable to speak, unable to direct the course of events?

It was the physical situation, however, that impacted her mental control, so she wrote *physical*.

With a sigh, she slipped her questionnaire into the envelope and sealed it. When she looked up, Morgan was already standing by the door, waiting patiently.

He took her arm as they left. "Let's leave your car here for the moment. We can have a nice, quiet dinner together, and then we'll fetch the car and I'll follow you home."

It sounded like a great plan to her. Her stomach was growling, and they were around the corner from one of their favorite haunts, a French bistro with intimate candlelit tables and food to die for.

Morgan watched her as she ate, his gaze so intent that she finally put down her fork and glared at him. "What are you doing?"

A corner of his mouth curled in a grin. "Remembering."

Her face flamed red, and she buried her nose in her

water glass, drinking thirstily. Even now, the dry taste of the gag lingered. "Well, stop it."

He chuckled and cut into his chicken. "You're blushing." He said it mildly, but she bristled.

"It's hot in here."

"If you say so. But on the other hand, it might be the memory of me striping your ass."

"Morgan, for heaven's sake." Her gaze darted wildly from side to side, trying to see if anyone had overheard his outrageous remark.

She shook her fork at him. "Behave." She twirled her fork in a slender piece of pasta and put it to her mouth. As she opened her lips, chewed, and swallowed, his eyes followed every move.

She moved restlessly in her seat. "Stop it."

He raised an eyebrow. "What?"

He sucked at portraying innocence. "You know what." She gulped a mouthful of wine and felt her nipples harden beneath the sheer fabric of her bra. Morgan noticed... of course. She leaned forward, hoping to catch him off guard. "Tell me about some of your questions."

He shook his head, his smile strained as he adjusted himself beneath the tablecloth. "Nope."

"Just one?" The curiosity was eating her alive.

"Don't be so nosy."

"I don't like secrets."

He sobered. "There are a lot of things you don't like. And I'd say today was one of them."

She looked away, slightly abashed that he would refer to it so carelessly. "Parts of it were okay."

He took her hand in one of his, drawing her attention back to his face. His gentle grip stilled her restless fingers where they played with breadcrumbs on the tablecloth. "I'd like to say it was difficult for me, as well," he muttered. "But I have to be honest with you."

She cocked her head, studying his look of shamed, mulish defiance. "By all means. Be honest."

He ran his free hand through his hair and rubbed his thumb in the center of her palm. The slow caress was surprisingly erotic. "It was bloody fucking awesome."

8

Morgan figured she deserved to know the truth. He wasn't an enlightened male after all. Scratch the surface, and he was a horny bastard like all the rest. And it had seriously gotten his rocks off to tie her up and punish her.

The shocked look on her face was priceless. She took a sip of her wine and continued to stare at him, apparently speechless.

He shrugged. "Not what you expected to hear, I guess." Now he felt guilty. He should have kept his mouth shut. He was supposed to be teaching her to trust him, not giving her reasons to toss his ring back in his face.

She leaned back in her chair. "What was so great about it? For you, I mean."

She appeared genuinely curious, so he tried to put his feelings into words, not exactly a guy strength. He shrugged. "At first I spent a lot of energy wondering if you were okay, mentally I mean. I knew I wasn't really hurting you. But soon, the whole visual scenario grabbed me. God, if you could have seen yourself." He swallowed, his tongue thick, and grabbed his water glass, feeling raw heat grip his package as the memories flooded back.

She licked her lips. "Was it just the nudity? Or the setting? Or the props?"

"It was all of it," he muttered. "Some kind of primitive male dominance thing."

Finally, she smiled. And the relief he experienced took on tidal-wave proportions. He felt her bare foot play with his shin.

She laughed at him. "Well, don't look so guilty. It's all that testosterone. It's bound to make you crazy sometimes."

Her humor diffused the near-painful postmortem, and suddenly they were back on even ground.

As they left the restaurant, she linked her arm in his. "Well, if there is any justice in the world, I'll get my turn. You wait and see."

Hannah worked hard on Wednesday. She was organized and efficient and productive. She filed tax receipts. She cleared her desk. She updated her calendar. She was on top of things.

But none of her ultra superwoman activities managed to erase the memory of being helpless and at the mercy of a man. Morgan. Her fiancé. Her big problem.

He continued to hint at meeting her parents. She continued to ignore him. In an attempt to deflect his single-mindedness, she had urged him to set up a dinner with *his* parents. So tonight— much sooner than she had anticipated—she and Morgan were off to Ocala to meet Mr. and Mrs. Webber.

Morgan had offered to take them all to dinner at a nice steak house, but his mother insisted on cooking. So the only thing Hannah had to do was pick out a dress that made her look like the girl every mom wants her son to bring home.

Easier said than done. She discarded four frocks that showed too much cleavage. The skirts on two more were too short. A trio of sundresses left her back bare—too racy. The sheer fabric in a handful of others showed her nipples.

It occurred to her that maybe she had too many clothes. It was definitely a weakness.

Finally, in desperation, she pulled out the dress she had worn to Grammy's funeral. Both of her maternal grandparents had died far too young. Hannah had been furious with God at the time. Lots of people lived to be ninety or a hundred. Why not *her* grandparents? How was it fair that they died in their early seventies? God had been remarkably silent, and eventually, her bitterness faded. She didn't have it in her to maintain such self-destructive anger.

And after all, she had filled the void with so many wonderful new surrogate family members, not the least of whom was Elda. The close relationship with the older woman shored up the emotional gap in Hannah's life.

Hannah stared in the mirror at the navy knit dress she wore. Its three-quarter-length sleeves and collar edged in white were suitably puritanical. The hem landed discreetly just across her kneecaps. With the appropriate bra, not a sign of a nipple. Perfect.

When Morgan picked her up that evening, he tried to suppress a smirk and failed. "Pearls, Hannah? Good Lord. Did I miss something?"

She slid into the passenger seat and waited for him to close her door and take his place behind the wheel. She smoothed her skirt. "I don't always favor the bohemian look," she said primly. "I felt it important to dress nicely for your parents."

He spared her one quick glance before returning his concentration to the hellish rush-hour traffic. "All you have to do is be yourself and they'll love you, sweetheart. They're very nonjudgmental people."

"No mother is nonjudgmental about her son's female companionship."

He chuckled. "If you say so."

It took just over an hour to make the trip. Which was good, because any longer, and Hannah's nerves would have reached the breaking point.

But her worries were needless. The elder Webbers turned out to be even nicer than she had hoped or expected. Stan Webber was much like his son in build, looks, and demeanor. Elaina Webber, also slender and tall, was a bit reserved at first, but warmed up as the evening progressed. Her frosted hair was cut in a simple bob and she wore black slacks and a colorful, dressy blouse. She had prepared fresh broiled redfish with a lime salsa and served it with new potatoes and a Caesar salad.

Over dinner, the conversation was general. Hannah suspected that Morgan had warned his parents in advance how to behave, because there were no awkward questions about Hannah's family or setting wedding dates.

Stan had retired recently and had sold his very successful car-rental business. Hannah sensed he was still coming to terms with the unaccustomed leisure time. The two of them bonded over stories of her many clients and their eccentricities.

Elaina had been a stay-at-home mom until Morgan went off to college. Afterward, she had renewed her teaching certificate and now taught eighth grade English. There appeared to be a bit of tension concerning Stan's desire to travel now that his time was free versus his wife's newly resurrected career.

After one or two snappish remarks were exchanged,

Hannah hastened to turn the conversation to a discussion of Morgan's theme park project. That did the trick. Both parents were justifiably proud of their son's success.

Stan stirred a third teaspoon of sugar into his coffee, despite his wife's frown, and grinned at Hannah. "You should have seen him in elementary school. One time he built an entire city out of pretzels, copper wire, and glue. The school had promised a new bicycle to whoever came up with the most original project design. Morgan was bound and determined to win. Even though he'd just gotten a bike for Christmas that year."

Morgan rolled his eyes. "It wasn't the bike, Dad. It was the competition. And I gave the bike to charity."

His mother patted his arm. "You always did like to win, son. Nothing wrong with that."

∽

Morgan sighed inwardly. He couldn't gauge the evening's success. Hannah was on her best behavior. Not a single anecdote about skydiving or reckless pursuits. If he didn't know better, he'd think she was the quietest, most conservative woman he'd ever met.

Not that she wasn't charming. She'd won over his dad instantly, and even his mother was now smiling genuinely and offering to share her sacred angel food cake recipe. But it was a bit eerie seeing Hannah dressed up like a Stepford wife. Where were her outrageous wit and her *to-hell-with-what-the-world-thinks* smile?

It was almost as if she was following a script, acting out the part of the perfect fiancée. It seriously freaked him out. No way did it compute that the erotically beautiful and sexy female he'd made love to in a jungle hut was in fact this same woman.

Hannah was quiet on the way home. Morgan drove in silence, with plenty to occupy his mind. He'd hoped that seeing his parents... witnessing their long-term, happy marriage might make her feel more secure about her own wedding plans. But with Hannah, who knew?

When she finally did speak, it was on an entirely different subject. She stared out the windshield at the sea of red and white lights on the interstate and wound a long strand of hair around her finger. "I wonder what tomorrow's session will be like?"

His dick surged to attention with a Pavlovian response that made it difficult to drive, much less carry on a conversation. "Who knows?" His voice came out sounding like rough gravel.

Hannah folded her hands demurely in her lap as though her conventional dress was actually dictating her responses. "I think it would be fun if I had a chance to tie you up." She said it nonchalantly, but his body got the message loud and clear.

He shifted in his seat. "We don't have to wait for some shrink to give us permission," he said. "Feel free to have a go at it tonight if you want."

She half turned to face him. "Really?"

He shrugged, trying to be cool about the whole thing. But the boulder in his throat made it tough. "I'm not a total Neanderthal. Turnabout is fair play."

When Hannah reached across the console and touched his thigh, he nearly ran off the road. She stroked lightly, almost as if she didn't realize she was doing it. "Don't you have to be up early tomorrow?"

"Doesn't matter." She'd reduced him to terse sentences. "I can sleep when I'm old."

She chuckled. "Men will do anything to get sex. I find that strangely endearing."

He kept his attention on the road. "It's not exactly breaking news," he muttered.

She moved her hand to his forearm, combing the light fuzz of hair with her fingernail. "I liked your parents."

Oh, God. "Could we please not talk about my folks when I have a boner?"

She giggled. "What *can* we talk about, then?"

He shuddered, his skin tight all over his body. "You could expand on the tying-me-up thing. Is that all? Don't you want to punish me?" *Please let her say yes.*

"Not so much punish as torture. You know… sexually. To see how long you can hold out without climaxing."

He cursed beneath his breath. Maybe he should pull off the road. His concentration was seriously compromised. Thankfully, he was now only minutes away from her driveway. When he made it there without wrecking, he put the car in park with a jerk and turned to face her, grabbing her and dragging her toward him for a desperate kiss.

She kissed him back for maybe thirty seconds before she wiggled away and opened her door. He grabbed for her hand. "Wait."

She slid from the car and bent down to peer at him through the open car door. "Anticipation makes things that much hotter, don't you think? I'll see you tomorrow at four thirty."

Hannah knew she was being mean. Perhaps it was payback for being tied up. Until now, she'd never thought of herself as a vindictive person, but the look of astonishment on Morgan's face when she left him hanging (or not) was sweet vindication for what he'd put her through.

True, he'd simply been following directions. But he'd had the gall to admit that he enjoyed her subjugation. So he deserved to suffer a bit, the rat.

As she showered and got ready for bed, she began to realize that her petty revenge might have backfired. She was jumpy and aroused and wishing she hadn't been so quick to send him away. Especially when he seemed willing to let her turn the tables and make him *her* prisoner.

She settled beneath the covers and picked up the phone. When he answered on the second ring, she made her voice a soft purr. "Are you naked?"

She heard the rough chuckle on the other end. "Is this an obscene phone call?"

She twisted the cord around her finger. "Define obscene."

"Naughty. Intended to serve as foreplay."

"Then yes."

There was a long silence and she heard him sigh, a ragged sound that conveyed more than sexual frustration. "Before we indulge in phone sex, my love, I think we need to talk."

She pouted, though he couldn't see her face. "Talk, talk, talk. Talk is cheap. I like a man of action."

"I'm serious, Hannah."

She gulped. She'd never heard that note in his voice before. "I'm sorry," she said quietly. "Of course we can talk."

"Did you like my parents?"

"Definitely. They're both lovely people, just like their son."

"Flattery, Hannah? You really must think I'm easy."

"A girl can try," she teased softly.

"They've been married a very long time, you know. And they're still happy. She looks after his health. He changes the oil in her car. They're devoted to each other."

She chewed her bottom lip. "Is there a *but* in there somewhere?"

"Not at all. I wanted you to see that I come from a family where marriage is for keeps. It's what I know. It's what I expect."

She couldn't think of a thing to say.

After an awkward pause, he coughed and muttered something she couldn't quite hear. "There's something else, Hannah, something I want you to hear loud and clear."

"I'm all ears." Her flippant response wasn't in keeping with the serious tenor of the conversation, but his dogged determination to make her see life his way was disturbing. He didn't seem to realize that *her* life experiences were the direct opposite of his. And it took two to make a marriage work.

"You don't have to set a wedding date."

Her heart dropped to her stomach at his terse statement. "I beg your pardon?"

"Our agreement," he said, irritation in his voice. But at himself or at her? "I wasn't being fair. We'll go through with the sexual counseling, because it's the right thing to do, and I think we'll learn something from it. But as of tonight it no longer has strings attached. I don't want a bride I have to badger into marrying me. If and when you're ready, you can set a date. But until then I won't nag you. Not anymore. And

I apologize for pushing you up until now. It wasn't fair and it was wrong."

He sounded humble and defeated. She was astounded. What had brought about this change of heart? Her hands trembled and she clenched the phone more tightly. "There's nothing to apologize for, Morgan. When a man proposes to a woman and she accepts, it's natural for him to expect her to choose a wedding date. I'm the problem here. I'm the one who should apologize." She swallowed hard. "Do you want your ring back?"

"God, no."

The knot in her stomach relaxed a fraction. "Then what is this conversation all about?"

"It's about me respecting you and your wishes. It's about me ceding control to the woman I love."

"Oh, Morgan." Tears welled in her eyes and trickled down her cheeks.

After a brief silence, he spoke again. "Good night, Hannah." And then he hung up on her.

She clicked out of the call and scooted down under the covers, pulling them to her chin. Her stomach felt funny and her chest was tight. What was she going to do about Morgan? She didn't deserve a man like him, and the gods were surely going to slice apart her happiness sooner or later. She couldn't let him get hurt in the process.

∽

On Thursday Hannah had lunch with Elda. Afterwards the two women set to work cleaning out one of the apartment's tightly packed closets. The center was having a group rummage sale, and Elda was determined to make a few bucks.

Hannah's adopted grandmother was unusually animated, and her cheeks were flushed with excitement. When Hannah pressed her for the reason, Elda grinned slyly. "I'm taking a cruise next spring with Arnie. We've signed up early, 'cause that gives you a good price break. The French Riviera..." She sighed blissfully, her face as dreamy as a girl's. "Do you think I can lose fifty pounds by then?"

Hannah frowned inwardly. "Do you really know Arnie all that well, Elda? And what if things between you cool off by then?"

Elda snorted and examined a fur wrap that was about as useful in Florida as an outdoor pool at the North Pole. She tossed it in the *get-rid-of* pile. "Sometimes you think too much, Hannah, my girl. Life is meant to be lived. My dear husband would have laughed his ass off if he thought I wanted to mourn him forever. He'd tell me to get off my butt and enjoy whatever time I have left. And I intend to."

"I'm not questioning your desire to have fun, Elda. I'm all for it. But what if Arnie turns out to be not such a great guy?"

Elda shook her head. "You young people are too damn scared all the time. Terrorists, global warming, bird flu... If I let myself dwell on all the bad stuff in the world, I'd never crawl out of bed. You have to take a few chances. And not just by jumping out of airplanes. You have to be brave enough to get out there and try to be happy."

"And if life kicks you in the teeth?" Hannah asked wryly.

Elda slipped her arms into a red satin blouse that was at least two sizes too small. "Then you're in good company, honey. Now open that big box and let's see what's in it. I need some vacation cash."

Hannah was not at all sure she was ready to meet

Morgan that afternoon. She'd planned on teasing them both with some titillating phone sex the night before, and instead, Morgan had sailed into deep waters.

What he'd said to her should have been a relief. The apology should have made her happy. And it did. On some level. But it also made her feel guilty as hell. She wanted to show him how much she loved him, but if she came clean—if she poured her heart out—he'd have her walking down the aisle in no time.

This time she didn't wait around in the parking garage. It was raining, and she was glad she didn't have to get drenched getting into the building. A line of thunderstorms rolled through the city, the brilliant flashes of lightning followed by loud cracks of thunder making her flinch. She did not like storms.

She also didn't like the thought of being locked in an elevator if the power went out, so she jogged up thirty-two flights of stairs. Perhaps the extra exercise would counteract the French pastry she'd had for dessert the night before.

When she saw Morgan in the office waiting room, she told herself that the breathlessness she experienced was a result of physical exertion. Every woman in the room looked at him, even the ones who were there with a partner. The Hursts shared this half of the floor with three other doctors, so there was a certain anonymity that Hannah appreciated. It would have creeped her out if everyone seated nearby knew what she and Morgan were about to do.

But on second thought, she didn't even know what was about to happen. She met her fiancé's gaze calmly and brought her lips to his for a quick kiss. "Do you have the key already?" she whispered.

He opened his palm briefly. "All set."

He steered her toward the door marked *exam rooms* and

they exited into the hallway of bland, unadorned doors. Their assigned spot was the same, room number six.

When they opened the door, Hannah actually glanced back at the number to make sure they were in the right place. No sign of a jungle hut remained.

Morgan whistled and rubbed his chin, an arrested expression on his face. "Now, this is a surprise."

Hannah surveyed the room with reluctant interest. "That's an understatement."

The room had been turned into a luxurious hotel suite. Flowers on a side table. A minibar. A nice sound system with music softly playing. And a king-size bed made up with a white linen comforter and ultrasoft white cotton sheets. The covers had been turned down invitingly. A chocolate strawberry encased in clear plastic wrap rested on each pillow.

When Morgan scanned the sheet of directions, his face went blank. He handed them to Hannah. "Take a look."

Hannah read the paper with a sinking heart.

Today you're to pretend you are enjoying the first night of your honeymoon. Hannah is to put on the wedding dress hanging behind the screen. Morgan can wear only the tux shirt and pants. Both of you are to imagine that today was your wedding day and that you had chosen to be celibate for the past month in preparation for your wedding night.

Hannah clenched the paper in her fist. This was far scarier than being bound and gagged. She stood irresolute, genuinely unsure if she could go through with this.

Morgan's jaw was granite. He wasn't a fool. She was doing a piss-poor job of hiding her discomfort. He shoved his hands in his pockets. "It's voluntary. No one is going to make you do this."

She tried to laugh. "It's way more luxurious than Tuesday's little play date. Wonder if we have to pay for the mini-bar. I bet that jar of macadamia nuts is at least nine dollars—"

Morgan stepped behind her, putting his hand over her mouth to stop her babbling, and wrapping his other arm around her waist. There was no way he could miss the fact that her heart was beating like a trapped wild bird. He nuzzled her ear. "Don't panic, sweetheart. This isn't real. Just breathe, Hannah."

His warm, comforting strength eventually broke through the utter confusion and anxiety that gripped her. She slumped against him. "I'm okay. I swear."

He released her and took her face in his hands, studying her intently. "You still look pale."

She bowed her head, for the moment unable to face the gentle understanding in his steady gaze. "I'm fine." She gazed at the decorative screen that sectioned off one corner of the room. "I can at least put on the dress."

"Only if you want to."

She'd needed to give him something. Anything. A shred of encouragement and hope. She made herself smile. "I hope it isn't all frilly. I look like crap in ruffles." Before she could change her mind, she evaded his hold and retreated behind the screen. Without looking at the dress, she stripped off her clothes.

She stood there in her bra and panties shivering, even though the room was plenty warm. It was just a dress, damn it. Not the holy grail of unwed young females everywhere. Nothing bad was going to happen just because she tried it on. To delay the inevitable for a moment, she took a brush from her purse and ran it through her hair until the heavy tresses lay silky and smooth against her back.

Finally, when she could dither no longer, she picked up

the heavy garment. Even the weight of the thing seemed threatening. She took a deep breath, slid the fairy-tale princess frock over her head, and struggled to zip the side closure. Then she looked into the cheval mirror someone had helpfully provided.

Her reflection was shocking in the extreme. She wiped her damp palms on her discarded jeans and tugged at the bodice of the dress. Then, with courage she didn't know she possessed, she stepped from behind the screen and confronted her patiently waiting fiancé.

He'd just slid his arms into the tux shirt and as he turned around, he sucked in a breath. "Oh, my God."

9

Hannah's face was troubled. "Does it fit?" Morgan felt like he was traversing a minefield. His throat was tight with all the things he wanted to say about growing old in rocking chairs and giving her babies to love and cuddle.

Instead, he leaned against the dresser and dredged up a lecherous smile. "It will do." He deliberately raked her from head to toe with a lustful gaze. "You look damn hot, Hannah."

She shifted from one foot to the other. Her hands played in the skirt's voluminous folds. It was a fairy-tale dress; strapless, the waist fitted, the skirt a billowing froth of virginal white. The tops of her breasts peeked invitingly over the embroidered satin bodice. Morgan imagined for a moment seeing her like this on their wedding day. Watching her walk down the aisle to pledge her love and commitment to him.

It was a painful image. Because he knew it might never happen.

Despite his mental turmoil, he kept his smile in place,

trying to play his part successfully "Aren't you going to comment on your groom's appearance?"

He was barefooted. Hannah had emerged before he had a chance to button his shirt, so it hung open, exposing his chest. He saw her eyes go from his face to his abs to the front of his pants. There was nothing he could do about the bulge there.

She swallowed visibly, and her tongue peeked out to wet her lips. "You look very handsome."

"And sexy?" He leered at her, trying to resurrect her sense of humor. She still looked extremely nervous and uneasy, and he sure as heck wasn't going to make love to a woman in her condition.

He closed the gap between them until his legs pressed into the fluffy netting that surrounded her with a cloudlike, chastity-preserving, no-go zone. Lightly he stroked one finger across the gentle swells of creamy flesh pushed up by the whale-boned edge of her frock.

The curves were soft. He tucked his finger in the shadowy gap between her breasts. "You didn't answer my question," he said huskily. He could smell her intoxicating perfume. And see the tracery of pale blue veins beneath her delicate skin.

She closed her eyes. "Sexy... yes." Her voice was slurred as his roving fingertip moved to one side and brushed a nipple. His progress was hampered by the close-fitting bodice.

Morgan bent his head, brushing a kiss across her cheekbone. "A month is a long time," he murmured, getting into his assigned part. "All day I've been imagining the moment when I'll finally be able to slide between your legs and take care of this ache."

She turned her head, trying to find his mouth with hers. "Kiss me."

He obliged her. But he denied them the hungry mating of lips they both wanted. He kissed her forehead, her ears, her nose, her chin. His hands grasped her shoulders, holding her up, or so it seemed. Her arms remained at her sides, her fingers still twisting and clenching restlessly.

He deliberately moved closer, using his height and size to intimidate her. "It's our wedding night," he muttered. "I want to make it last."

He scooped her into his arms and strode to the bed. Instead of joining her, he dropped her gently on the mattress and went to the bar, with shaking hands pouring them each a glass of champagne. In the distance, fierce rumbles of thunder roared, but the heavy drapes over the two small windows shut out the lightning flashes.

When he turned back to face her, she was propped against the headboard, legs outstretched as she unwrapped her chocolate-covered fruit. He lifted an eyebrow. "Is it wise to eat that while you still have on your dress?"

She stuffed the whole strawberry in her mouth, finally seeming to come out of her state of frozen anxiety. She smiled at him as she chewed and swallowed. "I have a big mouth, Morgan. You know that."

Her naughty innuendo made him grin. "Ah, indeed. I never should have doubted you." He perched on the bed beside her, hip to hip, and offered her a glass. "To my blushing bride."

She took it from him and downed the entire contents in one thirsty gulp. "I don't blush," she said breathlessly, wiping her mouth with the back of her hand.

He took a sip of the surprisingly good champagne and set his own glass and hers on the bedside table. "Do you have to get drunk to make love to your groom?" He asked the question idly, wondering what she would say. He sensed a recklessness in her and wished he knew how to coax her into relaxing and letting things take their course.

She shrugged and smiled. "Aren't all brides nervous on their wedding nights?"

"Maybe a century ago. I wouldn't think there are too many surprises now."

"There might be."

"Such as?"

"Married sex could be different."

He frowned. "You keep saying that. And maybe it's true. But if so, I see it as a positive. You don't, apparently." Despite his best efforts, the conversation had turned serious.

She pulled her knees to her chest. He caught a glimpse of bare toes, and now the damn skirt poofed out like an exotic mushroom. She wrapped her arms around her legs. Her protective posture cried *leave me alone*.

But he couldn't. Not now. Not ever.

He winced. "So you're not denying it. You do think married sex is a negative."

She thrust out her bottom lip, her expression mulish. "Did you know that statistically the average man has seven sexual partners in his lifetime?"

"And where did you get this information? Oprah, maybe? You watch way too much TV with those old people. They're poisoning your brain." He tried to get a rise out of her, but she didn't bite.

She frowned at him. "It's true. I read it very recently. It was the CDC or somebody like that doing a scientific survey."

"So what's your point?"

"Monogamy is an unnatural state for the male animal of the species."

"What about eagles and wolves?"

That stopped her for a minute. She shook her head. "I don't know. I'm not a biologist. And besides... we're talking about human males."

"You're the one who mentioned the word animal."

She glared at him. "You should have been a lawyer since you're so damn good at arguing."

He held up his hands. "I'm sorry. I'll be quiet and let you finish your pathetic theory."

"Pathetic?" Her eyes tossed daggers at him.

He fingered the edge of her skirt where it pooled on the bedspread. "Statistics mean nothing to me. Besides, for every man who's had fifteen partners in his lifetime, there has to be a guy like me to even out the average. A one-woman man."

She snorted. "You weren't a virgin when we met."

He didn't touch that one. "I'd be completely happy with you, Hannah, and no one else until they plant me in the ground." Shit. He was supposed to be keeping this light, and instead he was making vows like he was a damn knight heading off to war.

Her face softened. "You're a sweetheart, Morgan."

Great. Now she was patronizing him. He cleared his throat. "We're wasting time. Shouldn't we get on with this wedding night scenario? I'd hate to flunk our test. Dr. Sheila scares me."

Hannah wrinkled her nose, looking apologetic. "I don't think I can do it... at least not like this."

Disappointment churned acid in his gut. "I see." She couldn't even *pretend* to have a wedding night with him. So the chances of him ever getting the real thing were pretty damn slim. He tried to ignore his mounting frustration, but keeping his voice calm was hard. "What do you suggest? Playing rummy for the next hour and a half? Sorry, babe. I'm fresh out of cards."

Her eyes narrowed, and he realized he'd blown it. She sat up straight, deepening her cleavage and drawing his gaze away from her face, where storm clouds gathered.

She snapped her fingers. "Focus, Webber. My eyes are up here. And quit jumping to conclusions. All I was trying to say is that I can't pretend we really got married today. If and when that happens, it will be a sacred moment. I think it would be sacrilegious to make light of something so important."

The muscles in his neck loosened and he hung his head, sucking in a raw lungful of much-needed air. "Sorry," he mumbled. "Then what *did* you mean?"

She ruffled his hair. "Let's make a game out of it. Why don't you be the evil Scottish laird and I'll be the poor English girl you've stolen from her father's farm? It can still be our wedding night, but you've kidnapped me and forced me into a marriage that I either have to agree to or be branded as a fallen woman and banished from polite society for the rest of my life."

He struggled not to grin, "Lord save me from women and their romance novels." He chuckled when she scowled. It was fun provoking her, but in truth, he was fascinated by her playful, creative mind. He glanced around the pseudo hotel suite in all its luxury. "This is hardly a historically accurate setting."

She lifted her chin. "It's called improvisation. A skill many unimaginative men lack."

He stood up and stripped off his shirt. "Not me. I'm imagining all sorts of things already."

Her face registered alarm. "What are you doing?"

He shoved his hands in his back pockets. "No self-respecting Scottish laird would wear a shirt in his own bedchamber. And besides, I had the servants stoke the fire so my virginal bride and I would be comfortable."

She drew her lips between her teeth. "Oh."

He was beginning to like this new role. His lovely fiancée looked excited and apprehensive all at the same time. She was beautiful sitting there on the bed with her hair tumbled about her shoulders and her face flushed with rosy color. For a split second he wished fervently that it *was* their wedding night. But then he locked the unwelcome thought away. No time for futile what-ifs. Not when the here and now was so titillating. He rubbed the side of his face. "What shall I call you?"

"What's wrong with Hannah?"

He tilted his head. "I'm not feeling it. How about Angelique?"

"That sounds French."

"Perhaps your mother was French."

She grinned. "Maybe *you* could be a romance writer."

He crossed his arms over his chest. "Don't change the subject, Angelique."

She tried to rise to her knees, but the dress hampered her movements. She gave up with a huff and returned to her original position against the headboard. "So what do I call you?"

He smirked. "I'm not changing my name. Morgan is Scottish."

"Is not."

"Is, too. It means *sea warrior*. Kind of sexy, don't you think?"

She rolled her eyes. "Good grief."

He stroked his chin. *"Angelique and the Sea Warrior*, I like it. I see bestsellerdom in my future."

She shook her head. "I see *dumb*. And it's right here in front of me."

He put his hands on his hips, curling his lip in a sneer. "Enough mockery, wench. Let's get on with it. We've already wasted forty-five minutes. And a two-hour wedding night won't even begin to satisfy me." He put his hands on her waist and lifted her from the bed, grunting when his back twinged from the awkward angle.

Hannah giggled. "Being a romance hero isn't so easy after all, is it?"

He glared down at her, working on his Scottish brogue. "I can do anything I set my mind to, lass. Which is how I snatched you right from under the nose of those weak Englishmen."

"They weren't weak. You drugged their mead."

He rubbed her upper arms, smiling slightly. "I win by fair means or foul. Ye'd do well to remember it."

She made a dash for the door, but she tripped over her skirt, and he dragged her back.

"Where do ye think ye're goin', my shrewish bride?"

She struggled in his grasp, her chest heaving. The twisting and turning threatened to free one of her curvy breasts from its confinement.

Hannah cried out with convincing passion, "I'll never submit, you barbaric oaf. You'll have to force me."

He sank his teeth into the soft flesh at the side of her neck and then bit her earlobe. "There'll be no force, my sweet bride. Not on this night. But you'll submit. That's a promise."

He wanted to rip the dress from her body, but it didn't belong to either of them, and it looked expensive. Instead, he found the zipper, and despite his big hands, managed to unfasten it.

It took him long, frustrating seconds to gather up all of the damn skirt and lift the dress over Hannah's head. He tossed it on a chair and turned to face his scantily clad captive.

She wore nothing but a pair of black bikini panties. Across her breasts a thin red crease gave testimony to how the top of the dress had gripped her delicate flesh. Her dark nipples were tightly budded, either from excitement or from anticipation or both, and her long, slender legs were tanned and lovely.

He scowled down at her. "Don't fight me, lass. It will only make it worse. And if you'll recall, I've not had a woman in a month."

She shoved him hard, both of her hands planted on his chest. "I don't want to hear about your sordid past. I'm a gently reared lady. And my innocence is a gift I hope to give to the man I love."

He grabbed a handful of her hair and guided her mouth to his. "Then he's a sorry bastard, because tonight that innocence is mine." He ground his lips on hers, giving no quarter. Angelique struggled, biting and kicking. He hissed in pain when her knee came perilously close to his groin. He wrapped his arms around her and dragged her toward the closet door. Given the detail with which the room had been outfitted, it was no surprise that a hotel-type robe hung on a hook, waiting to be used.

Morgan tucked it around her. "Pretend it's made of animal fur," he whispered. He blatantly toyed with her breasts as he slid her arms into the sleeves. Then, before she had a chance to realize what he was up to, he removed the tie belt and bound her hands at her back.

"What are you doing?" The words were breathless.

He picked her up and carried her back to the bed. "Merely ensuring that no bodily harm comes to me in the course of your induction."

"Induction?" Her voice wobbled.

"Into the ranks of the fallen innocents."

Again she struggled, but he was bigger and stronger, and he had the element of surprise in his favor. She didn't know what he was going to do.

He left her face down on the bed while he stripped out of his pants and underwear. His erection was painful, almost as if it really had been a month since he'd explored a woman's body with his sex. His heart was pounding and his legs were weak. And the hunger in his gut was unfeigned and too damn real for comfort.

When he was nude, he stood by the bed for a moment or two. Her face was turned away from him. The curve from her spine to her ass was so beautiful he wanted to record it with paint and canvas.

On the wall above the dresser hung a small, rectangular mirror. He lifted it off the nail and brought it to the bed, resting it against the headboard. Then he rolled his captive to her back, somewhat awkwardly given her bound wrists, and smiled down at her. "Now, my lass. I'll be having that wedding night I've been promised."

Hannah winced as her shoulders strained in their sockets. She'd been afraid to act out a real wedding night with Morgan. But this crazy charade might be worse in some ways. Because Morgan was entirely too happy in his role as the evil laird. And she had a feeling he had several naughty surprises up his sleeve. Or he would if he'd been wearing sleeves.

She tried not to look at his big, gorgeous body. Seeing

him with his dark hair tousled and that rakish gleam of humor in his eyes made her stomach do funny little flips. Her intimate flesh was damp already, stimulated by the game they were playing.

The robe in which Morgan had dressed her was little protection without the sash. It gaped open in lewd fashion, allowing him to look his fill. He settled her across his lap, with his erection pressed against her ass. She squeezed her legs together. "What are you going to do to me? I'll scream if you force me. I swear it."

He had the audacity to laugh. "I own this land and these people. No one would dare defy me. And as for the screaming—well, my Angelique, you may scream. Indeed it is possible, but it will be a cry of ecstasy."

Her heart jerked in her chest. "You lie."

He traced circles around her nipples. "It's a promise," he said softly. The planes of his face were hard and determined. The laird, much like his modern twin, was accustomed to winning his battles.

They were positioned facing the mirror. She could see both of them. The image made her pulse race as her blood heated.

She pretended to struggle again. He subdued her easily, wrapping his hand in her hair and using his inexorable grip to make her obey. She was completely helpless.

He had seated himself behind her on the bed, with his legs spread wide. She was tucked up against his chest with his thick sex pressed intimately to her butt. In fact, unless she kept her elbows raised a bit, her hands were in danger of fondling him by accident. He took her chin in one big hand. "Look at us in the mirror, Angelique."

She closed her eyes stubbornly.

"So much passion," he muttered, his voice thick with arousal.

She felt his fingers on her leg. Her eyelids flew open. She watched, mesmerized, as both of his hands skated from her thighs inward.

His cheek pressed close to hers. "Look at us," he commanded. "See how I make your body weep."

Tremors shook her from head to toe as he parted her labia with his thumbs and gently probed with wicked precision. She clenched her teeth, resisting on behalf of her alter ego. But the shards of pleasure were seductive and sweet.

Seeing it all in the mirror magnified every sensation. The robe was almost completely off now, caught only at the elbows by her bound arms. Morgan's heat surrounded her as his arms enclosed her. His hair-covered legs bracketed hers. His forearms kept her thighs spread wide.

Softy, he stroked her aching center. She gasped, arching back into his embrace. He picked up the pace. She whimpered. Watching his fingers on her sex was unbearably erotic.

Even in the reflection she could witness the slick wetness that lubricated his path. He shifted sideways to reach her better. Now only one of his arms supported her. With his free hand, he played at her entrance.

She was breathing like a marathon runner, gasping for air, burning up. Sweating. Shivering.

He nipped her ear with his teeth. "Shall I stop, Angelique? Perhaps wait until tomorrow night to deflower you?"

His words were lazy, taunting. Rife with the knowledge of how close she was to reaching her climax.

She couldn't speak. Her mouth was dry. Her throat tight.

She turned her face into his shoulder, frustrated tears making her eyes sting. What did he want from her?

The wicked laird thrust two fingers roughly into her sheath, tickling the swollen flesh. "Beg me, Angelique. Beg me to satisfy you."

She cursed him.

He stroked her inner walls, probing and teasing, and all the while manipulating the center of her pleasure.

Just when she thought her orgasm was imminent, he removed his hands from her sex and went back to playing with her breasts. Her nipples were sensitive, swollen. He fondled her and cupped her flesh and toyed with her as though he owned her body and soul.

Fire clawed and writhed in her lower abdomen, demanding release. She fought him suddenly, half mad with hunger. "Let me go," she demanded weakly.

Again he stroked her sex. "Beg me, Angelique. I want to hear you beg."

He pressed down gently on the little knot of nerves and her breath caught in her throat with a keening cry. "Please," she begged. "Please."

He kissed her temple. "Please what? Shall I let you return to your people, chaste and pure? Or shall I make you weep with pleasure beyond your wildest imagination?" He turned her face toward him with firm fingers and thrust his tongue between her dry lips, simulating the sex act. "Choose, Angelique. Choose your virginal bed at home, or choose your new master. Which shall it be?"

"You," she cried, tormented by a knife-edge of hunger that wouldn't let up.

He skated over her nub and shoved three fingers inside her. Her back arched so hard her head caught him on the chin. But she barely registered the painful collision as shocking waves of pleasure gripped her pelvis and dragged her over the cliff of an intense orgasm that lasted for what seemed like hours.

She was barely aware when he turned her in his arms. Now her back was to the mirror. He lifted her, positioning her over his rigid penis. His face was dark with passion, his eyes narrowed in lustful concentration.

As the head of his shaft probed for entry, she cried out. "Release my arms... please."

"No." He growled the single word like a curse and shoved hard and deep, impaling her on his erection. Her inner flesh was supersensitive from her recent climax. The intrusion was almost painful. She fought him instinctively.

He cupped her head between his large palms and kissed her wildly. Again he surged upward. Their cries mingled with the sounds of flesh slapping flesh. His hands bruised her ass. She felt totally helpless, totally subjugated. Totally in thrall to the man who mastered her body.

For a moment, she *was* Angelique. Her untried body stretched by his broad length. Her previously virginal lips raw and aching from his passionate kisses.

She imagined the mirror behind her, creating in her mind the image of his hands on her ass, the way he held her carefully as he lowered her onto his prick without compunction. Possessing her repeatedly, forcefully, until for the second time in their brief fantasy encounter, her body tensed and exploded in sobbing, beautiful, blindingly sweet release.

⁓

Morgan fumbled with the knot at Hannah's wrists and finally loosened the tie and threw it across the room. He brought her arms forward and wrapped them around his sweaty neck. Their bodies were still joined. Inside her, he was still hard. He rested his forehead against hers, trying to regain his breath and his hold on reality.

He licked his lips, tasting her there. "You screamed, Angelique. I heard you. And there was no force at all. I want to hear you say it. Call me *my lord* and admit that I own you body and soul."

Silence reigned in the room. He was ready to go again, impatient for her answer. "Tell me," he demanded. "Else I will send you back to your father."

Her body drooped against his, her face buried in his chest. "You own me, my lord, body and soul. Do with me what you will. I am yours to command."

10

In the split second that followed her dramatic capitulation, a violent crack of thunder rent the air, loud enough to penetrate even their sexual haze, and the room went dark.

Hannah squeaked and dug her fingernails into his skin as she tried move nearer. Morgan held her close. "We're perfectly safe, my love."

She was trembling, and again he was taken aback by the odd dichotomy. Hannah could jump out of an airplane, but was scared of thunderstorms. She was a fascinating mix of contradictions.

He tightened his arms around her, ruefully aware that their bodies were still joined. He wondered if she noticed. In some rational corner of his mind, he expected the lights to flicker back on quickly. The fact that they did not meant that the trouble might be long lasting. A transformer perhaps, or even the building's power grid.

By now his eyes had adjusted to the lack of artificial illumination and he could see the faint evidence of daylight peeking around the edges of the drapes. He extricated one of his arms from Hannah's death grip and pressed a button to see the dial on his watch. They had about fifteen minutes before they had to be out of the room.

That knowledge was enough to take what was left of the starch out of his erection. Gently, he untangled their bodies. The storm sounded as if it was getting farther away. "Time's up, my Angelique. Let's get out of here."

He went to the window and drew back the drapes. Even though it was still several hours until nightfall, the heavy, sullen clouds cast a gloom over the city. But there was at least enough light to enable them to get dressed.

When they exited the room, the hallway leading to the lobby was lit at far intervals with emergency lights. The reception desk was empty, but the usual envelope awaited them. Morgan frowned. "Have you made our next appointment?"

Hannah nodded, still clinging to his arm. "It's not until next Tuesday."

"Then let's take the questions with us. I'd rather exit this building as quickly as we can."

The elevators were out of commission, of course, so they had to walk down flight after flight of stairs. It was a relief to finally step out into the main lobby and head for the parking garage on the other side of the building.

But even though the thunder had abated somewhat, the sheets of rain coming down were a problem. Driving would be a nightmare.

He sighed. "Let's go to your car and sit tight for a little while. There's no sense getting out in this mess if we don't have to."

Hannah squeezed his arm. "Look, Morgan. Isn't that Timmy and Rachelle?"

The young couple from their group appointment stood a couple of rows over in the mostly empty garage near a small, older model Saturn. They appeared to be arguing. As Morgan and Hannah approached them, Timmy lifted the hood on the car and peered inside.

Hannah called out a greeting. "Rachelle. Is that you? Do you guys need some help?"

Both young people turned around. Up close, Morgan could see that Rachelle had been crying. He decided to let Hannah deal with that. He looked over Timmy's shoulder. "What can I do, man?"

∼

Hannah took in Rachelle's distraught face and without second-guessing herself, went over and hugged the girl. Rachelle might be a wife and a mother, but she was painfully young, and Hannah thought she just might need a friend. At least for the moment.

She rummaged in her purse and handed the rail-thin girl a tissue. "Did you and Timmy have a session at the Hursts' office?"

Rachelle turned bright red, hugging her arms around herself. She was wearing nothing but a thin tank top and jeans, and the wind blowing through the garage was damp and cool. "Yeah. You, too?"

Hannah nodded. "What's wrong with the car?"

Rachelle glanced at the two men who were visible only from the waist up as they peered under the hood. "Don't know. It's a clunker. We need a new one. But with the baby and everything else, we're strapped."

Suddenly she started crying again. Hannah put an arm around her shoulders, feeling woefully inadequate to offer advice. "What's the matter, honey?"

The girl's bottom lip wobbled. "I want to get home to the

baby, and we're late. I'm nursing and my boobs hurt when I go too long."

"We could give you a ride." The storm still howled, but what else could she say?

Rachelle's face lit up. "Really? That would be awesome." Then her face fell. "But we'd better wait a minute. Timmy thinks he can get the car going, and he'll be pissed if he thinks I don't have confidence in him."

Hannah nodded and smiled conspiratorially "That fragile male ego—right?"

Rachelle managed a weak giggle. "Yeah." She wiped her eyes one last time and looked at Hannah. "This thing tonight sucked."

"The car breaking down?"

"Well, yeah. That, too. But I was talking about the counseling session."

Hannah blinked. She wasn't sure she was ready for a sexual tell-all.

"Oh?" How did one respond in a situation like this?

Rachelle nodded glumly. "We were supposed to pretend like we had hooked up at a bar... that we weren't married... that we didn't have a kid."

"And it didn't work?"

"Hardly. We had a big fight and Timmy pouted, so we ended up sitting there forever and then having a quickie right before we left."

"What did you fight about?" Now Hannah was curious.

"I was supposed to act like *I* was picking Timmy up in the bar for a one-nighter."

"And?"

"He got all mad and jealous and said I did it like I was used to doing it all the time. Like I had met a bunch of guys that way. Which was stupid, because I was a virgin the first night he made love to me on our honeymoon. I swear... guys are so dense sometimes."

Hannah chuckled. "I'm with you there, girlfriend." She patted Rachelle on the arm. "Don't let it get you down. I'm sure it will all blow over. Was this your second session this week?"

Rachelle looked guilty. "We only did one. I know Dr. Sheila and Dr. Pat wanted us to do two, but I don't like leaving the baby, and we had to get a sitter. It was all complicated."

Hannah gave her an encouraging smile. "I'm sure next week will be better. Don't you worry."

Morgan walked over to them, a wry grin on his face. "I think we've got it going, but we'll follow you guys home, Rachelle, just to make sure."

Twenty minutes later, Hannah and Morgan watched from the car as the young couple darted through the rain and up the steps into a shabby duplex that looked like it hadn't been painted in a hundred years. The small yard was choked with weeds and the duplex on the opposite side had broken-out windows and graffiti spray-painted in red and black on the siding.

Hannah frowned. "They have a lot of strikes against them. It doesn't seem fair."

Morgan put the car in gear. "They may be young, but they've shown some maturity even so. They both seem committed to each other and their baby."

Hannah wondered what Morgan would think of Rachelle's confessions, but she owed it to the girl to keep her confidences. "A lot of couples in their situation would end up divorced before their third anniversary."

"And some wouldn't," Morgan said bluntly, his jaw outthrust.

Hannah sighed. "I hope they beat the odds." Her cell phone rang suddenly. She'd had it off during the session and only remembered to turn it back on moments ago. When she glanced at the Caller ID, her heart gave a funny bump. Elda never called this late.

She punched a button. "What's wrong, love?" Her hand gripped the phone as she listened to the frantic stream of words on the other end. "We'll be right there."

~

Morgan kept an eye on Hannah as they pulled up into the parking lot at Fluffy Palms. He'd not been able to get much information out of her other than the fact that Elda wasn't sick. He had a feeling that Hannah would have been happier handling whatever this crisis was alone, but he wasn't going anywhere.

Elda met them at the door. She seemed calm, but her eyes were puffy and red, and she was twisting a handkerchief in her fingers as if she'd like to rip it into shreds.

When they were all seated, Hannah leaned forward. "Tell us what happened."

Elda avoided their eyes, and Morgan could swear that she was as much embarrassed and ashamed as she was upset. Finally she spoke in a shaky voice. "It's Arnie. He cleaned out my bank account."

Hannah's jaw dropped. "He did what?"

Elda shrugged, unhappiness etched on her wrinkled face. "He took everything and disappeared."

Hannah frowned. "But how?"

Now the shame was clear. "I gave him my account number so he could move the deposit for our trip. I feel like such a fool." Fresh tears welled in her faded eyes.

Hannah went to her and gathered her in a comforting hug. "I'm so sorry, Elda. We'll help you, I promise. Won't we, Morgan?"

He gulped. Tracking down embezzlers was not his forte, but whatever Hannah wanted... "Of course we will," he said firmly. "We'll nail his hide to the wall."

Elda laid her head on Hannah's shoulder. "I should have smelled a rat. No man wants to take an ancient gal like me to the Caribbean. I was a stupid old fool."

Morgan remained with the two women for an hour, and then sensing his presence was now superfluous, he went for a walk. Night had fallen. After the storm and the heavy rain, the humidity made the air feel like a sauna.

It had been a day of highs and lows. Remembering the moments with his lovely, sexy Angelique made it necessary to adjust his pants. But unfortunately for him, Timmy, Rachelle, and Elda weren't helping his case.

Hannah thought the younger couple would be kaput in no time, and Elda's experience had proven that some men couldn't be trusted. So what made Morgan think he could convince Hannah any differently?

He sighed and kicked aside a palm frond that had been shredded during the storm. When it all came down to it, Hannah either trusted him or she didn't.

She still wore his engagement ring. That had to say something. But in every other way her behavior and her words pointed to a bad fall for Morgan Webber down the road. A day would come when she handed back his ring and said goodbye. He knew it.

But he refused to accept it. The two of them were perfect together. In every way. All he had to do was hang on until Hannah realized that some love was meant to last. The best kind of love. The love they shared.

Which brought him back to the one thing that still haunted him. Did Hannah love him as much as he loved her? Or was she only attracted to him and didn't want to hurt his feelings?

He ground his teeth together and turned back toward Elda's apartment. If winning Hannah's trust meant doing things like running a scoundrel to ground and retrieving the old woman's money, then by God, Morgan would do it.

∞

Hannah fell into bed that night exhausted. After leaving Elda's, they'd had to go back to the parking garage to retrieve Morgan's car, and by the time they finally made it to Hannah's place (he insisted on following her), it was late. Because Morgan had left the site early for their appointment, he wanted to be at work by daybreak Friday morning.

He didn't ask to come in, and for once, Hannah was glad. She had a lot to think about... the wild session with Morgan, Elda's heartbreak, even Timmy and Rachelle's situation. None of those relationships was smooth sailing, and none had easy answers.

She and Morgan usually spent Friday evening together and either Saturday or Sunday as well, sometimes all three. But she had already decided to tell him tomorrow that she wanted to be free for Elda this weekend. Elda was frail both physically and emotionally. Hannah was worried that this latest blow might knock her back to where she had been after her husband died.

Friday flew by, a long busy day that kept Hannah's mind off her own problems and totally preoccupied with helping her many elderly clients. She spoke to Morgan briefly, the conversation was stilted.

Early Saturday morning, Hannah dragged Elda out of her apartment and insisted they go out for breakfast and some shopping.

Elda grumbled the entire time. "I can't afford to shop. I'm broke, remember?"

Hannah took her arm as they stepped down from a curb. "Quit feeling sorry for yourself. Morgan will get your money back. He promised. And besides, you told me you have three other bank accounts. Arnie didn't have access to those, did he?"

They entered a nearby department store where Elda paused to admire a large, gaudy straw hat on a slim mannequin in the window. "Of course not. I might have been foolish, but I'm not a total doofus. I only gave him the info on my smallest account, the one I use for cash emergencies. It was still a lot of money, but I'm not wiped out."

"Then quit complaining."

An hour or so later, Hannah was in for a shock when she and Elda stopped for a drink in the food court and Elda ran into a man she knew from one of the other retirement centers. The older woman flirted shamelessly. Soon she and her admirer were laughing and carrying on like teenagers.

Hannah watched them, stunned. What was going on? When she was finally able to pry Elda away from her gentleman friend, Hannah sat her down on a bench and gave her a firm stare. "What were you doing back there?"

Hannah shrugged, her lip outthrust as it was every time she got stubborn. "What did it look like? I was socializing."

"But what about Arnie? I thought you were sweet on him. I thought he broke your heart."

Elda's bright auburn eyebrows went to her hairline. "I never said that. I was just mad because he made me look like a fool. And because he bilked me," she added with her lip curled. "I hate being an easy mark."

"So you weren't in love with him?"

Elda's mouth and her eyes opened wide. "Lord, no. I'll never love anyone besides my husband. But that doesn't mean I can't have fun until I die."

Hannah gazed at her, troubled. "I don't understand you sometimes, Elda. I thought you wanted to find another man to love."

Elda winced as her arthritic knee made it difficult to stand. She held out a hand. "I've got you to love, Hannah girl. And as for the men..." She rolled her eyes. "At my age, conversation and companionship are enough. But let's talk about you."

Elda knew in general about the whole sexual counseling thing. When she pushed for details, Hannah was forced to come up with a G-rated explanation that seemed to satisfy her.

When Elda asked what Morgan and Hannah were doing that evening, Hannah grinned. "I told him you were my first priority this weekend. So what do you want to do between now and Monday? I'm all yours."

Elda scowled as Hannah tucked her into the car. "I want to hang out with my friends. Why do you think I live at Fluffy Palms, honey? You're a darling girl to care about an old lady like me, but you've got a life to live. We've had a great morning, but I want you to take me home now. And then I want you to think of about a dozen ways to make that man of yours happy."

Hannah dropped off Elda, finished up a couple of errands, and drove home in a pensive mood. For the first time, it dawned on her that Elda was not quite the weak, needy woman Hannah had envisioned. Had Elda changed, or had Hannah herself created an image of the old woman that was entirely false? Was Hannah the one who was in need? Was Hannah the one who *wanted* to be needed?

She was hot and tired when she got home, and she wished she hadn't been so adamant about waving Morgan off this weekend. It would have been lovely to curl up with him on her big comfy sofa and watch a movie this evening.

When she pressed the button to listen to her messages, the day went from frustrating to downright awful. Her mother's singsong voice filled the room.

"I've got news, Hannah baby. I ran into someone special this week. Your daddy—can you believe it? He wants to meet you, darlin'. I hope you're free tonight Please call me. We can drop by your place, or get together for dinner. Our treat. Don't forget to call me back. I haven't heard from you in ages."

The machine fell silent, but the little red light continued to blink like a malevolent eye. Hannah dropped into a chair as her legs literally gave out beneath her. Her hands trembled, so she clasped them tightly in her lap. Her mother was bad enough. But her father?

For a split second, she wondered if her mother was trying to pull a fast one. How would Hannah even know if this mystery man was really the chump who had donated his sperm? Why now, after all these years? Did he want money, too? Or was this a genuine overture?

She thought back to all those times when as a little girl she had woven fantasies about a man who would show up one day and scoop her into his arms for a big hug. The man never had a face. Well, now he would.

She shivered and reached for the phone. She needed to talk to Morgan. Needed to hear his voice and feel his arms around her. But she stopped short of dialing the number.

Did she really want Morgan to meet her parents? That was exactly what would happen if she told him about the phone call. She knew him that well.

And what about her? Did she want to go through the misery of an evening with her mother and a stranger? But the other possibility was even worse. What if they showed up on her doorstep? At least in a public venue she could control things. She could leave if she had to. If she wanted to. And either of those was a distinct possibility.

She knew she would never be able to rest until she resolved things, so she bit her lip and picked up the phone a second time.

By the time she hung up, her stomach was churning, but she had made arrangements to meet her mother and a man named Raymond Quarles at the Olive Garden on Francisco Drive at five o'clock. Hannah and Morgan ate there frequently. She was hoping the loud, cheerful atmosphere would mask any odd and unpleasant conversation that might take place.

Jumping off a bridge was a piece of cake compared to meeting a father she had never known. Hannah actually threw up in the privacy of her bathroom before rinsing out her mouth and forcing herself to get into the car for the short drive to the restaurant.

Vivian was easy to spot. Despite her wraithlike appearance, she was loud. She ran toward Hannah with her arms outstretched and embraced her daughter. "There you are. Come meet your daddy."

Hannah was mortified. Fortunately they had arrived early. The waiting area was mostly empty save for a few bored hostesses and a busboy who flirted with them.

Hannah looked past her mother. A slight man, mostly bald, stood hesitantly near a wrought-iron bench, his hands stuffed in the pockets of his blue plaid shorts. His white knit shirt had the logo of a famous nearby golf course stitched on the pocket.

He didn't smile and neither did Hannah. Vivian dragged her daughter in his direction. "Come on you two," she said, her tone shrill with manic excitement. "Hug each other. After all this time..." Her voice trailed off as she realized she wasn't physically capable of forcing the father and daughter into an awkward greeting they didn't want.

Vivian turned to the hostess for help. "We'll be seated now," she chirped. "A special occasion." Her eyes darted from side to side, never landing on anything or anyone. Her hands fluttered like little ring-bedecked butterflies, hovering between Raymond and Hannah, but never landing.

The hostess seated them in a booth. Raymond scooted as far to the inside wall as he could. Vivian followed him. Hannah took a deep breath, contemplated fleeing, and then forced herself to sit down. After the waitress took their drink orders and disappeared, Hannah looked at the two people who were responsible for her existence. "I gave you half of Grammy and Papaw's money, Vivian. That's all there is. If you're here because you think my fiancé is rich, you can forget it. He works hard and has a good job, but there's no gravy train. Sorry."

The animation drained from Vivian's face, and she actually looked uneasy. "Why would you say such a terrible thing?"

Hannah shrugged. "I've been engaged less than a month and already you show up with a man you claim is my father. What am I supposed to think?"

For the first time, Raymond Quarles spoke. His eyes were the same shade of brown as Hannah's. But they were bloodshot. He met her gaze squarely. "Whatever your mother's faults, she's not lying about this. I'm the guy on your birth certificate."

Hannah's heart gave an odd lurch. "It's hardly the love story of the century," she said quietly, her voice flat. "Or do you claim that it is?"

He shrugged. "Nope. We'd never met before that night. We had a little fun. We were careless. Vivian contacted me later and told me what happened. I agreed to marry her."

"But why?" Hannah had never been able to come up with a reason to explain that seeming aberration.

Raymond smiled for the first time, a faint, wry twist of his lips that seemed to indicate a dull appreciation for fate. "I was supposed to be sterile. I figured it was my only chance at leaving my mark on the next generation. And I was a bastard myself. Literally. It seemed like a hell of a title to put on an innocent baby girl. So we got married."

Hannah clenched her jaw to keep her teeth from chattering. She was cold to the bone despite the Orlando heat. "And divorced three months later."

Vivian put her hand across the table as though she was going to take her daughter's arm. Hannah leaned back, effectively dodging the possible contact. Vivian's gaze was pleading. "We tried to do right by you, Hannah."

Hannah felt her control slipping. She wanted to scream and yell and rage. These people were the worst parents on the planet. They had stolen her chance to have a normal childhood.

But suddenly, in the midst of her hurt and turmoil, she heard Grammy's voice in her head as clear as day. *Let it go, Hannah.* She tried to swallow the knot in her throat. She could see Grammy's dear face... and the warmth of her smile. In a flash of clarity she realized how much it must have hurt Grammy to have a daughter as emotionally dysfunctional as Vivian. For years Hannah had wallowed in her own self-righteous indignation over being the wronged one... the poor, unwanted daughter.

But what about Grammy? Hadn't she been hurt even more? Having a daughter who simply couldn't handle the demands of adult life?

Hannah took a deep breath, concentrating on the cheerful music playing over the unobtrusive speakers overhead. Pleasant tunes that summoned up visions of sun-dappled vineyards and peaceful farming valleys.

Bit by bit, she gained control of her emotions. The two across the table from her were conversing in lowered tones, turned toward each other, speaking earnestly.

Hannah managed to smile at the waitress when she returned with their drinks. It seemed as if the woman had been gone an hour or more. Suddenly the thought of ordering food made Hannah gag. She picked up her purse. "I think I'll head home. I'm not really hungry."

As Vivian began to protest vociferously, Hannah sensed someone standing behind her shoulder.

She turned, thinking it was the waitress ready to take their order. Instead she saw Morgan, his face puzzled. "Hannah. What are you doing here?"

11

Busted. Hannah opened her mouth, searching desperately for something to say, but the damage had been done. Morgan glanced at Vivian and Raymond, frowning. Then he looked back at Hannah. "I thought you were spending time with Elda this weekend."

"I was," she said quickly. "I did."

He waited for further explanation, his hands shoved in his pockets and his jaw tight. She felt at a disadvantage with him standing and looming over her. She tried to divert his attention from the two people she was hoping might disappear in a puff of smoke. "What are *you* doing here?" She asked it with a cheery attempt at a smile that stretched her facial muscles painfully and failed miserably.

Now he jingled his car keys in one hand, his eyes watchful. "I met a couple of buddies at the bar for drinks and appetizers. It's Julio's birthday."

She pressed her knees together beneath the table to keep them from shaking. "That's nice."

Morgan bumped her shoulder. "Scoot over. And introduce me." The implacable expression on his face spoke volumes. He wouldn't be dissuaded. Not tonight.

When he settled in the booth beside her with his big warm body crowding her personal space, he smiled blandly. "Hannah?"

The other two remained silent, clearly fascinated by the unspoken tension between Hannah and Morgan. She lifted her chin. What the hell... it was his funeral.

She waved a hand at the two older adults. "These are my parents, Vivian and Raymond. And this is my fiancé... Morgan." She could see the questions in his eyes. She'd told him she didn't know her father. She'd told him she was spending the weekend with Elda. Morgan must be thinking the worst.

He extended a hand to Raymond. "It's a pleasure to meet you. And you, too, Vivian." Normally that phrase might be followed by Hannah has *told me so much about you,* but in this case, nothing could be further from the truth.

The men shook hands briefly, and Vivian, surprisingly reticent for once, murmured polite inanities. Finally, an awkward silence fell.

Hannah stirred restlessly. "Actually, Morgan, I was about to head home. I had a big lunch, and really I was just here to touch base with Vivian and Raymond. If you'll excuse me, I'd better get going."

Vivian's face fell. "But we were having such a nice time." She gave Morgan a beseeching smile. "Can't you stay and eat with us? I know Hannah would enjoy it more with you here. I want her to have a chance to talk with Raymond. After all, today's the first time they've ever laid eyes on each other, and they have a lot of catching up to do."

Morgan tensed. Hannah felt it. He spared a brief incredulous glance in her direction before he pinned Vivian with a steady gaze. "And whose idea was this?"

Vivian managed to flutter, even seated. "Well," she said, shredding her paper napkin in tiny pieces. "I heard that Hannah got engaged, and I thought about how sad it was for a girl not to have a father to walk her down the aisle, so I sort of tracked Raymond down and convinced him to come here with me."

Hannah frowned. "So you didn't just bump into him by accident?"

Vivian's expression was vague. "I suppose not. But still. He's here. You're here."

Hannah's doubts returned. Was this scrawny man really her father or some bottom-feeder Vivian had convinced to help her with a scam? Her stomach churned and she felt the nausea return.

Morgan put an arm around her shoulder, drawing her close. He must have sensed how close she was to breaking down, because he took control of the situation. "It was nice to meet you both, but Hannah and I haven't set a date. And we might end up with a very small wedding. It's up to her. In the meantime, we've both had a long, hard week, so I think we'll say our goodbyes."

He stood up, and Hannah followed him, grateful to have his strength and determination to extricate her from an impossible situation. She glanced from her mother to Raymond and gave them a brief, impersonal nod. A smile was beyond her. "I appreciate the dinner invitation. But Morgan is right. We have to go. Goodbye."

Outside, she leaned against Morgan's car and closed her eyes. Her legs were weak, and she felt queasy and shaken. Why had she gone to meet her mother? After all the other painful encounters. Why?

It startled her when Morgan asked the same question

out loud. She looked at him, her eyes bleak. "Because a kid never gives up wanting to know her father."

He absorbed her answer, his dark glasses shielding most of his expression. Instead of responding, he ushered her into the front seat of his Yukon. "I'm getting tired of going everywhere in two cars," he muttered.

When he took his seat, he glanced at her. "Where to now?"

She shrugged. "I don't want to go home. I feel like walking."

"How about SeaWorld?" It was late in the day, and the crowds would have dissipated by now. Morgan's aunt worked there and often gave them one-day passes. Morgan kept them in his glove box.

He started the engine. "Whatever you want."

The theme park was full but not unpleasantly crowded. Hannah and Morgan strolled for a half hour, not speaking. They paused to look at Shamu. They watched the penguins. They admired the flamingos in the late-evening light.

Finally, Morgan tugged her to a stop. "I'm starving. Let's go to that restaurant near the shark tank."

She followed him numbly. It was one of their favorite places. The host seated them at a booth facing the big wall of glass. Sea creatures of every ilk glided past in a never-ending, entertaining show.

Hannah watched the colorful fish blindly, barely registering the fact that Morgan was ordering for both of them.

When the waitress left, he leaned back in his seat. "Do you want to talk about it?"

She winced. "I didn't lie to you. I spent the morning and early afternoon with Elda. When I got home, there was a message on my answering machine from Vivian. She was threatening to show up at my place. I figured that meeting them in a public venue was the lesser of two evils."

"And this is really the first time you've met your father?"

"I doubt that man is any relation at all to me. Vivian is always looking for a way to squeeze a few more dollars out of my checking account. I'm sure she thought a tearful reunion would be a good investment." She heard the bitterness in her own voice and wanted to snatch the words back. Morgan didn't need to be dragged into the middle of her sordid family drama. He sure as heck was used to something far less unsavory.

His eyes were hooded. He stared at the room-size tank, but she had a feeling he wasn't seeing it. He rubbed his jaw. "I have an idea," he said quietly. "I've already contacted a private investigator to get information about Arnie. Why don't I ask the guy to check out Raymond as well? It should be easy enough to find out if he's the real thing."

She picked up a roll and cut it open. Anything to keep from looking at Morgan. She didn't want to see pity in his eyes. Or God forbid, distaste. "He said he's the guy on my birth certificate. But Vivian might have lied to him. Who knows?"

"There's always DNA." His words were quiet, without inflection.

It was the only way she would ever know for sure. Vivian had twisted reality so many times in her life, it was doubtful if Hannah or anyone else could actually glean a kernel of truth from anything she said.

Hannah reached for Morgan's hand. This might be where he decided to cut her loose. But he deserved to know the woman with whom he was contemplating marriage. "The God's honest truth is... I don't care one way or another. I'd prefer not to have either one of them in my life. Perhaps that sounds callous or even cold, but it's how I feel."

Morgan didn't speak right away.

She hurried to fill the silence. "I'm sure you think I'll change my mind, but believe me, I've had enough misery over the years to know that I'm happier all around when I stay away from her."

"I wasn't going to criticize, Hannah," he said quietly. "I'm just sorry she hurt you so much."

She tried to force a smile, but it wouldn't come. "It was a long time ago. I'm over it."

He shook his head. "That's where you're wrong, honey. What she did still hurts you… every day. I'm not sure it will ever go away."

∽

Morgan watched her face. It hurt *him* to see her so emotionally devastated. His own childhood had been close to idyllic, so it was difficult to imagine what Vivian's fruitcake behavior had done to her young daughter. And as for the dad—if that really was him—Morgan would like to cram the man's teeth down his throat. What kind of jerk would turn his back on his own daughter?

But this wasn't about Morgan's feelings. He picked up a forkful of risotto and baby shrimp and held it to her lips. "Eat this. You've had a hard day."

She opened her mouth obediently, and as her lips closed over the tines of the fork, he felt a little sexual buzz. Great. Hannah needed Mr. Sensitivity, and instead Mr. Lecherous Lust showed up. By the time he finished playfully feeding her dinner, he was seriously primed for action. Hannah seemed to have relaxed. There was color back in her face, and she actually laughed at his stupid jokes. He kept the conversation teasing and casual, anything to make her forget her dysfunctional family.

By the time they walked back out to his car, the lot was beginning to empty. The park would close in forty-five minutes. Morgan stopped her when they reached his big vehicle. He looked at the tinted rear windows.

"How about we get in the backseat and make out?"

She looked up at him, her wide-eyed gaze shocked but interested. "Really?"

He grinned. "It's been a hell of a day. I thought maybe necking like teenagers would be a great way to unwind."

For the first time, he saw her smile reach her eyes... a real, honest-to-God flash of humor and enjoyment. "I could be persuaded."

He unlocked the back door and helped her in, then scooted in beside her. He leaned over into the front seat and turned on the ignition and the air so they wouldn't suffocate. Hannah was grinning now. He breathed an inward sigh of relief.

She touched his knee. "Exactly how far are we going to go? First base? Second base?"

He slid a hand beneath her hair and caressed her neck. "You tell me."

He pulled her close and settled his mouth over hers. Something about this adolescent scenario made him hot. She nipped his tongue. He groaned, feeling the tightness in his groin. He cupped her breast, and then, when that wasn't enough, trespassed beneath her blouse until he found bare skin.

They moaned in unison. He teased her nipple and at the same time slid his palm up her bare, smooth thigh and under her small denim skirt. Her panties were no barrier at all. He found her center, moist and heated, and probed gently with a steady finger.

Hannah gasped and pulled him closer. She said something, but the words were muffled in his neck.

He pulled back. "What?"

She stroked his length through his slacks. "I love you, Morgan."

She'd said it once or twice before, but not often. The soft sincerity in her words caught his heart and squeezed it. He swallowed hard. "I love you, too." It wasn't enough. He knew it. She deserved to hear sonnets, symphonies, anything to convince her that his feelings were neither temporary nor superficial.

He kissed her roughly, trying to show her without words how he felt. Suddenly his necking-in-the-backseat idea seemed foolish in the extreme. He'd underestimated how much he'd want to fuck her.

His entire body was one big ache. And they risked being caught at any moment.

Another ravenous kiss. Her hands on his zipper. Cool air brushed his erection mere seconds before her hot mouth engulfed him. His fists tangled in her hair. He struggled to breathe.

He glanced wildly out the front windshield. People milled around, but none were actually near the vehicle. It was damned hard to be a problem solver when the woman you loved had your dick in a mind-blowing suction with her talented mouth.

"Hannah." He cleared the gravel from his voice and tried again. "Hannah. Get all the way in the back."

She looked up at him like he was nuts.

He was desperate. "I'm serious. Climb over."

The back of the Yukon was roomy, but not really big enough for what he had in mind. But hell, a man had to make sacrifices. He waited until she tumbled over the seat and then followed. He whacked his head on the roof and caught his foot in the net pocket on the back of the driver's seat. At last, he managed to fold his long frame down beside her.

She was laughing at him, her face soft with pleasure. "Any suggestions on how to execute Act Two?"

He unbuttoned her blouse and shoved up her bra. His mouth latched on to a nipple and sucked hard. Hannah whimpered and writhed against him in the cramped space. God, this had to be one of his stupider ideas. But if he didn't fuck her soon, he would self-combust.

He tugged her skirt to her waist and ripped the side of her panties. "Spread your knees." He freed his sex and moved on top of her.

Hannah got with the program and guided him with her hand. It took a couple of tries and some Twister-type maneuvers, but suddenly he was in. Her passage clasped him tightly as he stroked deeply.

He had a cramp in his right leg, and the zipper on his pants was scraping his balls.

Hannah winced when her head banged against the side of the car.

The physical discomforts barely registered, at least for him. He felt his climax roaring upward like a rocket from Canaveral. He found her spot and stroked it, kissing her wildly as the smell of sex and sweat filled the small space. He felt her hands cup his ass. His back jerked and cramped as he rammed her with piston strokes.

In some corner of his brain he took note of her rough cry as she came, but even that knowledge was lost to him when agonizing pleasure gripped the base of his spine and his nuts and exploded in a sharp, blinding rush of release.

～

Hannah's butt was numb. And carpet-burned. Morgan lay like a dead weight on top of her. She tried to breathe. It seemed important. "Okay, big guy. Playtime's over." When he didn't acknowledge her hint, she shoved at his shoulders. "I need air, Webber, Now."

With a disgruntled murmur, he rolled to his side. She crouched on her knees and peered over the backseat. Through the front windshield, she could see one or two cars dotting the lot, but most everyone was gone.

In the far distance, a security car started making its rounds. "Morgan." She nudged him with her knee. "Seriously, Morgan. Get up. Now."

The urgency in her voice finally penetrated his postcoital fog. He grunted and reached to zip up his pants. She kept an eye on the car with the blue light on top. It was only a SeaWorld security vehicle, but still.

He rolled to his knees, his head bent awkwardly. She pointed out the window. "We've got about a minute and a half until he's close enough to see what we're doing."

Morgan shook his head and wiped a hand across his face. Then he registered alarm. "Shit." With no chivalry at all, he shoved her over the seat. "Get in the front, Hannah. Hurry."

Unfortunately, on the way over the next seat, her knee hit the horn. She winced and looked back at the rent-a-cop. "He's getting closer."

Morgan was not built to coast over seat backs. It took him precious long seconds to maneuver over first the backseat and then the front. His face was red. She bit her lip to keep from laughing. He tried to start the car and cursed when the gears protested. The engine was already running.

The patrol car was less than a hundred feet away when Morgan put the car in drive and eased out of the parking space. He headed slowly toward the exit. "Is he following us?"

Hannah craned her neck. "Oh, God. He is." Suddenly their situation wasn't so funny anymore.

Morgan gripped the wheel. "I can't go any faster. The speed limit is twenty." It felt like a half hour before they finally reached the main gates and eased into the street. Behind them the Sea World vehicle circled the edge of the lot and headed away from them on another slow circuit to check out the stragglers.

Hannah's head dropped back on the seat and she started to gasp and wheeze and laugh. "Morgan, ohmigosh. I should kill you for this."

He looked at her, his expression sheepish. Suddenly they were both hysterical. Morgan had to pull off the road. They sat in the parking lot of a 7-Eleven and laughed until they cried. Then they looked at each other and started up again. It was at least fifteen minutes before they could both speak and breathe normally.

She dried her eyes with a napkin from the glove box. The range of emotions the day had provided left her feeling spent and weak. But she realized with some amazement that the knot in her stomach was gone.

Nothing in her life was all that bad as long as Morgan was there to lean on. She considered herself a strong woman, but sometimes a girl needed a rock to steady her. Morgan Webber was her rock.

She put a hand on his knee and stroked his thigh. "Now, can we go home?"

He tugged a strand of her hair, wrapping it around his finger and pulling. "We'll pick up your car tomorrow. I have a sudden urge to make love to you in a boring bed."

She put her head on his shoulder. "Sounds good to me, Mr. Webber. I'm all yours."

∼

Rachelle glanced down at the baby suckling at her breast. In these precious moments, she was sometimes shocked by the depth of the love she felt for this tiny, fussy infant. That wave of emotion was invariably followed by guilt. Was she shortchanging her husband? Was she putting the baby's needs before his?

But that was how it was supposed to be—right? Parents had to deny their desires in order to care for the new life that had been entrusted to them. She closed her eyes and leaned her head back against the rocker.

It was all so confusing. The hunger she and Timmy shared for each other was what had created the tiny new life in her arms. And then somehow they were supposed to sublimate that hunger with middle-of-the-night diaper changes and walking a colicky infant and trying to make an already tight budget stretch. It was a lot to ask.

She eased her sleeping daughter down into the crib and held her breath until the baby's pudgy fist found her mouth and she settled into sleep. Thank God.

Then Rachelle lifted the bodice of her cotton nursing gown and sniffed it with a moue of disgust. It seemed that all the time now her clothes smelled like sour milk and baby poop.

She tiptoed back toward the bedroom. Timmy slept, dead to the world, sprawled on his back. With a sigh she stripped off her soiled nightclothes and went down the hall to their cramped bathroom. After a quick shower, she felt better. She opened the medicine cabinet and stared at the bottle of inexpensive perfume her husband had bought her for Christmas. She'd barely used any of it. While she was pregnant, the scent had made her nauseous.

She picked up the bottle and closed the mirrored door. Her reflection stared back at her. Tentatively, she lifted one of her breasts. They had always been small. But at least for the moment they curved nicely.

She put a spritz of perfume in her cleavage, on each wrist, behind her neck, and as an afterthought, around her knees. Her nipples tightened, and heat flooded her lower abdomen. Her breathing quickened. She felt energized by her shower, and the baby usually slept at least three hours after this feeding.

She replaced the spray bottle and tiptoed down the hall back to the bedroom. Timmy snored softly, his chest rising and falling steadily. He was a restless sleeper. The covers were tumbled to one side, leaving him uncovered except for his hidden feet.

She sat down on the bed, oh so carefully. His penis, partially erect, rested against his taut abdomen. She wondered if he was dreaming. It had been weeks since they had had made love for real. They'd done it once on the night of her six-week checkup, and then that half-angry quickie two days ago in the doctors' office. And that was it.

She leaned forward and gently grasped his penis. He murmured in his sleep and stirred. Looking at his dear face made her insides go all soft and gooey She'd fallen in love with him on their second date.

He was clumsy in bed their first time, and she hadn't asked if he was a virgin as well. She hadn't wanted to embarrass him. Things were different for guys. They liked to be macho. So she pretended to climax, and it wasn't long before Timmy caught on and learned what she liked. What made her come.

They had been so happy together, even though they worked long hours and money was tight. Every night they came home and had sex for hours, drunk on the fact that they could enjoy each other's bodies as much as they wanted.

The pregnancy was a surprise. But after the first shock, they had both been happy about it. Timmy was so sweet during those nine long months. And after the first trimester, the sex had been amazing. She'd been hungry for him all the time, and he liked to tease her with new and interesting positions. They were young and healthy and infinitely in lust.

But after the birth, she had been overwhelmed, and Timmy had seemed like another obligation she had to meet.

Perhaps her mother had been right to insist on the sexual counseling. If nothing else, it had awakened Rachelle to her husband's desperate need for her. And now suddenly, her own sexual hunger was back.

She stroked his sex firmly, smiling when it rose and thickened. The head was red and swollen and fluid oozed from the eye. She bent and licked it off. Timmy murmured. She swirled her tongue over and around the cap and then swallowed as much of his length as she could manage. His groan sounded as if he were in pain.

She moved over him and took him, with one swift slide, deep into her body. She loved the way he stretched her. She bit her lip at the sheer stinging pleasure of feeling his length pulsing inside her.

She rose up on her knees, and at that moment, his eyelids opened, his gaze hazy and confused. "Rachelle?" He stared up at her, probably wondering if he was dreaming.

She reached behind her and played with his balls. "I need you, Timmy," she whispered. "Make love to me."

She saw the moment his brain clicked into gear. His face darkened and his jaw set as he surged upward, gripping her hips and filling her again and again. She closed her eyes and leaned back, changing the angle, sharpening the stimulation to her aching sex. She moaned and let him move her as he wanted to, her body rigid with the nearness of her release.

He rolled them both and put a hand over her mouth. "Scream all you want, babe. I won't let you wake the baby."

With a muffled cry and fingernails scoring his back, she trembled on the precipice and plunged into the hot, wicked night.

12

Shaun was at his wit's end. It was Monday, six days since he and Danita had screwed in the stairwell of the Hursts' office building. In the aftermath of that incredible, unscripted experience, he'd been so relieved, so encouraged, so satiated and generally happy with the world, that he'd wanted to take out a billboard proclaiming the news. He'd found everything he had been looking for.

But that night... in their bedroom, the sexy woman who'd begged him to make her come was nowhere to be found. Danita had been quiet, distant, perhaps even troubled.

He'd assumed they would have sex. It was all he had thought about the rest of the day. Which meant that his return to the office that afternoon had been near useless. He'd been completely unproductive. But smiling... a lot.

That evening, Danita had fixed dinner as she did most nights. They ate on the screened-in back porch. The boys called. Shaun and Danita got on both phones so everyone could talk at once. It was nice.

The twins hadn't come home this summer. They had

jobs and girlfriends. They were full of stories. They were looking forward to fall break. Danita promised them their favorite meals when they came home.

Danita was animated on the phone, but afterward she seemed to fade inward. It made him crazy. He didn't know how to reach her. And when they went upstairs, she pleaded exhaustion and went to sleep. Leaving him to lie in the dark with his throat tight and a lump of dread in his stomach. Were they going to make it? Or was long-term marriage just not possible anymore?

The subsequent five nights followed the same pattern. Apparently, his wife did not find him sexually attractive. Without the naughty stimulation of the counseling session, she would rather sleep than screw.

It saddened him. And made him angry. So much so that he came within an inch of blowing off their Monday-afternoon appointment. Why put himself through this? Danita couldn't climax during vanilla sex with her husband. She had to have directions from a pair of shrinks to get turned on.

He was pissed when he met her downtown. He was pissed when they walked into their assigned room. He was pissed when he saw his wife's expression. She looked apprehensive. Scared. Goddammit. He was her husband. What did she expect? That he would yell at her if she didn't have a satisfactory orgasm?

He undressed in the thick silence, the tendons in his neck tight enough to pop. Danita read their instructions aloud in a hesitant voice, and now she undressed as well. It was actually the first time he had seen her fully nude in almost a week.

Her face was flushed. Again he was shocked by the absence of hair on her mound.

He put his hands on his hips, every ounce of testosterone in his body driving him in a dangerous direction. The room was outfitted to look like a cave. There were animal pelts on the floor and fake torches for lighting. Shaun couldn't have cared less if they were in the Hilton on Waikiki.

Danita's nude body had a predictable effect on his libido. He was hard and ready.

Her arms hung loosely by her sides, and he'd bet his last dollar she wanted to cover her breasts or her bare sex but didn't dare. She still held those damn directions in front of her like a paper shield.

He crossed the room, unable to erase the scowl on his face. "Give me those."

Her eyes widened, but she held out her hand.

He grabbed the sheet of paper and tore it into several small pieces. "I don't give a shit about what we're supposed to do," he said bluntly. "We haven't had sex in a week, and I plan to make up for lost time."

"Six days," she muttered. "But the last time we were in here you said we should follow the directions... that we've paid for it."

"Screw the directions. If the only way I can screw my wife is to pay for it, so be it."

She backed up a step. He didn't blame her. He was angry. So angry he was breathing hard. It took a lot to make him lose his cool, but he was there.

He stared at her, wondering if he was about to put the final nail in the coffin of their sex life and maybe their marriage. "Get on the floor, Danita. I'm going to fuck you as many times as I can without passing out. And don't worry..." His throat clogged suddenly with furious emotion. "I won't try to make you come. In fact, I'm not even going to pay attention to your needs. It's all going to be about me today."

She had gone so white, the little freckles on her cheeks stood out in relief.

He snarled. The sound was animalistic and shocked even him. He narrowed his eyes. "Any problem with that?"

She shook her head, her eyes wide. She was mute. And that suited him just fine.

Since she seemed frozen where she stood, he bit off a curse, grabbed her wrist, and tugged her down to the pile of soft furry hides. He reached for a conveniently placed tube of lubricating jelly and slathered it on his shaft. Then he got on top of her, plunged between her legs, and rode her hard.

He came in less than a minute. And he was still erect. He flipped her to her knees and took her from behind. This time his orgasm finished him off. He wasn't eighteen anymore. Afterward, they dozed in silence. Or at least he did. He wasn't sure about Danita.

He had avoided looking at her face. He didn't want to see pity, or revulsion, or even worse... long-suffering. He'd always enjoyed playing with her body, bringing her to climax. But for some reason, he didn't excite her anymore. It was only frustrating them both when he tried so hard.

He rolled to his back and slung an arm over his face. Danita was turned on her side, facing away from him. Now that he had time to process his surroundings, he realized that the makeshift bed was surprisingly comfortable, even if the fur did tickle his ass.

He reached out to touch her shoulder, but his hand hovered in the air. He drew it back. He'd behaved like a Neanderthal... literally. And caveman sex was no way to woo a woman like Danita. She was soft and refined and ladylike. He'd probably disgusted her.

He had no idea if she had even come close to an orgasm. He doubted it. Memories of last week hit him hard. He remembered her beautiful face flushed with passion, her husky voice begging him to let her come.

God, if he only knew what triggered that. Why had she climaxed in a dirty stairwell when he could never seem to satisfy her in their comfortable bedroom? Was there a man alive who understood the female psyche?

Thinking about last week's session made him hard... again.

His mind was a whirl of emotions and regrets. He was lost in a trackless wilderness without a map or a compass. The only hope he had of survival was the woman beside him. A woman who seemed like a stranger to him now.

He lubed up his dick and rolled to spoon her. Without speaking, he lifted her leg and entered her from behind. Her soft gasp gave him pause, but she wasn't fighting him. She wasn't touching him, but she wasn't rejecting him. At least not overtly.

This time was longer and slower. In another circumstance, he would have reached around and stroked her where he knew she needed it. But he couldn't bear the thought that she would tense up. And he didn't want to face the fact that he might not be able to bring her off. So he thrust from behind, impersonally, using his hand on her shoulder only for an anchor.

When it was over, he felt unutterably sad. He might as well have been screwing an inflatable doll.

He stood up and started putting his clothes on. Danita acknowledged him... at last. She rolled to face him, but her gaze fell short of meeting his. "Is it time to go?"

He shrugged. "I'm done."

Her bottom lip trembled before she clamped it with her teeth. "Okay."

Watching her get dressed was torture. Everything she did was sensual, graceful. He wanted to howl in frustration when he felt himself harden again. The hunger he felt for her was tearing him apart. Her colorful sundress left her back and shoulders bare. When she bent over to slip on her sandals, he lost it.

With his pants still unzipped, he lunged for her, grabbed her around the waist and shoved her, butt first, up against the nearest wall. He freed his dick from his boxers and impaled her, panting, desperate for release despite what had happened earlier. Her tiny, easily-shoved-aside panties were no barrier at all.

He avoided looking in her eyes. Instead, he concentrated on the place where their bodies joined. They were still linked physically, even though they seemed to have lost the emotional connection that had kept them together all these years.

He cupped her ass, lifting her into his strokes. His biceps and his knees screamed in protest. He fucked her repeatedly, feeling more pain than pleasure. He wanted some kind of response from her. But he was too damn scared to say or do anything but grit his teeth and thrust until he shot off again.

Right there at the end, he thought he felt her climax, but he was beyond thinking clearly, lost in his own groaning release. He lowered her slowly and actually felt his face go hot. God, he was such an ass.

Still, Danita said nothing.

~

She was shaking as they finally left the room. Shaun was so different today. Clearly, his unusual behavior was her fault. She'd been cold the past week. She knew it. The fact that her responses were beyond her control was no excuse.

But strangely, despite his brusque manner and the complete lack of tenderness he normally showed during sex, she'd been turned on. Certainly right at the end. Her climax had ripped through her like a flash fire. She hadn't been repulsed by his crude language or his rough lovemaking. If anything, she had enjoyed it.

And that shamed her. What kind of woman preferred angry sex? Was she broken inside? Had she lost the ability to respond to her husband's gentle caresses? What in the hell was wrong with her?

～

It took every ounce of self-control Shaun could muster to face the receptionist, take his own set of questions, and fill in the answers. He hoped the good doctors graded on a curve, because his choices on the A/B/C/D form were completely random. Afterwards, he barely even remembered reading the words on the page.

Their appointment had been late in the day this time. When they got off the elevator in the parking garage, he realized that he and Danita had parked on different levels. The irony did not escape him.

He ran a hand through his hair. "Would you like me to grab some Chinese for dinner and bring it home?"

When he glanced at her, she clutched her car keys and grimaced. "I'm not really hungry. Why don't you get whatever sounds good to you? I'll heat a can of soup later if I want anything."

He bowed his head for a moment, staring at an oil stain on the concrete floor. "We have to talk when we get home, Danita. Tonight."

He studied her face and saw her pallor, her air of complete emotional and physical exhaustion. The artificial lighting in the stark garage emphasized her somber expression.

She cleared her throat. "I know," she said quietly.

The look in her eyes haunted him as he drove home. He stopped for a burger and tried to eat it in the car, but after three bites, his stomach revolted.

At the house, he found Danita packing an overnight bag. For several seconds, his heart simply stopped beating. He cleared his throat. "What are you doing?"

"Mom called. Dad's not doing well. She asked me to come spend a night or two and help her decide if he needs to go to the hospital." She faced him with the width of their king-size bed between them. "I'm sorry, Shaun. I don't really have a choice."

He sighed, leaning against the doorframe. "Of course you don't." He continued to watch her quick, efficient motions. "When is our next appointment?"

Her sharp indrawn breath pained him, but she answered. "Thursday afternoon. And then the final group appointment on Friday night."

He nodded slowly, wondering if he was going to regret drawing a line in the sand. "We'll go," he said bluntly. "But it doesn't matter what they have planned for us. We'll use the room as neutral ground. And we'll talk. About every-thing." His heavy emphasis on the last two words didn't escape her, because he saw her body jerk as if his phrase had hit a nerve.

When she didn't respond, he felt his frustration start to

rise, but he tamped it down. "I can't go on like this, Danita. You have to talk to me. We either go forward, or we call it quits. It hurts too much. I can't stand by any longer and watch us destroy what it took a lifetime to build. So be ready. We're not going to leave that room until we clear the air. No matter the outcome."

It was a long speech. The words felt like razor blades in his throat.

Danita had stopped packing. She clutched a T-shirt in her hands, her face dead white, the expression in her eyes agonized. He refused to give in to the urge to pet her and assure her everything would be all right. Instead, he frowned. "Say something, damn it."

A single, fat tear rolled down her cheek, but she met his gaze steadily. "I understand," she said, her voice dull and flat. "I'll be there."

∽

Monday night Morgan took Hannah and Elda out to dinner at Kentucky Fried Chicken. He would have gladly sprung for something more upscale, but it was the old woman's favorite. He was content to eat his meal quietly as the two females chattered away.

It was a hoot to see how each of them tried to mother the other. And he doubted if either of them recognized it. Over dessert, Hannah finally got around to sharing the news that had prompted the evening's agenda. She told Elda about the meeting with Vivian and Raymond.

Elda put down her spoonful of pudding and stared. "Good Lord."

Hannah grimaced. "Yeah. It was ludicrous. I don't know why I went."

"Do you think he really is your father?"

Hannah shrugged, but her nonchalance didn't fool Morgan, so Elda probably wasn't convinced, either. "I don't know and I don't care. If I had to bet, I'd say no. Vivian's track record with the truth is lousy. And over the years it's occurred to me that she might not even *know* who my father is. She has always claimed it was this Raymond guy, but even that could be a lie."

Elda pushed her glasses up her nose, her rheumy eyes strangely gentle. "They say that bad parents are better than none at all."

Hannah snorted, her words cynical. "You'd need to prove that to me."

Morgan remained silent, content to monitor the byplay between the two women.

Elda sighed. "You have to think past the present, Hannah my girl. There are lots of things to consider... like having grandparents for your children. And what about having a dad to walk you down the aisle?"

Morgan saw Hannah's face register the memory of Vivian voicing a similar thought. Hannah frowned. "In the first place, I doubt I'll ever have children. And in the second place, if I get married, I plan to walk myself down the aisle. There won't be anyone giving me away. That is an antiquated notion at best."

Morgan lost track of the conversation for a moment. The knife lodged in his chest throbbed dully. *If*. Not *when*. One stupid little word. But the distinction was telling. Hannah had spoken without thinking, comfortable with Elda, not guarding her speech. In doing so, she had let slip a Freudian gaffe that even a moron could analyze.

Hannah still didn't think she was going to end up marrying him.

His fists clenched beneath the table. He felt paralyzed with emotions that were impossible to sort through. But the one clear constant was hurt. A real man never let that one show.

Elda caught his gaze, her own sympathetic. He lifted his chin and smiled stubbornly. It seemed a good time to change the subject. "Well, ladies," he said, needing to regain control of something. "I have good news."

Hannah looked puzzled. "You do? What is it?"

He avoided her lovely golden-brown eyes and grinned at Elda. "Arnie is no longer a free man. If all goes well, your money will be back in your account by the end of the week."

"Lord save me." Elda slumped back against her seat, her eyes wide and her gnarled hands trembling. Her voice shook. "Are you sure?"

Morgan nodded. "I hired an investigator, and actually, it was nearly an open-and-shut case. Arnie was a small-time crook and not too bright. He left a trail of bread crumbs every step of the way."

That seemed to bother Elda. "So he wasn't a professional con man?"

Morgan took a swig of his beer. "Well, if he was, he was lousy at his job. Or maybe he got careless. Either way, you don't have to worry about him anymore."

Elda sighed gustily. "I'll definitely be more careful next time."

Hannah raised an eyebrow. Morgan read the disapproval on her face loud and clear. "Next time?"

Elda grinned sheepishly. "That nice man we saw at the mall wants me to take a bus tour to Vegas with him."

"But, Elda, I thought you were swearing off men."

"When did I ever say that?" She patted Hannah's

hand. "There may be a lot of snakes in the world, but that doesn't mean I'm going to quit walking in the garden."

Morgan turned on the radio for the drive home. He was out of sorts, and didn't know if he could talk to his infuriating fiancée at the moment. She deserved his support, especially in light of what had happened over the weekend, but he was running out of patience.

He tuned in to an Orlando XM station that did weather updates on the hour, and he pretended to listen. But in a moment, he actually had to tune in mentally as well. There was a hurricane on the way.

The forecasters were predicting that the storm would make landfall as no more than a category one or two, but that it would almost certainly drop heavy amounts of rainfall over central Florida. They were recommending the usual laundry list of precautions: bottled water, flashlights, nonperishable foods.

Morgan groaned aloud. That was all he needed right now. The hurdles in his theme park project seemed to be mirroring the bumps in his personal life, aka the rocky road to marital bliss.

Hannah put her hand on his thigh. "That won't be good for you, will it?"

He wanted to ignore her innocent caress, but damned if his body didn't betray him. He wanted to be surly and rude and righteously indignant. But old habits die hard. Hannah couldn't help her feelings. She hadn't been intentionally cruel. It was his own damned fault for thinking anything had changed.

He kept his attention on the road, his spine stiff. "Yeah. This week is going downhill fast."

Hannah peered out the drapes Tuesday afternoon, watching for Morgan. Despite the looming weather crisis, he'd managed to get away from work as he had promised and would be picking her up momentarily. Today was their next-to-last session before Friday night's wrap up.

She couldn't really imagine what that final group appointment would entail. Surely they weren't all going to spout off about the intimate details of what had gone on in those rooms behind closed doors.

She was concerned about Morgan. He'd been awfully quiet the night before. Especially after the dinner with Elda, And though she had invited him to come in or even stay the night, he'd made some flimsy excuse and had left her on her doorstep with little more than a quick kiss.

She tried to let him know how much she appreciated what he had done for Elda, but he brushed off her thanks. It was clear that to him the whole Arnie thing was no big deal. Morgan was a man people could count on in a crisis large or small, and he didn't seem to understand how wonderfully comforting it was to have that kind of reassurance. He was such a protector at heart, and yet he didn't recognize what that meant to those around him.

She nibbled her lower lip, wondering what the Drs. Hurst had in store for Hannah and Morgan today. After clicking through a few *have-to* items on her list, Hannah had taken the afternoon off for some self-pampering. She'd sunbathed on her tiny terrace for a while, then showered and shaved her legs and taken a short nap.

The lazy afternoon should have relaxed her, but she'd spent far too much time brooding about her confrontation with her parents. Although she would die rather than admit to any curiosity about the matter, it was difficult not to wonder if Raymond really was her father.

But if he was, so what? A successful sperm and a drug-hazed quickie didn't make a man a parent. For that matter, it hadn't made Vivian one, either.

She twitched the curtain one last time, feeling jumpy and strangely apprehensive. A little while ago, she'd poured herself a glass of wine in hopes of calming her nerves. But the alcohol had done nothing more than make her feel all warm and woozy. Which in turn made her think of sex and Morgan, which in turn brought her thoughts back to what might happen in the next few hours.

After the bondage scenario and the even more challenging wedding-night charade, she was desperate to know what she might be facing. Her imagination was working at warp speed. When Morgan rang the doorbell, she jumped. Showtime.

He bussed her cheek and headed back outside, his demeanor distracted. In the car, she tried to break the tension. At least it seemed like tension on her part. Morgan hardly registered her presence.

She drummed her fingers on her thighs. She had dressed in a daring red sundress made of pseudo-bandana fabric. The hem fell in sharp points that flirted with her knees. Morgan barely noticed.

She sighed... loudly.

He muttered something when the car in the next lane cut them off. His attention never wavered from the traffic. And even if his devotion to driver safety was commendable, it was starting to piss her off.

She waved a hand on front of his face. "Hellooo. Morgan. Remember me?"

He slanted an irritated gaze her way. "What's the matter, Hannah? Am I not paying you enough attention? Is that it?"

She was shocked, speechless even. Witnessing Morgan

in a surly mood was such an unusual occurrence she didn't know how to react. She turned her head away, staring out the passenger window. She wasn't so touchy that one terse comment could hurt her feelings. But even so, her eyes burned with something she couldn't quite name.

After that, they didn't say anything at all. When Morgan pulled up in the now-familiar parking garage, she couldn't help herself. She put a hand on his forearm. "Have I done something to make you angry?"

His big hands gripped the steering wheel as if he would like to choke it... or somebody. His whole body vibrated with pent-up emotion. Finally, as the uneasy silence dragged on, she saw the tension begin to drain out of him.

She waited, wondering if she was entirely to blame, or if his mood was the result of a combination of factors.

He ran a hand across the back of his neck and turned off the engine. Almost immediately, the late-afternoon heat began to make the inside of the car uncomfortable. She felt a drop of sweat trickle down between her breasts as she shifted in her seat.

Morgan looked at her, his mouth twisted in a wry smile. "I'll shake it off before we get upstairs. Let's go. We're on the clock."

13

It no longer bothered Hannah to ask the receptionist for the key. It did, however, still make her stomach plunge to step into the hallway and approach the door to their appointment room. She fumbled with getting the lock to open, and Morgan nudged her aside. "Let me do it."

She stepped back and then crossed the threshold when he ushered her inside. They both stopped cold, three steps into the room. A large, rice-carved four-poster bed dominated the space. The mattress was covered with pristine white sheets and a white embroidered comforter.

The luxurious bedding was folded back, and a black satin blindfold had been tossed carelessly on one of the plump pillows. A couple of documents lay neatly near the foot of the massive bed.

Taped to one of the posts was a cream envelope marked *instructions*. Morgan reached for it. When he turned it over and lifted the flap, Hannah saw him extract two smaller envelopes. This was something new.

He handed her the one with her name on it. She frowned, but opened it and read the contents:

Hannah—

Please take a look at the papers on the bed. They are fairly self-explanatory. All the information has already been filled out, with the exception of your two signatures. The documents are real, but of course they are not legally binding unless you sign and file them. They need not leave this room. We have placed a paper shredder near the door for your convenience.

This afternoon, you are to take charge of the sexual agenda between you and Morgan. You'll find appropriate props in the dresser drawer. All the while, try to keep the documents in mind. Seek to understand why they frighten you so much. At the same time, we urge you to try and disappear so deeply into the encounter with your lover that the documents cease to have meaning.

If you wish, have Morgan sign the papers, both sets, before you commence. Then blindfold him and let the games begin. But do not tell him about any of this.

She refolded the note and put it back in the envelope. When she looked at Morgan, he was frowning.

He lifted an eyebrow. "What does yours say?"

She folded her arms at her waist. "I'm not supposed to tell you."

He didn't like that. His eyes flashed with displeasure, but he merely nodded. "Okay. But how am I supposed to know what to do?"

She licked her lips. "I'll tell you." She walked over to the bed and picked up the two sets of papers. Morgan stood behind her, reading over her shoulder. One document was an application for a marriage license. It was dated for Wednesday of the following week.

The thicker sheaf of legalese was divorce papers. Hannah's hand shook. They were dated for three years in the future.

Morgan cursed beneath his breath. "What kind of bogus shit are they up to?" Clearly he was still in his badass mood.

She picked up the pen on the bedside table. "Nothing here is real. You know that. It's part of the charade. Here, sign them."

He cooperated, but continued to grumble. "I don't like this one bit."

When he finished, Hannah followed suit and then put the papers on the dresser. She turned around and looked at him. "Get undressed."

Morgan's eyes narrowed. A shiver snaked down her back. He appeared neither amiable nor conciliatory. But he obeyed her blunt command. When he was completely nude, he faced her, his arms crossed over his broad, lightly hair-covered chest. He didn't speak.

Breathless, she tried to focus on her instructions. She waved an imperious hand. "Stand beside one of the posts. Put your back to it." She didn't wait to see if he would comply. Instead, she went to a drawer and pulled out some cloth ties. Her gaze fell on the papers. The divorce-related ones were ugly, but the simpler form was more daunting still. Why did it seem so threatening?

She poured herself a glass of water from the carafe left by unseen hands and downed it thirstily. When she approached the bed, Morgan was right where she had told him to be. She avoided looking at his penis, though she could tell it was not erect. Had his inexplicable anger overridden his desire for her?

She looked him in the eyes. "Put your hands over your head." He obeyed slowly, his gray gaze stormy as a winter sea. She knelt on the bed and tied his wrists tightly to the finial at the top of the bedpost. She pulled at the knot until she was sure he couldn't wriggle free.

Then she moved around him, retrieved the blindfold from the bed, and returned to slip it gently over his head. The sharp little puff of breath that brushed her cheek was his only outward response.

She settled the elastic band behind his ears and smoothed his silky hair. She was so close to him, she could feel the heat from his body. When he was blind and immobile, she left him and crossed the room.

She picked up the thicker set of papers she and Morgan had signed and read them carefully. The divorce decree hardly seemed applicable. Morgan was not the kind of man to admit failure at anything, especially marriage. And since she couldn't ever imagine wanting to leave him, the whole idea wasn't quite real. She tossed it aside.

The application for a marriage license, however, was all too persuasive. All it lacked to be legit was a quick trip to the courthouse. Sick anxiety gripped her as she visualized herself and Morgan doing just that, walking inside, papers in hand, to declare their intent before the great state of Florida. And if she didn't think Morgan would ever divorce her, why in the heck was she so scared?

She bowed her head, eyes closed, acutely aware of her captive and his helpless passivity. Thoughts and images whirled in her brain. Her mother, the man who claimed to be her father. Grammy and Papaw. The boy who had clumsily taken her virginity. The gynecologist who had looked at her with such naked disapproval. The goldfish Vivian had carelessly washed down the drain in the kitchen sink when she was supposed to be helping Hannah change the water in the dirty tank.

Hannah gripped the edge of the dresser. She had never let a physical fear stop her from doing something she wanted to do. Maybe it was time to let go of a few of her emotional fears. And Dr. Sheila was right. It was a fear. Hannah was afraid of getting hurt, because she knew just how terribly painful it could be when the people you loved let you down. Even Grammy and Papaw hadn't kept their promise. They had died when Hannah still needed them.

She sniffed and opened her eyes. She wasn't sure what she was supposed to do now, but she had to do something. Dwelling on the past was only confusing her.

She took a deep breath, gave herself a pep talk, and then began to get undressed.

∼

Morgan strained to hear any sound from Hannah. With his sight gone, his other senses were supposed to be heightened... right? Or was that only true with permanent sight deprivation?

He heard a rustle, and his pulse quickened. He was at least seventy-five percent sure she was taking off her clothes. About damn time. He was none too pleased to be blind and trussed up like a sacrifice, so the sooner they got started, the better. He figured that once things got rolling, Hannah would eventually let him go so he could pay some attention to her needs. He just hoped it wouldn't be too long.

His arms were already aching, and the carving on the bedpost was rough against his back and butt. The carpet beneath his toes was soft and plush, though. He imagined laying Hannah down on it and fucking her. Ah... he could only dream.

Strangely, now that he was at her mercy physically, his frustration and anger over her ambivalence about marriage faded away. He should accept his fate like a man. He was at her mercy emotionally, as well.

Either she would be his bride or she wouldn't. And apparently, given her stubborn nature and the burdens she'd had to bear because of her upbringing, it could be a hell of a long time before she trusted him enough to say yes.

But he could wait. He would wait. It was the only viable choice he had.

When a hand brushed his groin, he yelped. Then hot color flooded his face, partly from embarrassment and partly from what Hannah was doing to him. She fondled his balls, scraping lightly at the hair with her fingernails and testing their weight with her palms.

He locked his knees to keep his legs from trembling. His sex rose firm and eager in a throbbing erection. But she avoided his penis, choosing instead to concentrate on less volatile spots like his calves and his feet.

He heard the scrape of a lid and smelled a sweet, heady fragrance. Moments later Hannah smeared lotion from his lower thighs all the way down to the arches of his feet. The scent was overpowering, filling his head and his bloodstream and making him think about sex.

And then it dawned on him. He was going to have to walk out of here smelling like a damned flower. She rubbed the back of his knee, and a bolt of lust made him weak. His hips thrust forward in an unconscious effort to find her body and mate with it. But she must have moved out of range.

Moments later, she resumed her torture. He'd never particularly thought of himself as having erogenous zones anywhere below his sex... but his innovative Hannah was showing him some vulnerable areas that were a complete surprise.

She circled his ankles with her hands, squeezing lightly.

Then he felt her tongue on his ankle bone, and he groaned aloud. She wet the spot and licked it lazily, first one ankle and then the other.

His sex swelled and ached. He wanted to drag her by the hair up to his crotch and force her to eat him. But he hung there, helpless as a baby, while she played with him like a sex-shop toy.

Her thumbs rubbed his shinbones. Her teeth grazed his arches. Eventually she abandoned his lower legs and moved up his thighs. His entire body tightened in anticipation of the moment when her mouth would close over his prick and take him deep.

But he was dreaming. Hannah rubbed lotion into his skin from his knees to his hips, but she never touched his genitals, not even by accident. She reached behind him and caressed his ass, but though he felt her breath on his shaft, there was no physical contact.

His breathing grew ragged and his heart rate spiked. How much of this could he stand?

Now she was at his chest, stroking him in large, lazy circles. His skin absorbed the scent and his brain internalized it. From now and forever he would associate this particular fragrance with Hannah and sex.

Assuming he ever got to screw her. She tugged at his small, flat nipples and he shuddered. Damn. She was slowly destroying him.

He wanted her to speak, to say anything. But she kept up the slow, silent attack. Now she was at his throat, his neck. The tip of her finger traced the shell of his ear, delved deep to thrust inside.

"Hannah." Her name rasped from his throat in a moaning plea for mercy.

She ignored him. Now he felt her touch his face. She

moved carefully around the blindfold, measuring his cheekbones with her thumbs, toying with his chin. She didn't force lotion in his mouth, but she tugged his lips apart, and he felt the brush of her tongue against his.

He responded wildly with a surge of adrenaline, trying to suck her tongue, but already she was gone. Helpless anger and frustration washed over him, but he couldn't hold on to them, because now she was doing something to his arms. He felt a weird tickle and then bit down on a cry when he placed the odd sensation. She was touching the sensitive flesh of his underarm with a feather.

"Hannah." He said her name again. "Let me go," he said urgently. He was afraid suddenly, afraid he wouldn't be able to withstand her erotic torments indefinitely. "Let me go, baby. Let me love you."

Her silence was complete. He couldn't even hear her breathing. The damned feather moved slowly, retracing the path her fingers had taken with the lotion. Lust swelled and tightened in his loins, making him weak and dizzy. Every inch of his skin was sensitized. When he thought he couldn't bear it a second longer, she arrived back at his feet and finally ceased her torture.

Then he heard the rasp of a match and smelled smoke. A new odor permeated the room, even apart from the acrid aroma. She must have a candle. Something musky and heavy with Middle Eastern overtones. Hallelujah. Maybe she was setting the stage for some romantic lovemaking. And then he jerked in shock when he felt hot wax on his nipples.

"Holy hell." The exclamation ripped from his throat. The mild burn shocked him more than anything. The sensation cooled quickly. But she repeated it on his feet, his knees. And then he got a bad feeling. "Jesus, Hannah. No."

Sharp stings dribbled over his balls. He shrank back instinctively, trying to escape the possibility that his manhood might be permanently damaged. For the first time he heard her laugh softly. The wicked, sensual satisfaction in the low chuckle made the hair on his body stand up. He was one fucked-up dude.

She didn't plan to release him anytime soon.

Thank God she stopped short of his prick with the hot wax business. He sensed her move away, and the smoke smell grew stronger, so he thought she had blown out the candle. Or he hoped she had. He strained his ears, listening for a clue, any clue at all.

He sucked in a breath when he felt warm, feminine flesh from his chest to his knees. She was snuggling up against him, pressing all her delightful body parts to his. He would have whimpered if it hadn't have been an unmanly thing to do.

His arms tugged futilely at their bindings. He wanted to hold her, damn it. He wanted to cup her ass and caress her tits and rub between her legs until she writhed and begged him for mercy

He almost cried when she left him. It was impossible to gauge time. How much of their two hours had passed?

It startled him when he felt something at his mouth and realized it was a bottle of water. He drank gratefully, not comprehending until that exact moment how dry his mouth was. Moments later the water bottle was gone. Then he felt cool liquid dribbling over his aching sex.

The sensation was indescribable. She hadn't touched his prick at all, not even one accidental graze. And now the water on his tight skin both soothed and pained him. He felt the drops fall onto his thighs and run down his legs. Then a soft towel blotted up the excess. But not from his most intimate flesh.

For long moments nothing happened. He could hear his heart beating in his ears. If he tried really hard, he thought he could detect faint noises outside the room, but it might have been his imagination.

Music filtered into the room. It dawned on him that Hannah was responsible. It was a jazz CD, one they had made love to on several occasions. His pulse skipped a beat and his anticipation grew. He bit back a howl of shocked pleasure when he felt the feather tease his balls again and then move to his shaft. She touched him so lightly it was almost as if he were imagining the contact.

He shifted his feet uneasily, unclear as to whether he wanted to lean in to the featherlight strokes or back away. But before he could decide, the game changed. A sharp prick on his hard-on made him flinch. She was using the opposite end of the feather now. He felt it trespass ever so gently into the opening at the head of his shaft.

He groaned and shuddered. It was too much. He'd concentrated fiercely on holding back his inevitable orgasm, but now the terrible stimulation raked him with shivers of need. He moved restlessly. The teasing feather followed. Hannah scraped at his balls, retreated to his nipples momentarily and came back to the swollen, sensitive head of his sex.

He craved her hands on him. "Please," he muttered, his masculine pride long since consigned to the dust. "Please, Hannah."

The wicked little pricks and scrapes ceased. Silence reigned but for the low, sensual notes of music stealing into his head and making his lust grow and deepen.

He heard something being dragged across the floor. But

the noise made no sense. A hard object bumped his shins. Hannah murmured an apology. Then he bit out a curse when he felt her sex brush his groin. *What the hell?* She was standing on something, a chair maybe?

Her hands landed on his shoulders and her legs bracketed his waist just as she lowered herself onto his erection. The excruciating pleasure paralyzed him for a moment. He held his breath, deathly afraid she would move away... that she was only playing with him.

But the tight, slick caress of her body remained, enclosing his pulsing shaft in heat and bliss. His hips thrust wildly, and her nails dug into his shoulders. "Don't move." The words were a breathless hiss. "Stay perfectly still. I'll do all the work."

It was agony to obey. He clenched his fingers around the post and braced his feet. Somehow, her legs wrapped around him and she lifted and lowered herself on his rigid sex. The sensation, the knife-edged jolt of fire tearing him in half, increased. He gasped for breath, the muscles in his arms strained beyond endurance.

Her sex milked him steadily. Her unorthodox position made hard thrusts impossible, even if he had been allowed to participate. She rode him slowly, grinding down on him to increase her own pleasure.

Even without the blindfold, he would have been blind with the red haze of insanity. Even with the desultory pace of her movements, his climax threatened. "I'm gonna come," he muttered.

She froze. "No." It was unequivocal.

He sucked in deep breaths, trying to ignore the urge to shoot off. He doubted his ability to obey any longer. When she started to move again, sweat dripped into his eyes, causing the blindfold to stick to his face.

He could feel her breasts mashed to his chest. In his mind, he pictured her, nude and lascivious in her carnal attack. He wanted desperately to regain his sight, even more than he wanted to touch her.

She bit his ear. He jerked, driving his sex an inch deeper. His hips moved in a primal rhythm, but she chided him. "None of that," she taunted. "I'll do this."

His head dropped back against the post, and his chest heaved. He would never survive.

But then it got worse.

She disengaged their bodies. He heard her ragged breathing. "Sorry," she muttered. "This position is impossible."

He felt her move away, and then the bed behind him moved slightly. "What are you doing?" he asked, his words husky, his throat raw.

She didn't answer. Moments later, he heard the unmistakable sounds of a woman playing with herself, sliding her fingers over slick, wet flesh, moaning with pleasure, crying out in feverish joy when her hips arched off the sheets and she came with a long, moaning cry.

He hung there in shock, his wrists and his emotions numb. No way. No fucking way.

He ground his teeth, almost doubled over with the pain of his abrupt inability to climax. "Hannah. God, honey. Help me."

He waited for her to come back, to mount him, to finish what they had started. But she was always two steps ahead of him in this impossible-to-predict, endlessly long, incredibly frustrating miscarriage of sexual justice.

The water bottle came to his lips again, and he spat it away. "Untie me. Now. I've had enough."

She didn't answer him. His blood pressure notched into

the danger zone. "Hannah." He tried for a cajoling tone, but it sounded more like a humble entreaty. Then he felt slim fingers close around him intimately. His heart lodged in his throat. Oh shit, not like this. But his wishes didn't amount to a hill of beans, and his traitorous dick was giving an enthusiastic yes to the new plan. Anything was better than nothing.

Hannah knew what he liked. And she was damned good at it. His eyeballs rolled back in his head, his entire body went catatonic, and he gave a hoarse shout as he jetted his release into her warm, caressing palm.

He lost a few chunks of time after that. Nothing so dramatic as losing consciousness. Merely a sort of out-of-body experience that made him completely unaware of what his devious fiancée might be doing.

The noise of the paper shredder brought him back to reality. It was a shock to feel his wrists being untied. Instinctively, impatiently, as soon as he was free, he lifted a hand to the blindfold and ripped it loose.

He was shocked by what he saw. Hannah was fully dressed. She was sitting in a chair, watching him with dark, wary eyes. No one examining her demeanor would ever have believed her capable of planning what had recently transpired in this room. He felt uncomfortable in his nudity, so he turned away suddenly and reached for his clothes, donning them with clumsy haste and tucking in his shirt.

When he was back to normal... socks, shoes, and all, he glanced at his watch. They had eight minutes left. He raised an eyebrow. "Cutting it kind of close, weren't you?"

She lifted an eyebrow, her grin smug. "Are you complaining?"

He considered the question for a moment. "Hell, no," he said, theatrically rubbing his wrists. "I enjoy a little bondage and torture as much as the next guy."

He stalked toward her, enjoying the moment when her eyes flared wide and feminine outrage brought her to her feet. "Don't try intimidating me with your big self," she whispered, coming up on tiptoe to align their mouths.

He caught her close, holding her tightly and stroking his hands over her back. It felt so good he wanted to groan aloud, but he contented himself with cupping her ass and nibbling her lips. "I'm too scared of you to try," he teased, moving his tongue lazily on hers.

She trembled in his arms. His gut said to scoop her up and carry her back to the bed. But they were down to four minutes. He checked.

He let her go reluctantly. She picked up her roomy tote bag as they prepared to leave the room. The woman could carry all sorts of scary things in there. But was one of them a marriage license? Or was that particular piece of paper at the bottom of the trashcan? He had a hunch she had shredded the other.

The divorce decree had merely been a smoke screen... a gentle dig by the good doctors to test Hannah's resolve. No one really thought she and Morgan would end up divorced.

The question was—would he and Hannah ever get married to begin with?

He followed her into the reception area and almost lurched to a halt when an uneasy thought occurred to him. What kind of answers had Hannah filled in on the last questionnaire that could have prompted this afternoon's scenario? It boggled the mind.

They spent longer than usual on today's post-session assignment. Hannah concentrated fiercely, her brow furrowed, as she bubbled in choices and wrote in answers. His own paper was straightforward. All of his responses were easy and, in fact, almost automatic.

He was a man who had known from the beginning what he wanted and how to get it. The fact that it was taking longer than he might have liked was irrelevant.

Hannah loved him. He knew it in his bones. All he had to do was wait her out and everything would be fine.

14

Wednesday, the city sweltered in the grip of uneasy dread. The bad weather threatening off the east coast of the state had been upgraded to a tropical storm. Her name was Constance.

And Constance was making life miserable for a lot of people.

Hannah knew that all three retirement centers where she worked were top-notch and would take good care of her elderly clients. But still she felt responsible for their mental and emotional well-being.

She worked flat-out all day, trying to make at least minimal contact with every person in her database. It was a frustrating task, not because of traffic or the frantic weather reports or even the crowds at the supermarket. But because each of her charges in one way or another was anxious and more than normally verbose.

Some worried about family members elsewhere in the state. A few fretted because their prescription medications were running low. Hannah was able to help with the second concern, but getting in touch with relatives who couldn't be bothered to pick up a phone made her furious.

People who were fortunate enough to have grandparents and great-grandparents and yet didn't appreciate them ought to be smacked. Maybe that would drill some sense into them. But then again, maybe not. Human nature often meant taking blessings for granted.

Elda didn't ask for anything out of the ordinary when Hannah stopped by late in the afternoon. But she was concerned. She drew Hannah into her warm, fragrant kitchen and pressed her into a chair at the table. "Here," she said, holding out a plate. "Eat a cookie. And then promise me you're about to go home and get your own place ready. I don't like you out driving in this mess."

Hannah bit into the peanut butter bar with alacrity and mumbled around a mouthful of sugar and calories. "Don't go all dramatic on me, Elda. The sun is still shining. Remember? They aren't looking for landfall until the wee hours of Friday morning."

Hannah sniffed. "That's barely thirty-six hours from now. And what about your windows? Have you picked up plywood? Do you have plenty of nonperishable food? What about Morgan? Will he be there with you? You shouldn't be alone."

Hannah rolled her eyes. "This isn't a soap opera, my love. I'm not boarding up any windows, because Constance is not supposed to be more than a category one. My cabinets are full, thank you very much, and as for Morgan, I'd say he's got his hands full out at the site. I'm a big girl. I'll be fine in my apartment, I swear. Unless you want me to ride out the storm here with you."

Elda frowned. "Of course not. But I don't like the idea of you being on your own."

Hannah stood up and hugged her. "I've been on my own a long time now. I'm perfectly capable of dealing with one barely impressive weather pattern. And as for Morgan, I sure as heck am not going to add to his stress by whining like a sissy girl. He has to make all sorts of preparations and take tons of precautions at work. We didn't even get to eat dinner together last night, because they called him out to the site unexpectedly. I doubt I'll see him tonight, either. But quit worrying. I'll be fine."

∽

Rachelle turned off the Weather Channel. It was making her nervous. She couldn't seem to stop looking at the stupid graphic that showed a swirling eye bearing down on Florida. She still remembered the terrible hurricane that had ripped a swath of devastation through her neighborhood when she was only seven years old, and even though Constance was barely up to speed in terms of being a powerful storm, the very uncertainty of it all scared Rachelle.

She heard the front door open and knew Timmy was home. He was expecting them to leave for their appointment as soon as the sitter arrived.

Rachelle bit her lip. She felt guilty and confused and ready to cry.

He found her in their bedroom. She held a finger to her lips. "I finally got her to sleep. Please be quiet."

She knew he'd been about to scoop her up in one of his enthusiastic hugs, but her body language warned him off. He shoved his hands in the pockets of his jeans, his expression troubled. "Why aren't you dressed, babe? Beebo's sister will be here in twenty minutes."

Rachelle winced. Beebo was a longtime buddy of Timmy's. A beer-drinking, loud-mouthed, motorcycle-riding hulk of man. She was terrified at the thought of leaving her innocent baby in the care of the guy's unknown sister.

Her face must have been easy to read, because Timmy frowned. "What's wrong?" He stared at her, almost belligerent, it seemed.

She shrugged, tightening the sash of her thin nylon bathrobe. She'd showered, but that was as far as she had gotten. "I'm not sure I can do this, Timmy. You know I don't like leaving the baby."

His face softened. "I went over and talked to Beebo's sister. She's a very nice lady, two years older than him, and enrolled in college. She wants to be a teacher. We can trust her, I swear."

Rachelle knew he was telling the truth. And she knew she wasn't being fair. She had promised Timmy she would try to book them two appointments this week, but somehow, it just hadn't happened. And now with the storm coming, the late-morning time slot reserved for them today was their last shot before Friday night's group session.

She wrapped her arms around her waist. "We could make love here," she said. She smiled at him, even though she didn't feel at all amorous. It didn't take much to coax her young, hormone-driven husband into bed. And surely she could convince him to send the sitter home.

Timmy froze in the act of peeling off his T-shirt. His typical buoyancy faded, and suddenly he looked at least ten years older.

He dropped the shirt on the floor, his face pale. "I *need* this, Rachelle. And I'm not talking about having sex. I know that being parents means we have to sacrifice for the baby, for our family. But I need to know that I come first with you sometimes. I have to know if you still want me. I can't be on the edges of your radar indefinitely. Please don't break this appointment. I'm begging you."

The raw vulnerability in his voice, on his face, shocked her. Timmy was not a deep man. He worked and played and loved with abandon. He was a happy person. But the boy looking at her now, a boy far too young to have a wife and a child, seemed haggard and desperate.

She swallowed the lump in her throat. "Of course I want you. You're my husband."

His jaw firmed, his eyes turbulent with emotion. "Then show me, Rachelle. Today."

The sitter's arrival was almost anticlimactic. Beebo's sister, all supposition to the contrary, was clearly a capable person. She *oohed* and *aahed* over the baby with endearing enthusiasm. Rachelle assumed the woman thought Timmy and Rachelle were off to see a movie and have lunch... the things most young parents love to do when given half a chance. So Rachelle didn't disabuse her.

Thankfully, their clunker of a car cooperated. They made it downtown right on time and headed upstairs to claim their key and find the room. After a brief stop at the reception desk, they went down the hallway and paused in front of room four.

Timmy reached out to put the key in the lock, and Rachelle laid her hand on his. "I love you, Timmy. And I *do* need you... so much it hurts. I'm sorry."

His crooked, goofy grin flashed, making his eyes light up. "I know you do, sweetheart. Same here."

Timmy's chest was still tight, and his knees were knocking. He didn't know where he'd found the courage to lay down an ultimatum. It wasn't his style at all. And he felt like a pussy for being so damned needy.

But this fatherhood thing was tough to take. The six weeks of post-delivery celibacy had been bad enough. But watching Rachelle bond with the baby and at the very same time shut him out made everything inside him feel sick and uncertain.

Did other women do this? Did they turn all their love toward a helpless little bundle of need and in the process forget the husbands who adored them?

He felt shame for not being able to be a better man. For not rising above the physical demands of his body and being able to go cold turkey on fucking until life got better. Or at least easier.

But what if nothing ever changed? What if this was the new status quo? That's what scared him shitless. He could handle the responsibilities of fatherhood. But he couldn't bear it if his young wife loved their baby more than she did her clumsy, not-all-that-smart husband.

He looked around the room with interest. It was dark and somber today. A couple of leather chairs sat in front of a fake fireplace complete with realistic gas logs and a small, crackling flame.

One wall had been outfitted with bookshelves, all full of leather-bound volumes, and somehow the good doctors had squeezed in a small pool table, as well. The whole place had a masculine feel to it.

Rachelle picked up the instructions and read them with a puzzled look on her face.

He peered over her shoulder, "What's the matter?"

She turned to face him. "Nothing. It says I'm supposed to pretend you're my very rich, very successful husband. You've been away on an extended series of business trips, and you've been ignoring me. I'm supposed to entertain you and seduce you."

Timmy's eyebrows, and his dick, rose. "Sounds fun to me. When do we start?"

"We're supposed to put on costumes."

He didn't waste any time waiting to see what she would do. He turned to the pile of masculine clothing on the nearest chair and started putting it on. The tweed jacket, dark slacks, and dress shirt were top-of-the-line. He doubted whether he'd ever be the kind of guy who wore such clothes, but he was prepared to do so if it meant hurrying this along. He wanted his wife.

When he was properly clad down to his thin, expensive socks and highly polished wingtips, he felt ridiculous. But he sat in one of the high-back chairs and glanced in Rachelle's direction. His breath whistled between his teeth and his body tensed. Sweet heaven.

She was already outfitted for her part in a black satin maid's dress trimmed with white collar and cuffs. Her long, sexy legs were covered in fishnet stockings, and she wore black stiletto heels. The scanty frock was cut out on the tits to show Rachelle's nipples. When he dragged his gaze to her face, she was flushed with embarrassment. He shifted one of his legs to hide his boner. No need to be too blatant about his pressing need.

He cleared his throat. "You look hot, babe."

She smoothed the small skirt. "I feel silly. Does this kind of thing really turn men on?"

He chuckled hoarsely. "Oh, yeah. No worries there." He

started to stand up and then belatedly remembered that he was supposed to be bored with his wife.

Fat chance. He picked up the newspaper on the table beside him. He opened it and pretended to read. Occasionally, he surreptitiously peeped over the top to monitor Rachelle's behavior.

She stood irresolute for long agonizing seconds. He gripped the paper so hard that the side of one page tore. His hands were sweaty, and the newsprint rubbed off on his palms. Finally, Rachelle approached him.

His heart was pounding, but he kept his eyes on the headlines. He felt her at his knee. And then she spoke, her voice tentative.

"Timmy?"

He lowered the paper half an inch, his expression deliberately stern. "Call me Tim. I'm a grown man, not a boy."

She bit her lip. "Right. Of course. You're the man of the house." She said it absently as though trying the words on for size. She wiped her hands on her tiny apron. "I missed you." The statement was hesitant.

He folded the Times. "Did you keep busy while I was away?" He tried not to look at her lips. They were shiny and wet, and he wanted to lick the gloss. It tasted like peppermint. He knew. It was her favorite.

She smiled. "I've been going to aerobics. You know. To keep in shape. I know men like their wives to be thin and beautiful."

In her words he heard something that rang a bell in his head, even through the haze of sexual hunger. Did Rachelle think her body was no longer sexy? She was a few pounds heavier after the baby, but mostly in the breasts and ass. Two places a man enjoyed a bit of curviness.

And even if she'd gained a lot more, why would it matter to him? She would still be his beautiful Rachelle.

He leaned back in his chair. "You look great. What else have you done?"

With grace, she went to her knees and put her cheek on his thigh. "Mostly I missed you," she said huskily. Her hands stroked his calf. Even through his pants her touch felt hot and suggestive.

He was embarrassingly close to coming, and they hadn't even made it twenty minutes into their session. He moved her hand away from his body. "Stand up." His tone was bland. "I want to look at you."

She was clumsier this time, staggering when one of her heels caught the carpet. He reached to steady her and they both gasped when his fingers accidentally made contact with her bare nipples. He jerked back, feeling sweat gather on his forehead. The damn tie was choking him. He closed his eyes for a split second and then tried to emulate boredom as he ran his gaze from her head to her toes.

He nodded brusquely. "Why are you dressed like a hooker?"

She gasped, looking hurt. "I was trying to entertain you."

His fingers gripped the chair arms. "Why?"

She licked her lips. "You've been gone a long time. I thought we should spend some time together. You know. In bed."

He spread his knees and reached for her hand. "Come closer." When her thighs were trapped between his, he leaned forward and caught the nearest nipple between his teeth. Rachelle cried out. He groaned deep in his chest as he worked the nipple with his teeth and tongue until he felt the gradual loosening of her entire body.

She had been tense and stiff since they entered the room, and he sure as hell didn't want sex unless she was prepared to enjoy it, too. He put a hand between her legs. Her head fell back as she shivered.

She wasn't wearing any underwear. His fingers delved into her slick, moist warmth. He bit back a curse as he felt his sex tremble and spasm. God, he was close. And it was stupidly embarrassing. A man needed staying power to satisfy a woman. In that respect, he was still too damned young. He had to gain control of the situation or this was going to be all fucked up.

He reached for his belt buckle and undid his zipper. Rachelle had backed up a step or two as soon as he released her. She watched, her gaze riveted on his lap, as he freed himself and deliberately jerked off. It didn't take much. His breath caught, his eyes squeezed shut, and a violent, wonderful shudder of release ripped through his aching dick and balls.

He caught the come in the paisley silk handkerchief from his jacket pocket and when he could move, laid it aside. As calmly as he was able with his chest still heaving, he spoke steadily, "Let's try that again."

He beckoned her a second time, and this go-round, he was at least able to touch her intimately without desperately wanting to climax. He fondled her sex, keeping his deliberate assault teasing, light.

Rachelle had her eyes closed. He stopped what he was doing and leaned back in his chair.

Her eyelashes flew open, her mouth slack. "What's wrong?"

He had to stifle a grin. He tucked his hands behind his head, studying her provocative appearance. "I believe *you* are supposed to be seducing me."

She ran her hands through her silky blond hair. "Right. Okay."

It pleased him that she was clearly rattled. He lifted a finger and circled it in the air. "Face away from me. And strip. Give me a show."

Her eyes flashed, but she obeyed. She put her back to him, and he knew she was unbuttoning the little excuse for a dress. When she turned around, his eyes bugged out. Her tits played peek-a-boo with the partially open bodice. The full, lush curves of her breasts made his mouth water. He grabbed the edge of her skirt and reeled her in. "That's enough."

His voice was slurred, all his attention on the dark shadow of her cleavage. He drew the sides of her top together and positioned the cloth so that once again, her nipples poked through. He bent forward and suckled them, tugging with his teeth and lips.

Something warm and slightly sweet spurted against his tongue. Rachelle jerked and struggled. It took him a few seconds to process her groan as anguish and not pleasure. Her face was red, her mouth trembling. "Damn, Timmy. I'm sorry, I didn't mean for that to happen."

Her milk had let down. For a second he, too, was embarrassed. They had not played like this since their daughter was born. Was he an ass for getting turned on? Was this twisted?

And then he looked at Rachelle's fresh, beautiful sensuality and knew the answer. He stood up and gathered her into his arms, holding her with every ounce of tenderness he could muster. "You're the mother of my child," he said softly. "That's a miracle. And you're also my hot, gorgeous babe of a wife. I can't help it if everything about your body turns me on."

She pulled back enough to see his face. "Everything?" In her eyes he saw a plea for reassurance.

He touched her nipple lightly, gathering a bead of milk on his fingertip. He licked it off. Then he ran his finger in the sticky wetness a second time and rubbed it on her lower lip. "Everything," he muttered.

He kissed her roughly, thrusting his tongue in her mouth and crushing her to his chest when he felt her respond. For weeks it seemed like she had done no more than tolerate him out of guilt or duty. Today he wanted her passion, her hunger.

And she gave it to him, thank God.

He ripped the dress from her body, tearing buttons and lace in the process. But he let her keep the shoes. He was hard again, and the stupid dress clothes that made him seem like someone he wasn't chafed suddenly.

He frowned at her. "Undress me, woman. We're supposed to be having a seduction, right?"

Rachelle's face lightened, and she actually giggled, a light-hearted, girlish sound that made her seem the age she really was. Her hands wrestled with his belt, his buttons, his stifling jacket. Her task took her longer than his, but eventually they were both nude. He resisted the urge to tumble her to the carpet. He was pretending to be a successful man of the world. A man who had made fucking an art form. He put his hands on his hips. "Go bend over the pool table. And close your eyes."

Those very same eyes widened in interested shock and anticipation. She sashayed over to the baize-covered game surface, deliberately twisting her hips as she walked. Her mouthwatering ass was curvy and firm, her legs long and slender. She paused to pull her hair over her shoulder. Now the back of her neck and the line of her spine enticed him beyond endurance.

He watched patiently as she picked up a pair of balls, cupped them in her hands, and sprawled over the table, her butt in the air. The naughty high heels were icing on the cake.

Good God Almighty. Had any man living ever seen a more delectable sight? He stalked her, his fists clenched, his groin aching. How to start? His brain was fried suddenly, probably by the incredibly carnal visual stimulation. For a guy barely out of his teens, it was the equivalent of a nuclear power surge.

He stopped just behind her and placed his hands on her ass. The skin was soft and warm. He rubbed her bottom, sliding his thumbs down her crack and plumping the flesh. Then he settled his erection in that same divide and massaged her with his dick.

With a little sigh and moan, her fingers relaxed, and the two brightly colored balls she held rolled away lazily. One found a side pocket and dropped into it with a quiet *thunk.*

He grinned. Nice shot. He urged her up on the table, hoping he wasn't desecrating an expensive item of furniture. When she was on her hands and knees, he removed the dangerous shoes. He picked up the pool cue and used the grip end to tease her.

He spread her stance an inch wider and arched her back. He rubbed the slick enameled surface between the folds of her sex, almost but not quite penetrating. He leaned forward and bit her gently on her ass.

Rachelle cried out and pressed toward his face. He abandoned the pool cue and reached between her thighs to stroke her intimately. She was swollen and so wet it made him dizzy with the driving urge to take her.

He pinched her ass. "Stand up."

She tried to obey, but her movements were uncoordinated. He helped her to her feet and made her step to the edge of the table. Now he could lick her with ease. He tongued her, nibbling her sensitive flesh and anchoring her against his face by gripping her ass.

She was breathing harsh, sobbing breaths, her fingers clenching and unclenching in his hair until she was in danger of jerking him bald. She came suddenly with a wail and then went boneless so that he had to gather her up in his arms to keep her from falling.

He carried her to the chair, seated her carefully, and then dropped to his knees and buried his face between her legs for round two.

He would have liked to pleasure her a third time, but he couldn't wait. The tremors of her second climax had barely subsided before he dragged her to the soft rug, spread her thighs, and entered her with one strong surge.

It was heaven and it was hell. His whole body went rigid, even the cells in his skin were supersensitive, trembling on the edge of reason.

He rode her slowly at first, lifting her lax body into his thrusts over and over again. He tried to concentrate on the visuals, her tightly furled nipples, her taut, full breasts, the beauty of her face washed in passion.

But a man's body will always betray him in the end. He was sweating, panting, holding onto her hips like a lifeline, when a sudden, jagged arc of fire seized his spine, shook him like a helpless puppet, and flung him into a burning lake that closed over his head and dragged him under until even drowning seemed like a blessing.

He slumped on top of her, near exhaustion at the end.

Time had lost all meaning. They might have been in this room for days, weeks.

Something hot and gritty pressed at the back of his eyes. He recognized the emotion and the almost-tears as stunned relief. He hadn't lost his wife. Not at all. It was too much to absorb.

So he pressed his face to her breast and tried to remember that he was a man.

15

Shaun glanced up as Timmy and Rachelle appeared in the reception area. He was about to greet them when he realized they were in a world of their own, Timmy had his arm around Rachelle. She had her head on his shoulder. They were smiling into each other's eyes, and their post-coital glow was unmistakable.

Whatever they had done in the room down the hall had left them satiated and drunk on their love for each other. Timmy whispered something in his wife's ear as they exited the suite of offices. Rachelle's soft giggle lingered as the door *whooshed* shut.

Shaun felt the bitter taste of envy in his mouth, and it wasn't a repast he'd ever really been exposed to. His life had been damn close to perfect. Oh, with a few bumps along the way, but nothing major.

Now he was reduced to being jealous of a barely-past-adolescence boy who still had zits, for godsakes.

Shaun glanced at his watch... again. He and Danita had a one o'clock appointment. He had offered to meet her for lunch beforehand. She had declined. Today was *it* for them.

Their last shot. It must have been Timmy and Rachelle's final experience as well, because the two lovebirds had not paused to fill out a questionnaire.

Shaun dreaded the Friday night wrap-up. How could he sit in front of six other people and confess that the sexual counseling had been a bust? How could he admit that he was no longer able to satisfy his wife in bed?

It was two minutes before one when Danita walked through the door. She wore a more casual outfit today, pink cotton shorts and a pink and white knit top. She was beautiful and put together as always, but for the first time in his memory she seemed haggard, beaten down.

She managed to smile at him, but it was a weak effort. He had already picked up the key, and it took only a few moments to find their assigned room and go inside.

He had told her it didn't matter how the room was set up. That today wasn't about sex. But it was going to be a hard promise to keep. Three TVs on three walls of the room were turned on with low-budget porn flicks running. The carnal sounds of panting and cries and other overtly sexual noises filled the room.

Shaun locked his jaw and quickly turned them off. The rest of the room was not much better. A collection of S and M toys littered the bed, including a riding crop, handcuffs, and silk scarves. Presumably this was what a man got for blowing off last Monday's questionnaire.

Unfortunately there wasn't a single chair in the room, unless you counted the low stool beside the case of dildos. He looked up at the ceiling, closed his eyes, and reminded himself that a lot was riding on today's session. Riding. Ha. He looked at the whip and quickly averted his eyes. He shouldn't be getting any ideas.

Danita fidgeted, her gaze darting around the room

nervously. She still held her purse in front of her, gripping it as if she dared not let it go.

He sighed. "I'll clear off the bed, and we'll sit there to talk. Is that okay with you?"

She nodded briefly, but didn't respond otherwise. It didn't take him long to gather up all the provocative sexual equipment. He dumped it en masse on the hot-pink shag rug that had been turned into a love nest with mounds of purple and black throw pillows.

When the bed looked more utilitarian than erotic, Shaun held out his hand. "Shall we?" Feeling Danita's small hand slip into his gave his heart a jolt. He needed her. In every way. It was as simple as that.

When they were settled side by side with their backs against pillows and the headboard, he stretched out his long legs. Danita had preserved a distance of eighteen inches or so between them, but he didn't protest.

He raised his arms above his head and rolled his neck, feeling the tendons pop and crackle. Then he put his hands on his thighs. "I'll start."

"Okay." Her quiet whisper held relief.

He drummed his fingers. "I'm a one-woman kind of man. From the first day I saw you, I knew you were my other half. And in all these years, that has never changed. But *you've* changed, Danita. And I don't know what to do or how to act. It seems to date back to when the boys left for college, but I thought you handled that ..." He trailed off, not really knowing where to go from there.

He'd expected her to be reluctant. He'd anticipated having to drag information out of her. But she surprised him. Her voice was low but steady as she started to speak.

Danita had rehearsed what she wanted to say. It was important that she make him understand. She wet her lips. "I know you think I don't want sex anymore."

His eyes flashed with an emotion she couldn't name. "Well, do you?"

She exhaled on a long, ragged breath. This wasn't going to be easy. "Do you remember the week the boys went off to college?"

He frowned. "Of course. You cried for three days. I think that was when I started losing you. I tried cheering you up, but nothing worked."

She shook her head. Men, even the good ones, were blind at times. "Do you remember how you tried to cheer me up?" she asked wryly. She could talk about it dispassionately now, but at the time it hadn't been at all funny.

He propped up one knee and slung an elbow over it. "As I recall, I told you how sexy and desirable you were."

There was indignation in his voice. As if he couldn't believe she hadn't appreciated his heavy-handed efforts. She smiled briefly, though the memory wasn't the least bit humorous. She clasped her hands in her lap and stared at them. "It seemed to me that you were glad the boys were gone. And that made me angry."

"Glad?" He said the word with a blank look of confusion on his face. "God, no. My heart was breaking."

Her fingers clenched tighter, her knuckles white. "Well, you sure didn't show it. As far as I could tell, it was good riddance and don't let the screen door slam your butt on the way out."

He was genuinely shocked. She could tell. "You thought I didn't love our boys? That I was happy to see them go? Hell, Danita. It was tearing me apart, but I was trying to be strong for you. You were grieving. I couldn't bear to see you so unhappy."

She half turned to face him. "That's not the impression I got at all," she said somberly. "All you could talk about was how much sex we were going to have and what a novelty it would be to walk around the house naked. You claimed we would be like newlyweds again. Having sex all day long. It seemed to me that you thought our children had been cramping our style all these years and now that they were finally gone, we could screw our brains out."

"And that made you—"

"Angry. Hurt. Confused."

He ran a hand over his forehead, his expression troubled. "Good Lord. All I was trying to do was get your mind off the fact that our big, noisy house was suddenly empty and quiet as a tomb."

She shrugged wryly. "Well, you failed. Nothing was going to make me forget. It's called *empty nest*. All parents go through it. And I dealt with it. I found new interests, made adjustments, changed along with my life."

"But?"

"But I couldn't get past the anger and the hurt. I had poured my life into raising those two wonderful boys and when you seemed to bid them goodbye without a single qualm, it was as if every bit of mothering I had ever done was worthless. Even worse than that, you apparently wanted a sex goddess at your beck and call, and I was nothing more than a middle-aged housewife."

His face was easy to read. He was appalled, shocked, sick at heart. Well, too bad. He'd wanted the truth. So there it was.

He grimaced. "No wonder you didn't want to have sex. I wouldn't have wanted to have sex with me, either."

She picked at a piece of lint on the sheet. "It's not all your fault. Part of it was me. I woke up one day and realized I wasn't young anymore. Then our friends started getting divorced, and I got scared. I knew I needed to spice things up in the bedroom, but the harder I tried, the more frozen I felt inside. Which is a hell of a way to approach sex. But I was afraid if I didn't entertain you, you'd be long gone."

She saw him swallow. His gaze was steady when he spoke. "I would never divorce you, Danita. Some days when I look in the mirror, I still can't believe you picked me. I love you. Nothing in my life matters more to me than you and our boys. I should have told you that when they left, but I thought it would make you feel worse."

She winced. "I wish you had. I needed you to hold me and share the pain. But I thought you weren't experiencing what I was feeling. And that hurt almost as much as losing my babies. It seemed as if the three men I loved most had abandoned me all at once. I was devastated."

"I'm sorry." His face was gray... haunted.

She drew her knees to her chest. "I always loved having sex with you. It scared me when my body stopped responding. But they say the brain is the most powerful sex organ, and I guess my head was in control. I should have tried to explain what was going on inside my thoughts. And for that, I owe *you* an apology."

He dropped his head, his posture defeated. "Where do we go from here?"

She closed her eyes and leaned back against the wall. "I'm so scared," she whispered, her throat tight. "What if we can't get back to where we were?"

"I don't think we can."

Her heart froze in her chest. This was it, then. Love wasn't always enough. "I see."

His rough laugh was not amused. "I don't think you do. We can't go back, my love. But we can go forward. At least I hope we can."

The raw vulnerability on his face pained her. When she was silent, he continued. "But you have to promise me honesty, Danita."

She took his hand. "I could have faked orgasms all those times, but I didn't. Even when it was painful and awkward for both of us." She said it simply. So he would remember the disappointing nights and understand. She saw in his expression that he did.

He linked their fingers, his big hand warm on hers. "I have to know one more thing, sweetheart. During our second session here, when our directions said we were *not* to have orgasms. What happened? The stairwell. You were..." He stopped, clearly at a loss for words.

She felt her face heat, but he was right. He deserved an explanation. Especially since every time after that she froze up again. She broke the clasp of their fingers and put her hands to her face. This was hard to talk about. "The paper said I was not supposed to climax. Suddenly, I didn't have to worry about pleasing you. I wasn't going to seem sexually defective. It was okay if you played with me and nothing happened."

"But something *did* happen," he said softly. She could feel his gaze on her down-turned face. "You went wild in my arms."

"Because there was nothing to prove, I guess."

He sucked in a shocked breath. "Good Lord, Danita. I never expected you to be a trained monkey. Sex is about mutual pleasure. At least it used to be."

She stood up, no longer able to be so near him. But now she had to face all the titillating furnishings in the room.

Gulp. So she decided it was safer to keep her gaze on her husband. "I didn't want to disappoint you. The harder I tried, the worse things got."

He ran a hand through his hair. "Tell me something. On Monday, when I took you like a caveman... literally... Did that excite you? Did you come?"

She nodded, remembering his quasi-rough treatment. "It was erotic and unexpected. You were so... animalistic. The novelty of it all stunned me. And yes... I did have an orgasm."

It was his turn to wince. "Well, that's just great," he said sourly. "If I handle you with respect and tenderness, you can't respond. But if I act like a selfish bastard, you can get off. That sounds kind of sick and twisted to me. Maybe we've gotten so fucked up we don't even know how to do this anymore."

Her jaw dropped. "You don't mean that."

Now he stood up as well. "I'm screwed, Danita. I can't touch you without wondering if I'm doing it right. What would you suggest?" There was quiet despair in his voice.

She looked around the room to give herself time to think. "We have to break old patterns," she said finally. "We'll start over, sexually speaking. No second-guessing each other's motives or thoughts. If we want to know, we'll ask. You can't take it personally if I don't climax. I'll do my best, but no promises."

He raked his hands through his hair. "God, Danita, I don't care if you have a bloody orgasm." He shut his mouth abruptly, his expression comically chagrined. "That came out wrong."

She giggled. "I hope so." Then she sobered. "I want to concentrate on making love to you without worrying about the ending. I want to feel sensual and sexual and relaxed. I want to have fun."

He nodded slowly. "Agreed."

They faced each other with the bed between them. She kicked off her sandals, pulled her top over her head, and flung it aside. Clad only in her bra and shorts, she teased him. "So no trying to make me come."

He held up his hands. "I swear."

"And no hiding your feelings. If you're sad and upset, I want to know it."

He shoved his hands in his pockets. The fabric of his pants tightened across his abdomen, and she could see his erection. "I swear I'll cry on your shoulder every chance I get."

She grinned, feeling her heavy heart lighten. "Smart-ass."

He rubbed his neck. "Smart? Doubtful. Sexy? Maybe... you want to check it out?" He stripped off his clothes so rapidly that she blinked and had to clear her throat. He was a man in his prime... hard-bodied, tough, intensely masculine. And his penis. She tried to drag her gaze from it, but the thick column of flesh was mesmerizing. Particularly with her own hunger building by the minute.

He was waiting for her to say something, but a sudden, inexplicable shyness paralyzed her vocal chords. When she didn't move, he came around the bed and gently removed her bra. But he didn't touch her breasts otherwise. They stood there, breathing the same air, the room fraught with overtones of sexual hunger, painful uncertainty, and a fragile blossom of hope.

He brushed her cheek with the pad of his thumb. "Why don't you take control, my love? Make me your sex slave. Do with me what you will. Then my giving you an orgasm will be a moot point."

She shook her head, knowing instinctively that it was the wrong approach. "No," she said simply. "I want you to be sexually dominant. It has to be that way. At least until I can unlearn this stupid internal mechanism that shuts down all my responses at a certain point."

He frowned. "You think that will work?"

She placed a palm on his warm chest, feeling the steady beat of his heart beneath the layers of skin and bone. "I don't know. But I'd like to give it a try." She linked her arms around his neck. "Take me and make love to me. No holds barred. Give it your best shot."

∾

Shaun had known real fear a time or two in his life. The night his twin sons were born and Danita's blood pressure spiked. The day a child ran in front of his car on a rainy street. The time his mother tripped and fell down a partial flight of stairs.

But all those terrible moments faded into the past in light of this new and heart-stopping challenge. Was he man enough to risk it?

He remembered their recent pledge about honesty. "I'm scared," he admitted hoarsely. This woman was his life. The thought of hurting her in any way, mentally or otherwise, was unbearable.

She kissed him softly. "I trust you, Shaun. And I'm not going anywhere."

He took a deep, ragged breath and scooped her into his arms. It was the work of minutes to fold back the covers, deposit her on the bed, and secure her wrists with handcuffs. Apparently his quick motions startled her, because her eyes widened to a wary gaze.

With her upper body immobilized, he stripped off her shorts and panties. He paused to kiss her sex, lingering to nuzzle her with his nose and breathe in her erotic scent. Danita moved restlessly, but he ignored her.

Next, he turned on all the TVs but lowered the volumes so that the sexual soundtrack didn't intrude overmuch. He saw Danita's eyes go to the nearest screen. He grinned inwardly as he watched her cheeks flush. Her teeth worried her bottom lip. Her nipples tightened and hardened as she monitored the action on the set.

With his lovely wife temporarily occupied, he was able to go about his business unobserved. He gathered up the case of dildos and carried it to the bed. When he sat down by her hip, the mattress dipped.

She looked up at him, and then she noticed what was in his hands. Now she turned beet red. Her breathing began to come in short, sharp jerks.

He made a big show of selecting a specimen from the velvet-lined box. It was a nice collection, no expense spared. The one he finally picked was surely an antique. It was realistically carved ivory, and the warm cream shade of the shaft suggested another era.

Danita tugged at her wrists. He ignored her. He picked up a tube of lubricant and spread his wife's thighs. Gently, he smeared the sticky substance all over the folds of her sex, but he was careful to avoid the spot that controlled her release.

Then he took the ivory implement, tested its weight in his hands, and began to press it deep into his wife's pussy. Danita cried out, and he stopped. "Am I hurting you?" It was a genuine question. The thing was big and hard.

Danita shook her head. "No." Her barely audible response reassured him. He moved the dildo deeper, probing gently, twisting so the carvings in the ivory would stimulate her sensitive inner flesh.

He used it like that for long minutes, slowly most of the time, but occasionally with quick sharp thrusts. He saw in her face the instant she neared her climax. He withdrew the toy and put his hand over her mouth. "You must be completely quiet," he hissed. "You don't want the people out there to hear you."

Again he entered her. His own shaft was nearly as hard as the fake one. But he ignored the need to fuck her. This was too much fun.

Danita's hips lifted an inch from the mattress as she sought the relief she needed. He'd been careful to avoid a certain place. The omission had drawn out the torture. Danita would climax. He was sure of it. But without deliberate stimulation of that tiny bundle of nerves, the impending explosion would be postponed.

He moved the shaft more quickly still with his hand over his wife's mouth. Her eyes were large and frantic. She bit his fingers. He jerked them away with a curse. "Naughty girl," he whispered. "You'll pay for that."

He left the ivory penis in his wife's pussy and moved up on the bed. Now he teased her breasts. Danita had lovely tits, full and round with rosy nipples. He nipped the tips one at a time with his teeth, laughing softly when she cried out and called him names.

Seeing the lewd object protruding from her body made him crazy. He bent and kissed her roughly, devouring her mouth and squeezing her breasts at the same time.

Her lovely eyes pleaded with him. "Let me go."

He studied her nudity, the complete sexual abandon of her pose. "No," he said simply "I'm not finished."

He straddled her waist and rested most of his weight on her. He took his shaft and rubbed it from base to tip. The stimulation was almost too much. He was on the edge.

She watched him, her face flushed, her chest heaving. Slowly, he began to work his sex with one hand, closing his eyes and giving in to temptation. With his free hand, he reached behind him and moved the dildo in his lover's body. It was difficult to concentrate on both tasks at the same time, but he was extremely motivated.

Danita tried to escape, but he had her pinned down. He moved the ivory more briskly. Her legs twisted restlessly He pumped his shaft, groaning aloud at the raw pleasure. Suddenly, he gripped the head of his prick and rubbed her nipples, shouting as his come shot over his wife's chest in warm, gushing spurts.

He lifted his leg and rolled to the side, settling on his knees and gasping for breath.

She landed a blow on his hip with her knee. "Do something," she wailed.

He moved between her legs and grasped the dildo. Their eyes met, hers wild with hunger, his implacable. "No one but me... ever."

She nodded, jerkily.

"And sex every night if I want it."

Another nod, but he was losing her.

He pressed the thing deeper into his wife's slick passage. "And you'll enjoy sex, even if I have to torture you like this night after night."

He twisted one last time, and covered her mouth with his hand just as she screamed and went rigid in a long, shuddering orgasm.

He rotated the ivory shaft slowly as she shivered into relaxation. Then he removed it and kissed her most intimate flesh. He nudged her sex with his tongue. Danita protested faintly.

He lifted an eyebrow. "Too soon?"

She glared at him. "Too sensitive."

He took her ankles and held them apart. "I have seven more dildos to try. And forty-five more minutes to use them. I can't afford to waste any time."

She struggled wildly, her hair falling in her face, her skin damp with perspiration. "Don't you dare."

He studied the box of toys intently. Then, keeping a straight face, he looked back at his desperate wife. "I don't know. It seems a shame to waste them."

Her chest heaved, doing interesting things to her dewy breasts. "Let me go," she panted, "and I'll make it worth your while."

He reached up without ceremony and unlocked the handcuffs. Danita tumbled into his embrace, wrapping her arms around his waist and covering his throat and neck with kisses. "I love you, Shaun."

The lump in his throat made it tough to respond. "I adore you, angel," he said gruffly. "Your mind, your body, the way you say my name when you want to come."

She took his soft penis in her hand and played with it gently, her eyes downcast. "Are we going to be okay?"

He could barely hear her voice. He stroked her hair. "You tell me."

When she looked up at him, her eyes sparkled with unshed tears. But she was smiling. "I'm not a twenty-year-old sex goddess."

He squeezed her in a bear hug. "Thank God. I'd never be able to keep up with you."

She kissed him softly. "I loved being a mother, but not as much as being your wife."

The quiet conviction in her statement hit him hard. "I'm not asking you to choose," he said, feeling guilty for some reason.

She had played with him until he was fully erect and ready to go. Now she bent and kissed the head of his sex. "Motherhood is a temporary job. But I'll be your wife forever. And that makes me very happy."

He groaned and fell back on the bed as she started in on an enthusiastic blowjob. "God, I hope so, my love. Because I can't live without you."

16

Hannah wandered around her apartment in a crappy mood. It was late Thursday evening and the first bands of rainfall from Constance were moving over the state. Already, some streets with poor drainage were flooding.

Morgan had called midafternoon and begged off from their final appointment at the Hursts' office. He was apologetic, but the crew at the theme park site was going crazy trying to outwit the coming storm.

She reassured him, of course, that she understood. And she did. But it didn't stop her from being disappointed. She was rapidly becoming addicted to those sexual sessions, and she wondered how he would feel about signing up for another two-week block. Tomorrow night was supposed to be the group wrap-up, but because of Constance, the meeting had already been postponed until Saturday afternoon at three, weather permitting.

Sadly, the delay meant that Friday would be one long day cooped up inside. Hannah hated inactivity. She would never have survived in a nine-to-five office job. That's why she loved working with her elderly clients at all three retirement center locations. It kept her out and about and so busy that the days flew by.

She microwaved some popcorn around nine o'clock and ended up not eating it. Her stomach hurt, probably from PMS. That only added to her general blue mood. And she missed Morgan. He had eased his way into her life and made himself indispensable. Despite her best efforts to keep some personal boundaries in their relationship, she now realized that although she *could* function on her own without a man, she no longer wanted to.

She stared at the TV blindly as the truth hit her. She loved Morgan. And she wanted to be his wife. Wow. When had she stopped being scared of that idea? Had those counseling questionnaires and sessions really worked, or was she simply coming to a conclusion that should have been clear to her a long time ago?

Morgan was a man for the long haul. They complemented each other. And the love they shared was strong enough to last. Even if things got rough from time to time, as they invariably would.

She realized that she was smiling a goofy, excited smile. She wanted to tell Elda. Heck, she wanted to tell the world. But Morgan deserved to be the first one to hear her confession. Hannah Quarles was tired of being a coward. She'd been a physical daredevil from time to time, but that was only to cover up her basic insecurities.

Now she no longer had to hide. She was ready to be in love. She was ready to be part of a couple. She was ready to take the plunge, white dress and all.

Everything inside her went all mushy and soft as she imagined gliding down a long, carpeted aisle, wearing a fairy-tale gown and walking toward the handsome man who waited for her. He would be so happy. She couldn't wait to let him know.

But he was in the middle of an extremely stressful situation at the moment. She would wait until the storm was over to have the *big talk*. Maybe on Saturday, after the final group thing, the two of them could go out to dinner and she would tell him she wanted to set a date.

She grinned to herself, imagining his face when she broke the news. Then she looked at the beautiful ring he had placed on her finger. Mrs. Hannah Webber. It sounded pretty darn good. This was going to be a great weekend.

∽

Morgan rolled over on the hard, narrow sofa and groaned as he tried squinting at the clock on the far wall of the trailer to check the time. The faint gray light of dawn told his internal body clock it must be around six thirty, even if he couldn't quite read the numbers. Every bone in his body protested the idea of moving. Because of an insane need to monitor the rapidly deteriorating weather situation overnight, he'd camped out in this stifling metal box along with two of his best guys who were now sprawled out in sleeping bags at his feet.

It had been sometime after midnight when they all fell comatose into bed, or what passed for bed at the moment. The pounding rain on the metal roof, along with the shrieking winds, had sounded like a glimpse of hell. For several hours beforehand they had worked like dogs making preparations, but the storm would have the last word. He just hoped they'd be able to clean up the mess in a day or two and get back on schedule.

He nudged his cohorts one at a time with his foot. "Hey... you two... let's go see how bad it is."

The scope of the disaster was appalling. Morgan swallowed the sour taste of defeat and scrubbed his hands over his face. It was still raining, of course, but the water falling now was a gentle shower compared to what had gone before.

The radio stations were reporting that fourteen inches of precipitation had pounded the central part of the state in as little as six hours. The site for the next great theme park no longer existed.

Morgan was stunned. And angry. And tired to the point that his hair follicles ached. As far as the eye could see there was nothing left of his months of hard work but a sea of mud littered with palm branches and debris. The underground pipes that had been so painstakingly laid out in grids were mostly exposed. Worse than that, they were broken, twisted, crumpled by the whims of Mother Nature. In another month or so the paving and planting would have begun. But the site had been at its most vulnerable moment, and now it was nothing more than a wet, mucky garbage heap.

He reached desperately for perspective. There was no loss of life. This wasn't his personal money at stake. And there was insurance, of course. But the sheer waste made him sick. He walked over to where the other two men stood and stared at them grimly. "Start making phone calls. Get as many of our guys back out here as you can. We might as well get started."

It killed Hannah to hear the defeat and misery in Morgan's voice Friday morning and not be able to help him. He had called primarily to check on her, but he'd been unable to disguise his frustration. She had dragged all the details out into the open. Maybe knowing she was waiting for him could be enough to get him through this tough spot.

She knew it would be tomorrow at least before she would see him again. He had promised to meet her for the last group session. In the meantime, she would stay busy and try not to worry about him constantly.

She called Elda to make sure things were okay at Fluffy Palms. The report was good. Some downed trees. A few cars damaged. But nothing major. The two other retirement centers fared about the same.

Hannah kept the Weather Channel on as she puttered around the apartment. Constance had moved out into the Gulf and would soon be causing problems for Louisiana or Texas. Occasionally one of the roving reporters did a location update from Orlando. Many streets were flooded and some power lines were down. Law enforcement had requested that the public cut out all but the most essential trips by car. Traffic light outages and debris on the roads made travel dangerous.

Hannah still felt slightly nauseous, and she wished her period would start. Food was not at all appealing, but she made herself eat soup and a grilled cheese for lunch. Afterward, she decided to clean out her bedroom closet. That would keep her occupied until dinnertime, and then maybe a movie and a long talk on the phone with her fiancé would round out the evening.

She rubbed her tummy and grimaced. What she really wanted to do was veg on the couch all day, but that seemed self-indulgent in the extreme. She had plenty of chores she had been putting off. And today was the perfect time to play catch-up.

~

By Saturday morning, Morgan was ready to drop. He wasn't authorized to approve overtime, and besides, until the land started drying out, he'd done about all that was in his power to ameliorate the situation. The crew had spent hours yesterday shoveling up the detritus from the storm, and now all they could do was wait.

The sun was supposed to make an appearance this afternoon, so surely by Monday there would be some improvement in the soil conditions. In the meantime, he would go home, clean up, and sleep for a while before meeting Hannah downtown.

He never got past the shower, unfortunately. His mother phoned, and he could tell from her voice that something was wrong. His still-young, self-reliant parents rarely contacted him for any kind of help, so despite the poor timing, he felt like he had to go.

He stopped by Hannah's on the way. She opened the door, and a smile lit up her face. "You're early," she said, pulling him inside for a hug and a kiss.

He held her tightly, feeling some of his tension drain away.

"I hate like hell to tell you this, but I've got to go to Ocala. My mom called, and something is wrong. She wouldn't tell me over the phone, but I'm wondering if the house has been damaged."

Her face fell, but she managed a smile. "It's okay, Morgan, really. I'll go on to the meeting without you. And they'll all understand. You take care of your parents. Make sure they're okay."

He covered her mouth in a long lazy kiss that threatened to lead to something else. Even as tired as he was, his body was primed and ready. Holding Hannah had that effect on him every time.

Finally he broke the kiss and simply held her. He would give just about anything to walk down the hall to her bedroom, make love to her for an hour, and then sleep with her... sweet, blessed sleep.

He straightened and brushed a kiss on her forehead. "I'll make it up to you, sweetheart. I promise."

She followed him to the door and pinched his butt. "I'm counting on it," she teased. As he stepped into the hall, Hannah put a hand on his arm. "Wait a minute."

He lifted an eyebrow, his gaze roving over her face, her hair, her soft, wonderful body. "Yeah?"

She touched him in an intimate location, causing him to suck in a quick appreciative breath. "I have a special surprise for you tonight," she purred, her fingers bold and dead on. Much more of this and he'd be taking her in the hallway and to hell with anything else.

He cleared his throat. "Will I like it?" he asked, trying to remember why he had to leave.

She gave him one last naughty caress. "I can guarantee it. You'll be a happy man."

∽

Morgan's parents lived in an upscale two-story colonial at the fringes of his dad's favorite golf course. Grandpa Webber had opened a rental car company back in the early sixties when tourism was beginning to boom, and had amassed a respectable amount of money from his efforts.

Morgan's dad took over in the early eighties, and the family fortune had continued to grow. When Morgan evinced no interest in the business, his dad kept right on working. Finally, a year ago, he took early retirement, and now he enjoyed his daily golf games and his well-earned, relaxing lifestyle.

When Morgan pulled up in the driveway, everything looked fairly normal. A couple of the trees had lost small branches. And junk still littered the street and yard. But other than that, he couldn't see a problem.

Of course, the roof might have leaked. That wasn't always obvious from the outside. Then he gave himself a mental kick and climbed out of the car, his muscles aching. He wasn't going to solve the puzzle by sitting out here doing nothing.

His mother answered the door, and on first glance, seemed her usual self. She herded him back to the kitchen and offered him lunch. Since he'd skipped breakfast, and his stomach was growling, he jumped on the invitation. His mom's chicken salad was legendary.

His dad joined them moments later, his demeanor distracted. He was even quieter than normal. Morgan's mom was the talker in the family. The three of them chitchatted idly until the meal was complete, and then Morgan tried to figure out what was wrong. "Mom... Dad... is there a problem from the storm? Do you need me to go up on the roof and check things out?"

Morgan's mother paled. She looked down at her hands folded in her lap. His dad shoved back from the table and stalked to the sink, staring out the window at the wet, messy yard. His back was stiff.

Morgan swallowed a fillip of unease. "Mom?" He would start with her since it was obvious his dad wasn't inclined to be communicative. Or maybe his mom had called Morgan without informing her husband, and his dad was pissed. His pop hated being coddled, especially if there were any hints about him getting older.

Morgan was tired, his usual patience at a low ebb. "Mom." He repeated the single syllable forcibly. "What the heck is going on?"

She raised her head, tears glittering in her eyes. For the first time he could remember, she looked her age. "Your father and I are getting a divorce."

Morgan heard a ringing in his ears, like that one time during high school wrestling when a two-hundred-pound classmate had knocked him flat on his ass.

He blinked rapidly and realized his vision was not quite right. He coughed and fidgeted in his chair. "Excuse me?" His stomach hurt with a sharp pain that might have been bad mayonnaise.

Suddenly, his father whirled around, his face grim and resolute. "You heard her. We're getting a divorce."

Morgan gaped at them as his world crashed at his feet. This was it, then. Hannah would never marry him now.

That ludicrous thought was completely out of context. He should be worrying about his parents… their well-being. He should be doing something to make this right.

But he sat, paralyzed, in the cheery yellow and white kitchen and managed the only word he could formulate in his shock, "Why?"

His dad turned back to the window. His mom folded and refolded her cloth napkin. His mom always used cloth, whatever the occasion. She thought paper was low-class and showed a lack of hospitality.

He wanted to get up and leave. He felt a pressure in his chest and an urge to vomit. But he gripped the edge of the table and said it again. "Why?"

His mother faced him, her chin high and her eyes bright with defiance. "Your father and I have nothing in common. We've grown apart. We no longer want the same things in life."

He leaned forward, desperation and an oddly juvenile sense of loss eating him alive. "But you still love each other... right?"

His father finally faced them both, his arms crossed over his chest, his lips twisted in what was almost a sneer. But his eyes held suffering. "Apparently not, son. It seems that we've used up that particular commodity, and it's not a renewable resource."

Morgan felt like a stuttering fool. He was not prepared for this, had no training for this. How did you tell your parents they were acting like idiots? He cleared his throat and glanced in anguish from one to the other. "But what will you do?"

His mother spoke up without missing a beat. "Your father will keep the house since he's so attached to his golfing buddies." Her voice dripped venom. "I plan to move... maybe get an apartment in New York. I've always wanted to enjoy the cosmopolitan lifestyle."

Morgan's dad let out a vicious curse his son had never heard him use in thirty years. Then he gazed at his only child. "We had to tell you first. Before gossip got out." He stopped suddenly, real contrition marking his face. "I'm sorry, Morgan. But this is for the best. And you'll just have to accept it."

Hannah felt a bit awkward walking into the group appointment alone, but when she explained about Morgan and the theme park site and his parents, everyone nodded. You couldn't live in Florida and not understand how a hurricane could turn life upside down.

The other two couples had arrived before her, and she was surprised to see a noticeable difference in their behavior since the last time. Both sets of spouses were practically sitting in each other's laps, smiling and touching and generally looking like honeymooners.

Hannah hid a frown as she got comfortable on her one half of a loveseat. Had she and Morgan missed out on something the rest of them had discovered behind closed doors?

Thankfully, Dr. Pat and Dr. Sheila hadn't changed. They were friendly and professional. After inquiring about how everyone had fared during the storm, they got the ball rolling.

Dr. Sheila smiled coyly. "Well," she said, raising her eyebrows. "Were you all happy with how your sessions unfolded?"

Shaun leaned forward, his gaze intent. "I have a question about that."

Dr. Pat waved a hand. "Go ahead."

"How did you know or how did you decide what kind of scenario to set up for each individual session since you had two sets of responses every time to work from?"

Dr. Pat nodded. "Good question. We made judgment calls. Sheila and I read both sets of answers and together we decided what aspect of your relationship had been called into question on that particular day. Sometimes both of you headed in the same direction with your answers, and our job was easy. Other times, you gave divergent comments, but even then we could usually pick out a theme or a point of conflict. We tried to address those as well."

Shaun sat back in his seat and Dr. Sheila smiled, encompassing the five of them in her gaze. "So who wants to be brave and tell me what you learned about yourself and your spouse? You can avoid specifics. We don't want you to kiss and tell." A quiet titter of embarrassed laughter filtered through the room.

Timmy and Rachelle were holding hands. The young woman grinned at her husband and then looked shyly at the group. "I was able to step back and see how I was making our baby the center of my life. That's not healthy, and it sure isn't fair to Tim or our marriage. Plus, I'm cheating myself when I feel only like a mom and not like a wife."

"A very sexy wife," Timmy cut in with a loving glance at his spouse. "I learned that even though parents make sacrifices for their kids, the most important thing we can do for them is to create a committed, happy relationship with our partner and to keep our love alive and strong."

Dr. Sheila clapped her hands softly, practically bouncing in her seat. "I'm so proud of you. This is a tough and crucial time in your marriage, and I see you both growing and changing in the best possible way."

Dr. Pat smiled indulgently at his wife's enthusiasm. He turned to Shaun and Danita. "What about you two? You certainly have the most experience at this marriage thing. Do you have any insights for us?"

Danita rubbed her husband's thigh and then clasped his hand in hers. "I'd like to tell these young ones that it's not ever completely smooth sailing. And even love takes work. Shaun and I both thought we had all the answers. We made it for a very long time with no real problems. But then our boys went off to college, and we *both* grieved. Change is difficult. But you have to communicate with the one you love in order to get through it."

Dr. Sheila made a note on her clipboard. "You two have set a fine example for the rest of this group. And I can see from your faces that you've crossed a hurdle or two." She paused and shifted her attention. "Now you, Hannah. You're on the hot seat, I guess, without your partner, but I'm sure you can speak for yourself at least, even if you don't feel comfortable sharing Morgan's feelings."

Hannah had thought this part would be easy. But with all eyes on her, her brain went blank. Suddenly all she could think about was the wild, naughty sex she and Morgan had engaged in just down the hall.

She felt her cheeks flush, and she grimaced. "Well, I'm really sorry he's not here. But on the other hand, it makes me a little more at ease in mentioning some things. For instance, I've been reluctant to set a wedding date. I had this terrible chip on my shoulder about marital longevity. And I was so afraid that if I let myself say yes to Morgan that somehow my happiness would be snatched away when I least expected it."

Dr. Pat narrowed his eyes. "That sounds like the voice of experience, my dear. Would you care to elaborate on the subject?"

She shrugged. "My parents were married for about five minutes. My mother shoved me off on my grandparents for them to raise. They both died a few years back. It's difficult to trust in the future when you know firsthand how quickly things can change."

"But you're willing to take a chance now?" Dr. Sheila's face was nakedly hopeful.

Hannah laughed, feeling a lightness in her chest that

was new and precious. "Definitely. I'm planning to fix a romantic dinner tonight for Morgan, and over dessert, I'll tell him I'm finally ready to set a date."

They all cheered and teased her and for the first time in a long time, she really could see a rosy future ahead. For her. For Morgan. And possibly even for one or two of those tiny, squalling bundles of joy.

The group appointment wrapped up not long after. The doctors urged all of them to make use of another round of sexual sessions anytime it seemed necessary or even for just plain fun.

Dr. Sheila hugged them one at a time. "Sometimes we all need to do something special for ourselves even when things are going extremely well."

Hannah stopped by the store on the way home and picked up steaks to grill. Morgan usually took care of that, but since she wanted to surprise him, she planned to cook early and have it all ready when he arrived.

She was a little surprised that she hadn't heard from him. She'd called his cell once after she left the Hursts' office, but apparently Morgan had his phone turned off. It worried her. She hoped the situation with his parents was nothing serious. Their home was lovely. She'd hate to think anything had been ruined.

In between working on the evening's special meal, she showered, shaved her legs, and put on a flattering, gauzy sundress, one Morgan hadn't seen. She dried her hair and brushed it until it bounced and crackled around her shoulders. Then she pulled it up in a high ponytail on the back of her head. It was unbearably hot and muggy outside, and since she'd been in and out to the grill, her small kitchen was not cooling down much despite the valiant efforts of her air-conditioning unit.

Her stomach was still bothering her—well, her abdomen really. Kind of a low, dull ache. One she still attributed to PMS although it wasn't exactly what she was used to. As good as the food smelled, she wasn't very hungry. If her period started, she would feel funny about having sex. So maybe it would hold off for another few hours.

By five thirty, she was really getting concerned. She'd checked her phone a thousand times, but no text messages appeared, and the special ring tone she had for Morgan never sounded.

To keep herself from getting completely frazzled, she filled the sink with soapy water and decided to go ahead and wash the dirty grill. The steaks were keeping warm in the oven and all the other food was ready.

Before she picked up the scrub pad, she went to the kitchen table and removed her watch and engagement ring, dropping them with a little clink into a small china dish that had belonged to Grammy. Hannah was ultra-superstitious about losing that gorgeous diamond down the drain, so she was always careful to remove her jewelry anytime she cleaned up the kitchen.

Another half hour passed. The grill was shiny clean, the countertops dry and neat, and still no Morgan.

Finally, at ten after six, her doorbell rang.

17

Morgan could have used his key, but he didn't. It was too much of an effort to fish it out of his pocket. When Hannah flung open the door, her expression was a mixture of pleasure and pique. "Morgan, for godsakes. Where have you been? I was getting worried."

He allowed her to draw him inside, but he evaded her embrace, pretending instead that he had a pressing need to shrug out of his rain slicker. He hung it on the back of a chair and faced her.

His heart thumped against his ribs and his mouth was dry. Hannah looked as beautiful as he had ever seen her. She was wearing the kind of dress that begged a man to strip it off, and her face was flushed from spending time in the kitchen. Her feet were bare. She often kicked off her shoes when she was cooking.

Fortunately, she didn't seem to notice his silence. She was talking enough for both of them. The timer on the oven dinged. Hannah walked out of the room, motioning for him to follow. "I thought you might be starving. Everything is ready."

He stood just inside the doorway and watched her flit from stove to table. Maybe he was trying to memorize how she looked, how she moved. He felt like he was suffocating. His forehead was damp and his stomach churned.

She set the plate of steaks on a hot pad and frowned. "So tell me about your parents. Is the house okay?"

He nodded slowly. "The house is fine." In his ears his voice sounded rusty and old, but Hannah didn't seem to notice anything out of the ordinary.

She went to the fridge and removed a bottle of white wine. "So why did they ask you to come?"

His fists clenched. He relaxed them deliberately. "Some travel plans they wanted to talk about," he said vaguely. "How's Elda?"

Hannah pulled the cork from the bottle and poured two glasses. "She's great. They're having a post-hurricane party tonight. Can you believe it?" She handed him a goblet. "Oh, and by the way, the session with Dr. Pat and Dr. Sheila was very interesting. I'll have to tell you all about it. But first things first. Have you heard any more news about your mess at work?"

He shrugged. "Hurry up and wait. That's about it." Suddenly he couldn't bear to drag this out any longer. A quick, sharp slice was the best.

He set his glass on the table. "I know you've gone to a lot of trouble, Hannah, but I'm sorry. I'm really not hungry. Mostly, I just came for this." He watched himself, as if in slow motion, lean over and pluck the sparkling engagement ring he had given her from a little china dish.

Hannah stared at him. "I thought we agreed we'd wait on resizing it until later. It's not all that loose, honestly."

He saw puzzlement in her big brown eyes. He looked down at the ring. "I'm taking it back," he said slowly.

Still she didn't understand. She frowned and studied his face.

He dropped the ring in his pants pocket and faced her, his expression deliberately blank. "It's over, Hannah." There. He'd said it first. Before she had a chance to be the one. This way he was in control. This way he could avoid the pain of being dumped. Which was, of course, bound to happen when Hannah heard the validation of what she had believed from the beginning.

He saw her go pale. "What's over?" she asked carefully. She leaned against the sink, her arms circling her waist.

Misery filled his chest. Grief squeezed his lungs and made it hard to breathe. "My parents are getting a divorce," he said dully. "So you were right all along. Nothing is permanent, least of all marriage. Besides, admit it. You never wanted to marry me in the first place. You took the ring that day I proposed, because you didn't want to hurt my feelings. You felt sorry for me, like I was some charity case loser."

He laughed hoarsely. "I thought you would change your mind eventually. I was sure I could make you see things my way. But you were a hell of a lot smarter than me. I can be a stubborn ass. Sometimes it takes me way too long to see the truth."

He wanted to kiss her one last time, to remember the feel of her soft body and lush breasts nestled against his chest, but he didn't have the guts. He was barely holding it together.

She took a step toward him, her hands outstretched. She smiled cajolingly "You're exhausted, my love. And this thing with your mom and dad must have hit you blindside. Sit down and relax. It will be okay. You'll see. Let's have dinner. We'll talk about it."

He backed away from her, his movements uncoordinated, his Norman Rockwell world in ashes. "I'm sorry, Hannah." And then he fled.

∼

Hannah was too stunned to follow him. What had just happened? For a brief moment she wondered if this was one of those odd dreams that seem very real until the alarm clock goes off. But she looked at her bare left hand and she looked at the dish on the table, empty except for her watch, and she knew. This was no dream. It wasn't even a nightmare. You could wake up from those.

Given the look on Morgan's face, she was not going to open her eyes tomorrow morning and discover that everything was back to normal. He wasn't a man to fool around. He was serious.

Nothing hurt yet. She was still numb from the sheer absurdity of it all. She'd been planning to set a wedding date tonight. To tell Morgan she would be his wife and love him forever. They were going to have wonderfully spontaneous, hot, messy sex. They were going to make plans. They were going to snuggle in the dark and paint visual dreams of their future life together.

Suddenly, she started to shake. Hot tears leaked down her cheeks. She dashed them away angrily. She wouldn't accept this. She couldn't. A sharp pain in her side made her gasp. She stumbled to the bathroom and threw up, feeling wretched and more alone than she ever had before, even after her grandparents died.

She made herself return to the kitchen and put the food away. She turned off the stove and emptied the wineglasses into the sink. She worked mechanically, afraid if she sat down she would crumble into nothingness.

In fifteen minutes the room was spotless. But she kept stopping to wipe her face. She hurt all over. As if she'd stood outside in the midst of the hurricane and been pummeled with flying debris.

Weaving on her feet, she stumbled to the bedroom and crawled beneath the sheets, completely dressed, with all the lights still on. She was scared of the dark, afraid if she closed her eyes, she would disappear into the well of despair that was sucking at her feet.

She lay there for hours. At first, she thought her phone would ring. Morgan would laugh and apologize and tell her he'd overreacted. He'd tell her that his parents' fight had blown over and that they weren't really getting a divorce at all. He'd come over and hold her and make love to her and give back the ring.

She kept her left hand curled beneath the pillow. She couldn't bear to look at it.

But the phone never rang, and sometime before dawn, exhaustion claimed her.

∼

Morgan had to get through Saturday night and all day Sunday. After that, he would be back on the job. Busy. Busy enough to wear himself out so that he didn't have to think or feel. He could just work and work and work and fall into a coma at night.

In the meantime, he needed some help with his plan to court total, shit-faced, oblivion. He pulled into a liquor store, went inside, and bought enough Jack Daniel's to make a grown man pass out.

When he got home, he set the bottles on the counter and stared at temptation. He wanted to drink them, but his damn sense of responsibility kept him from opening even the first one. What if Hannah needed him for something? What if his parents called back? What if the big boss decided to come check out the disaster firsthand?

Morgan turned his back on the prospect of unconsciousness and flopped, dry-eyed, face down on the sofa. Anyone as sheer, bloody stupid as he was deserved to suffer.

∽

When morning came, it had the audacity to be clothed in blue skies and sunshine. Hannah much preferred the sullen hurricane. She wasn't prepared to face a perky, bright, cloudless day. She dragged herself out of bed and stared in the mirror. She'd looked better after having the flu. Her hair was matted and tangled and the dark circles under her eyes made her haggard.

She stripped off her dress, the dress she had imagined her lover's hands removing, and tossed it in the bottom of her closet. After a quick shower, she put on shorts and a T-shirt. She had work to do.

She hadn't paid too much attention to directions the night Morgan took her to dinner at his parents' house, but she was able to retrace the simple route. She parked in the driveway, not caring one whit if it was impolite to show up without calling.

She got out of the car, walked up the flower-trimmed walkway and pounded on the door, giving free rein to her frustration and her anger. Morgan's father opened the door. He had a roll of packing tape in his hands, and behind him she could see a stack of empty boxes.

She didn't wait for an invitation. She shoved past him and stopped in the foyer. "Where's your wife?"

He gaped at her. Hannah put her hands on her hips. "Get her down here. We have to talk. Now." She stalked into the beautifully appointed living room and picked a chair at random. Then she waited.

It didn't take long. Morgan's parents walked into the room with identical looks of confusion and defiance on their faces. She pointed to the sofa. "Sit there. Both of you." When they complied with her blunt command, she stared them down. "Have you lost your minds? Do you have any idea what you've done to your son? Do you know how stupid it is to throw away almost forty years of marriage?"

They sat, mouths agape, and stared at her.

She waved her hands, agitation and heartbreak making her sick. "He's built his entire world view around your loving marriage. He believes in permanence and trust and the faith you have in each other. You *can't* do this to him!" she wailed, feeling tears trickle down her cheeks again. "It's cruel and unnecessary and I won't let you."

Morgan's father found his voice at last. "I don't understand, Hannah," he said slowly. "Our problems are between the two of us. Why are you here?"

She rubbed her hands over her face. "That's just it," she said, forcing her words past a tight throat. "Those problems are between all *four* of us. Your son dumped me last night. Because of you."

Mrs. Webber gasped, her hand at her throat. "Oh, no, he couldn't," she cried.

Hannah stared at her grimly, feeling no sympathy for the older woman's distress. "Oh, yes, he did."

Mr. Webber cursed and got to his feet. "This is all your fault," he shouted, glaring at his wife.

She faced him angrily. "Don't you dare yell at me. You've been a complete jackass."

Hannah hissed. "Listen, you two. I work with ninety-year-olds every day who are cranky and eccentric and stubborn as hell. But they've earned that right. They're at the end of their road, and if the only pleasure they have left is acting like horses' asses, they're entitled. But you two have every blessing imaginable, and whatever this stupid argument is about can't possibly be all that important. You're not sick, are you? Nobody's dying? Neither one of you has had an affair?"

They both shook their heads, looking for all the world like guilty children.

She flung herself out of the chair and paced. "You're healthy; you're monogamous; you have a wonderful, loving, successful son, a fabulous home, and enough money to indulge your interests. So tell me, please. What in the hell do either of you have to be unhappy about? Because I really want to know."

Morgan's father winced. "It's complicated."

Hannah put her hands on her hips and glared at him. "Then *uncomplicate* it. Because up until dinnertime last night, I was the woman who was going to give you sweet, beautiful grandchildren. And believe me, if you pass up this chance, it will probably be a long, cold day in hell before Morgan decides to risk his heart again. I guarantee you."

Mrs. Webber was sobbing now. In an interesting development, her husband put his arm around her automatically, like he had been comforting her for years. No doubt he had. He frowned at Hannah. "Can't you see that you're upsetting my wife?"

Hannah rolled her eyes. "Well, join the club. Because I'm

pretty damn upset myself." She shook a finger at them. "I'll give you twenty-four hours to think about what you've done, and then I'm coming back. I'll keep coming back until you fix this. If that doesn't work, I know a couple of doctors named Hurst who can knock some sense into both of you, so don't make me get tough."

She strode to the door, her blood pressure through the roof. "I mean it," she said, her words steady even though her knees were shaking. "Get past this. Do what you have to do. But come hell or high water, you're going to get your act together or else face the wrath of Hannah Quarles."

She drove around the block a couple of times, because she was afraid to get out on the interstate in the shape she was in. She had never been so terribly scared and confused and angry and determined, all at the same time. It was a toxic combination.

When her breathing returned to normal, or close enough, she circled the perimeter road in the Webbers' subdivision. Despite the storm's fury, dozens of die-hard golfers were already out on the course. The litter Constance had scattered on the fairways had disappeared as if by magic. The pristine greens baked in the midday sun.

It must be nice to have an unseen army of workers who would take care of any unsightly problems. Too bad real life wasn't as easily restored to normal.

She glanced at her watch. It was lunchtime... and she had skipped breakfast. But her appetite continued to be nonexistent. Her stomach still hurt. She'd left her shirt untucked to cover the fact that the snap on the waistband of her shorts was undone.

She drove toward home slowly, just above the minimum speed limit. She felt odd, and the discomfort in her belly had moved down into her right side. She thought about pulling over to take some aspirin, but she'd forgotten to bring a water bottle with her.

She was just about on the outskirts of Ocala when she realized she couldn't make it. The pain in her side was worse, and she was shaking, maybe even feverish. All she wanted to do was lie down. She couldn't call Morgan. She wouldn't call his parents. Grimacing in discomfort, she dialed 911 and asked for directions to the nearest hospital. The woman on the phone offered to send an ambulance right away, but Hannah figured it would be quicker to grit her teeth and make it under her own steam.

By the time she pulled up in front of the emergency room, she was barely able to stumble inside. A nurse took one look at her and ran for a wheelchair.

From that moment on, things were a blur. They took her back to an exam cubicle and made her strip down. The room was cold, and putting on the hospital gown made her feel worse. They poked and prodded and asked a million questions. "When did you last eat?" "Sometime yesterday afternoon," she mumbled. That made her think of the beautiful celebratory dinner that had gone to waste, and she had to blink back tears.

The nurse was kind. "I know it hurts, but we can't give you anything for pain until we're sure what's wrong."

Soon they wheeled her down at least four long hallways to the ultrasound room. That part wasn't so bad. At least the lighting was dim and the technician wasn't inclined to talk. Though it didn't feel great when the woman pressed on Hannah's stomach and abdomen.

Once they took her back to her cubbyhole in emergency, she must have dozed for a little while, because when she glanced at her watch as the doctor came in, she saw that forty-five minutes had passed. The lab-coat-clad man was in his late thirties, harried, but kind. He held her newly constructed medical chart and smiled professionally. "Well, Ms. Quarles. You have an appendix that's nasty and swollen. We're going to have to jerk it out before it bursts."

"Jerk?" Hannah made a face.

The doctor grinned. "Sorry. Bad choice of words. Someone will be here in a moment to take you upstairs and admit you. Dr. Kent is the surgeon on call. She's excellent, so you'll be in good hands. If you have family you need to contact, I'd suggest calling them now, because a nurse will be starting IVs and whatnot when they get you into a room." He reached for her purse on the chair beside the exam table. "Here you go."

Hannah pulled out her cell phone and stared at it with indecision. She knew in her gut that Morgan would want to know. But part of her was so hurt and so sad, she couldn't bring herself to call him. After all, it was just appendicitis. It would be done laparoscopically unless—-as the doctor had pointed out—they ran into problems. If it weren't so late in the day, they probably would have let her go home this afternoon. And even if she had to stay overnight, she was a big girl. She would survive.

Instead of dialing the number that begged to be punched in, she called Elda. Hannah downplayed her situation and assured her worried older friend that she would call her as soon as the anesthesia wore off. Hannah wasn't entirely sure how she would get home from the hospital or who would collect her car, but she was in too much discomfort to worry about it.

Being admitted to the hospital, even in an emergency situation, was not quick and easy. There were forms to fill out, information to give, and the requisite plastic bracelets to put on. After that, they wheeled her down yet another hall for a chest X-ray. By the time she was finally installed in a standard, bland, beige room, almost two hours had passed since she had talked to Elda, and Hannah was near to tears. She was also second-guessing her decision not to call Morgan. She wanted him by her side holding her hand.

They got her settled into bed and stuck a needle in her arm, and soon some kind of wonderful medicine soothed all her hurts and fears. She watched drowsily as the nurse bustled around the small space. The other bed was empty. Hopefully it would stay that way.

When the woman hooked up a monitor that beeped quietly, Hannah murmured to her, "I thought they might wait until tomorrow morning to do this."

The nurse straightened her blanket. "We don't like to waste time with the appendix. Too dangerous. You can relax now and let the medicine do its trick. An orderly will be in to get you shortly."

∼

Morgan pressed down on the accelerator and whipped past two cars. His speedometer crept toward eighty-five. He was scared and trying not to think about what might be happening in some strange hospital in Ocala. Thank God Elda had called him.

She had been suspicious when Hannah never mentioned Morgan during the course of their phone call. So Elda had called Morgan to make sure things weren't more serious than Hannah was letting on. It was a toss-up as to whether Elda or Morgan had been more shocked that Hannah hadn't contacted her fiancé. Morgan had jumped in his car, still on the phone with Elda getting details, and flown toward Ocala. Try as he might, he couldn't come up with a reason why Hannah wasn't in the hospital in Orlando. It didn't make sense.

But he didn't really care. He had tried to call her as soon as he and Elda hung up, but Hannah had already turned off her phone. It made his heart ache to imagine her all alone, getting ready to go into surgery.

He eased his speed up to ninety and checked for cops in his rearview mirror. Surely if they stopped him, they'd cut him a break. But then again, with the way his life had been going lately, maybe not.

Once he made it to the hospital, he wasted precious time locating Hannah's room. The privacy restrictions were tough, and apparently Hannah had not listed any next of kin on her form, not even her mother.

He begged, he pleaded, he gave every bit of Hannah's personal information he could remember, and finally the woman at the desk relented, apparently realizing real panic when she saw it. She glanced at her computer screen. "Ms. Quarles is in room three-oh-nine, but there's a good chance they've already taken her into surgery," she warned. "If the appendix bursts, it can be serious, even fatal. I'm sure they didn't waste any time."

That was not helpful information for a man who had recently made the most colossal mistake of his life. The woman he loved more than life was in peril. He refused to wait for an elevator, choosing instead to run up the stairs. He skidded down the hall like a character in a movie and burst through the door of Hannah's room.

Several people stood around the bed, lifting her onto a gurney. Hannah's eyes were closed, her face pale, her gorgeous hair tucked into a thin, elastic-edged head cover. His heart stopped.

"Hannah." He spoke her name urgently, loudly. Her eyelashes fluttered, opened slowly, and she turned her head in his direction. "Morgan?" She seemed confused. But even drugged and half-asleep she was the most beautiful woman he had ever seen.

"I'm here, baby." He stood close to her side, trying to stay out of the way of business, but unwilling to be pushed aside completely. He took her hand, the one that wasn't taped to an IV. "Listen, sweetheart. Everything's okay. I swear. I don't want you to worry about any of it. And here... I have something for you."

He tried to slide the engagement ring on Hannah's finger, but the nurse frowned. "She can't wear that into surgery, sir."

"But I—"

"It's for her own safety." The nurse's steely-eyed gaze was adamant.

He drew back his hand, still clutching the ring. "Hannah. Did you hear what I said?"

She had zoned out again, but she made a valiant effort to focus on his face. She blinked, her lashes at half-mast. "I didn't call you," she said. "Why are you here?" There was no malice in her words, only tired curiosity.

In that moment, Morgan felt like the lowest form of life on the planet. He had to clear the lump in his throat before he could answer. "I'm the man who loves you," he said, his voice thick. "I'll always be here."

He squeezed her hand. He thought she squeezed back, but he couldn't be sure. The gaggle of medical professionals finished their preparations. The nurse looked at him with a modicum of sympathy. "I'm sorry, sir. We have to get her into surgery. You're welcome to wait in here. There's a snack machine down the hall. The doctor will come speak with you after it's over and she's in recovery."

Then they took her away from him and left him to ponder his failings in an empty room that smelled of alcohol and fear and uncertainty.

18

Time crawled in slow motion, but in reality it was only a little over two hours when a female doctor clad in green scrubs appeared in the doorway. She glanced at the chart in her hand. "Are you with Ms. Quarles?"

He nodded, his heart in his throat. "I'm her fiancé. Is she okay?"

The woman nodded. "She's in recovery... and she did very well. It was a close call, though. That appendix may have been bothering her for some time. It was about ready to blow. So I'm glad she came in when she did."

Morgan nodded, trying not to think about the what-might-have-beens.

The doctor looked at her watch. "Since it's almost dinnertime, I'd like to keep her overnight. And then, assuming everything is okay, we'll release her first thing in the morning. If you have any questions, you can check with the nursing station. I'll be back to check on our patient before I leave the hospital this evening."

"Thank you."

The door closed. Morgan slumped in his chair, his face

in his hands. He was numb except for an overwhelming sensation of gratitude. Hannah was going to be okay. That was all that mattered.

Thirty minutes later they wheeled the woman he loved into the room. Her eyes were closed and she was still hooked up to the IV. Once the nurses and orderlies had everything settled to their satisfaction, they left.

Morgan pulled his chair beside the bed and took Hannah's left hand. The one that was unfettered by medical equipment or even the sign of a man's commitment. He winced. Should he slide the ring back on before she woke up? Maybe if he were lucky, the anesthesia would have given her temporary amnesia. Maybe he could pretend that the scene in her kitchen last night never happened.

Hannah moved restlessly in the bed and groaned softly. Her face was pale. She looked infinitely small and helpless in that sterile bed. He squeezed her hand. "Easy, baby. Are you awake?"

Her tongue came out to wet her lips, and she grimaced. Gradually she opened her eyes. "Thirsty."

～

Hannah's throat was raw. Below her waist, she hurt in several different places. She reached a hand between the blankets and winced when the needle in her hand jabbed uncomfortably.

Morgan lifted her arm into a more comfortable position. "Don't mess with anything. Here, I've got you some Sprite over crushed ice."

He slid an arm beneath her shoulders and lifted her so she could capture the straw in her mouth. The cold liquid tasted like nectar. She drank greedily and finally sank back into the bed, exhausted. "What time is it?" Her head was muzzy, full of random images.

"Seven o'clock."

"At night?"

"Yeah."

She turned her face toward the window, but she couldn't see out.

Morgan was already on his feet. "You want me to open these?" He pulled back the ugly drapes and raised the mini blinds.

Hannah sighed. It was still daylight. Somehow that made her feel better, but she wasn't sure why. After that, an uncomfortable silence fell over the room. She pretended to doze. She was painfully aware of Morgan's big, solid presence at her side. His tenderness made her teary, but she couldn't read too much into it. Nothing had changed.

She had a vague memory of hearing his voice before she went into surgery, but that might have been wishful thinking. At the moment she couldn't think of a thing to say to him, so she continued to play possum.

Nothing was ever quiet for long in a hospital room. First a nurse came in to check her vitals for the umpteenth time. Then an aide came in with a supper tray, and Hannah was forced to acknowledge the fact that she was awake... and wonder of wonders, even hungry. Ravenous, in fact.

The woman raised the head of the bed, and when she left, Morgan helped Hannah uncover everything on the platter. She ate the chicken and peas and potatoes and roll without complaint. Even the orange Jell-O tasted wonderful. Afterward, she wiped her hands on the napkin and sipped more of her Sprite. Neither she nor Morgan spoke more than a few words in the process.

It was surprisingly embarrassing to have her ex-fiancé

escort her to the bathroom. He'd seen her naked, for Pete's sake. But even so, her face flamed as he bent to wrap the stupid gown around her hips and help her push the monitor at the same time.

When that awkward interlude was over, she felt like sleeping again, but Morgan took her free hand, his eyes dark with emotion. His clothes were rumpled, and he looked as if he hadn't slept at all the night before. Maybe he hadn't. His grip was tight. "We have to talk, sweetheart."

She wrinkled her nose. "Geez, Webber, kick a girl while she's down, why don't you?" She wasn't sure she was up for a big confrontation.

He chuckled, stroking her fingers. "I'm sorry, Hannah. I freaked out last night. And I hurt you. Will you forgive me?"

She scowled. "That depends. Are we still engaged? And I mean the real thing. Not some pity arrangement because you thought I was dying."

His face sobered. "God, don't joke about it." In his voice and on his face she registered how worried and upset he had been. For a moment she imagined how she would have felt if the situations were reversed. Pretty scary.

She would have reassured him, but he was busy slipping a familiar piece of jewelry onto her ring finger. She couldn't help it. She started to cry. She waved a hand in the air. "It's just the drugs," she sniffed. "Don't mind me."

He bent down and kissed her, despite her wet face and the fact that she hadn't brushed her teeth in forever. "I love you, Hannah," he whispered. He was warm and dear. The scent of his aftershave was familiar and comforting. He moved from her lips to her cheek to the side of her neck just beneath her ear. The wretch knew she was sensitive there. Even in her condition, her heart began to beat a bit faster.

She pulled back, smiling through her tears. "Be careful, stud. They're monitoring my blood pressure."

He grinned and smoothed the hair from her face. "Duly noted." His smile faded, and he grimaced. "Listen, my sweet. I promise you everything is okay. I panicked. I was afraid you'd hear about my parents and dump me."

"So you decided to beat me to the punch," she said wryly, not yet completely able to remember that dreadful moment with humor. Even now, the thought of it made her stomach clench. And the pain she experienced wasn't entirely from her incisions, though they were definitely contributing to the ache she felt from head to toe.

He released her fingers and scrubbed his hands over his face. "What my parents are doing hurts. I can't deny it, but it has no bearing at all on you and me."

"You're positive?" She wanted to make sure he believed in the two of them. She needed him to believe.

He met her gaze steadily. "Without a doubt."

It was almost like a wedding vow.

He handed her another fistful of tissues as the tears started up again. She blubbered and blew her nose and felt happier than any woman should who had just had part of her insides removed.

All the while, he stroked her arm, as if he couldn't bear to break the physical connection. Finally, he lifted his shoulders in a sigh. "I called my parents and told them you were here."

Hannah froze. "Um, what did they say?"

"Nothing about the divorce, so don't worry. I'm sure they'll come to see you and we'll all be very civilized and avoid the awkward topic."

Hannah was saved from answering when the door opened and Elda came in followed by her latest smitten swain who just happened to be fifteen years her junior and was still allowed to drive.

Elda carried a huge bouquet of flowers. She set it on the bedside table and hugged Hannah carefully. "Lord, girl, you scared us. This is from all of your admirers at Fluffy Palms. You'll be getting something from the other two centers as well, but I wanted to bring ours in person."

Hannah slipped the card from the small envelope and read it. *For Hannah, the light of our lives. Get well soon. Love, the gang at Fluffy Palms.*

She got all weepy again, and Morgan chuckled. "You'll have to excuse my lovely fiancée. The drugs are making her loopy."

The older couple stayed for only twenty minutes or so. Elda rolled her eyes and whispered in Hannah's ear, pointing surreptitiously at her companion. "He can't drive after dark because of his cataracts, but I pretend I don't know. It hurts his pride."

When they were gone, Hannah looked at Morgan. "You need to go down to the cafeteria before it closes and get something to eat."

He started to protest, and she shushed him. "Don't be stubborn. I'm sleepy. I'll close my eyes while you're gone. I promise."

He still looked unconvinced, but he went.

Moments later, Hannah sighed inwardly as she heard the quiet sound of the door swinging inward. This was like Grand Central Station. But maybe the nurse was going to take out the IV. She lifted her eyelashes, though it took an effort, and her dinner congealed in her stomach. Vivian hovered in the doorway, her eyes big and her hair in its usual disarray. Behind her stood Raymond. He urged Vivian into the room and shut the door.

Vivian tiptoed closer. "You okay, honey?"

Hannah lifted a shoulder. "I'm fine." She looked past her mother to the man who was supposed to be her biological dad.

His ordinary face was placid, pleasant. Not memorable at all. The kind of guy no one would ever pick out of a crowd. He answered her unspoken question. "Morgan called us. He thought we would want to know."

"And we did," Vivian said dramatically, her eyes shimmering with theatrical tears. "Hannah, you could have died."

"Well, I didn't," Hannah said dryly. Her fiancé had a lot to answer for.

Vivian held out her hands. For the first time, Hannah realized that the slight, ditzy woman held a narrow glass bowl filled with water. Vivian smiled hesitantly. "We brought you a goldfish. You know. On account of that time that—"

"I remember." Hannah interrupted her bluntly, not sure how to categorize the emotions she was feeling at the moment. Imminent, hysterical laughter headed the list.

She took the bowl of water and gazed down at the brilliant orange fish. Suddenly her bottom lip quivered and her eyes were wet again. She had to clear her throat before she could speak. "Thanks."

She handed the gift back to Vivian. "Why don't you put it on the windowsill for me."

Vivian seemed disappointed. Maybe she expected Hannah to hold it all night and play with it.

Raymond put his hand on Vivian's arm and steered her into the chair beside the bed. Then he stuffed his own hands in his pockets and looked at Hannah, his expression determined. "I'm gonna get one of those DNA tests. I'll pay for it. If you're my girl, I want to know."

Vivian glared at him, "I wouldn't lie about something like that, Raymond."

He patted her head. "No offense, my dear. But you were high a lot of the time back then. I'd prefer not to take chances."

Vivian subsided in her seat, resignation marking her expression. She looked up at the man by her side. "So... are you going to tell her or do you want me to?"

Hannah wanted more drugs. Desperately. And where the heck was Morgan? How long did it take to eat a hamburger? "Tell me what?"

Vivian's face brightened. For a split second she looked like a young girl. "Raymond and me are getting married. But not yet," she said hastily. "We won't rush it this time. We'll take things slow and easy. But there's a spark," she said coyly.

Raymond refused to be baited. He remained sober as he looked at Hannah and spoke. "We want to be here for you and our grandchildren."

The lump in Hannah's throat grew. "I'm not even married yet," she said, trying for humor. Though she had never felt less like laughing.

Raymond nodded. "You will be. We saw how your big fella looks at you. And he's a good man."

Hannah nodded. "Yes, he is," she said softly.

They left soon after. Hannah barely had time to process her feelings about their visit before the door opened yet again and *Morgan's* parents walked into the room. Sheesh. Was she paying for all her sins at once?

Her shoulders tightened. She wanted to pull the covers over her head. Even drugged, she had a fairly clear memory of standing in this couple's lovely living room and blasting them.

Morgan's mom carried a potted begonia and a cookie tin. "We brought you some peanut butter fudge," she said brightly, not quite meeting Hannah's eyes. "For when you're feeling better."

Neither of the Webbers sat down, so Hannah felt at a distinct disadvantage. She bit her lower lip. "I probably should apologize," she muttered.

Morgan's dad frowned. "Not at all. Although it pains me to admit it, you were right on several counts. We've each been petty and mean, and yesterday after you left, we both agreed that we need to see a counselor... at least for a while. To get our marriage back on track. As you so emphatically pointed out, forty years is a long time."

Hannah was saved from having to find a diplomatic response when her handsome fiancé reappeared. He stopped short in the doorway, his expression guarded. Then he came in and hugged his parents.

The tension in the room dissipated a bit when he spotted the fish and started to laugh. "Good grief. Who brought you that?"

Hannah gave him a stern look. "My mother."

He didn't even have the grace to look abashed. "So they came by, then. I thought they would."

"You could have warned me," she said glumly. "I'm not sure I had enough Demerol in my IV."

He perched on the edge of her bed and grinned at his folks. "Hannah's mom is a bit of an original."

Hannah snorted. "That's an understatement." She looked at Morgan's refined, well-dressed, dignified parents and realized with sudden insight that even their conventional appearance might hide some of the same quirks other people had. But Stan and Elaina were simply a bit less likely to flaunt their eccentricities in public.

When she tried to sit up farther in the bed, Morgan helped her. She put her head on his shoulder for a fleeting moment. It felt good to lean on someone else for a little while. Then she sighed. "I was just telling your parents that I owe them an apology."

Morgan's dad frowned. "Don't be ridiculous. I told you. It's not necessary."

"I was rude," she said, her face growing warm. "I could have gone about it differently."

Morgan stiffened slightly. "Gone about what?"

His mom smiled. "Your darling Hannah came to see us yesterday."

"So that's how she ended up in an Ocala hospital." He looked at all of them one a time, suspicion etched on his face. "Anyone want to explain?"

Stan grimaced. "She came to express her discontent about our plans to divorce."

Hannah felt Morgan go rigid. So much for avoiding the awkward topic. "He's being kind," she said. "It wasn't one of my finer moments."

Elaina chuckled. "She might have been a tad vocal, but her heart was in the right place." She stepped closer to the bed, leaned down, and kissed Hannah's cheek. "We owe her our thanks."

Morgan seemed more confused than ever, so Hannah patted his hand. "I'll give you the dirty details later. But for now, can we move on to something else? I'd rather not relive my nuclear meltdown, if you don't mind."

By unspoken consent, the conversation moved to less volatile ground. Soon Hannah started to fade. The older

Webbers made their farewells. Morgan left briefly to walk them out to their car.

When he returned, Hannah was barely awake. But she struggled to sit up in the bed. "We need to talk before you go," she said urgently.

He frowned. "I'm not leaving you here. That chair by the window pulls out a little bit. I'll camp out there and be just fine."

"You're too big."

"Thank you, baby," he said with a leering grin.

She huffed and pretended to be insulted. "Oh, good grief. Is that all you ever think about?"

He sat on the bed again and picked up her hand, kissing her fingers. "Around you? Yes. Sorry, but I can't seem to help myself."

She didn't protest any more. She was bone weary and very sore, and she didn't want to be alone. She scooted closer to him. "Hold me," she said.

Her voice cracked on the last word. Morgan frowned. "What's wrong, love? Do you need more pain medicine? I saw the nurse in the hall. She said they would probably come in and remove the IV in a little bit, so you'll rest more comfortably."

She snuggled into his arms as best she could. "Thank you for loving me."

He snorted. "Like it was a choice. From the moment I saw you running down the steps of that church, I never had a chance."

She smiled into his shirt. "You were relentless."

"I was head over heels in lust and in love."

"I notice you said lust first."

"Well, I was trying to be honest. I didn't think you'd buy the *love at first sight* theory."

Hannah closed her eyes as he stroked her hair. "I must look like a wreck," she mumbled.

He reached for her purse on the bedside table and extracted her hairbrush. "How 'bout I take care of that? It will make you feel better."

She straightened her spine and bowed her head as he carefully pressed the bristles down through her tangled waves. It was almost better than drugs. Over and over, with the utmost care, he brushed gently until every strand of her hair was silky and smooth. She was almost asleep by the time he finished. He finally abandoned the brush and hugged her tightly, careful to avoid the tubes and paraphernalia that kept her prisoner. "Let's make one last trip to the john and then get you settled for the night."

This time she was too tired to feel anything but grateful that he was there to lend his support, literally. In brief moments he had her to the bathroom and out and tucked between the sheets and blankets once again. She lay back with a sigh and reached for his hand. "Sit on the bed with me for just a few more minutes. Please."

She pulled the ring from her finger and held it out to him. "I want you to take this back."

He sucked in a sharp breath, and his face went white. She cursed herself for being so stupid. "It's not what you think," she said rapidly. "Sorry. I'm not explaining myself very well."

He seemed to recover, but his eyes were wary.

She tucked the ring in his pocket. "I had big romantic plans for last night. Needless to say, they didn't quite turn out like I wanted them to."

He dropped his head. "Sorry. Again."

She played with the fine, dark hair on his forearm. "I would really like it if we could start all over again. Let's give me a few weeks to get well, and then I'll fix another special dinner, and you can put the ring back on my finger. What do you think of that?"

His frown was black. "I think it sucks. Why won't you wear my ring?"

She met his surly gaze with a beseeching one. "You said last night that I took the engagement ring from you because I felt sorry for you, that I didn't want to hurt your feelings. There might have been a shred of truth in that. I knew in my heart I wasn't ready to get married. But I also *wanted* that ring as much as I was afraid of it. So I'd really like another chance to replay that moment. It would mean a lot to me."

His eyes were stormy. He glared at her for several tense seconds. Then a corner of his mouth tilted up in a wry grin. "Do I have a choice?"

She pretended to consider that. "No."

He laughed and smoothed the blanket over her stomach with a feather-light touch. "Are you hurting?"

She shrugged. "Not as much as when you walked out of my kitchen. Promise me that was a one-time deal."

"It was," he said fervently. "I swear. It felt like ripping my heart out."

She closed her eyes. The stuff in the IV was making her very sleepy. She spoke without looking at him. "Your parents told me they're going to see about some marriage counseling. They seem much better than when I visited them yesterday. I'm glad."

"You mean when you screamed at them like a fishwife? God, I wish I had been there."

She smiled, still with her eyelids shut. "You might have been so appalled, you'd never want to speak to me again. I was scary."

She felt him brush her eyebrows with a fingertip. Then

he moved on to her nose, her lips. When he kissed her softly, she whimpered.

He rested his arms on the bed and put his head on her breast. "Thank you, Hannah."

"For what?" Her words were slurred now, despite her attempt to speak clearly.

"For caring enough to go talk to them."

"I wasn't sure it would work. It still might not," she cautioned.

"Well, either way," he said firmly, "the important thing is that you tried. You believed."

She made one last effort to look at him. His face was turned away from her. She ran her hand through his silky dark hair. "I believe in us. I'm sorry it took me so long. I was a coward."

He sat up suddenly, his eyes intent. "You're one of the bravest women I know. And I'm not talking about the bungee jumping or the surfing or anything else you might have gotten up to. By the way, promise me you'll keep your feet on the ground when you're pregnant with our babies."

"Babies?" She said it with a grin.

He twisted a strand of her hair around his fingers. "My mom can't keep a secret worth a damn. She told me outside a minute ago that you offered to bear their grandchildren."

"I was in a tight bargaining position."

"So it was an empty promise? I'm shocked, Hannah. Lying to my parents?"

She took his hand and placed it carefully on her poor, abused abdomen. "I'll make you a deal. You promise not to lose that ring during the next month, and I'll let you knock me up."

19

Hannah smoothed the edge of a place mat and examined her kitchen table with a critical eye. The steaks were warming in the oven, along with a potato casserole and some yeast rolls from the corner bakery. The salad was waiting in the refrigerator for a last-minute toss with her homemade Italian dressing. Everything was exactly as it had been four weeks ago.

She was even wearing her flirty sundress, the one she'd rescued from the floor of her closet and had dry-cleaned. Unfortunately, Morgan, Saturday notwithstanding, had spent most of the day out at the site with his boss who had flown in from Miami. Hannah was keeping her fingers crossed that things had wrapped up when they were supposed to.

She bent to pick up a piece of lettuce from the floor and was heartened to realize that she felt barely a twinge of discomfort. She'd had her post-op appointment yesterday, and the doctor had professed herself extremely pleased with both Hannah's overall health and how the incisions had healed.

All in all, the day was going according to plan.

At five thirty, Hannah got antsy. At six o'clock, she fretted. At ten after six, her doorbell rang.

∽

Morgan stopped in the doorway and sighed. Seeing Hannah in that dress again, not to mention inhaling the aroma of his favorite meal, made the long hours out at the site all worth it.

She went up on her tiptoes for a hug and a lengthy kiss. They were both breathless when it ended. She smoothed her straps back into place and took his hand. "Tell me all about it. What did the big guy say?"

Morgan tugged her into his lap on the sofa. "He was very pleased at how much progress we've made in getting the project back on track. And he's providing extra crews so we can work double shifts and still possibly make our deadline."

Her smile lit up her face. "That's wonderful. But I never doubted you for a minute."

He ran his hand over her hip, testing the thin layers of brightly colored fabric. "Are you wearing any underwear? I'm asking strictly in the interest of keeping the conversation going, that's all. I really don't care."

She raised an eyebrow. "I see. I was hoping you'd applaud my efforts to conserve water, you know—by not dirtying as many clothes."

He put a hand on her thigh and headed north. They both groaned when he hit the jackpot.

Hannah nibbled his neck. "I thought you'd be hungry after working all day."

He caught her lips and devoured them in a desperate

kiss. He and Hannah had been celibate during her recovery, first so as not to cause her pain, and then later to make tonight even more special. "Will the food spoil if we wait?" He tugged at the fragile straps of her dress.

She shrugged, as much as she could with his mouth teasing her nipples. "Not irretrievably," she panted.

He found her zipper and made use of it, groaning in appreciation when he dragged her dress over her head and disposed of it. She was already barefoot. Without what appeared to be her single item of clothing, she was now completely nude.

He laid her back on the sofa and knelt on the floor beside her. Carefully, he traced the three small scars from her surgery.

Hannah wiggled her hips. "That tickles."

He mapped her body with his hands, caressing every plane, every amazing curve. "You're beautiful," he muttered.

"You're horny," she teased, her brown eyes warm and bright with happiness. "I've missed you." She said it simply, quietly, smoothing his hair with a soft touch.

He nudged her legs apart. "I think I've forgotten what to do."

She gasped when he brushed a super sensitive spot. "It will come back to you. I'm counting on it." Her words were breathless, excited.

He wanted to pounce on her and ram his throbbing sex into her wet, slick heat until they both went crazy. But overriding his hunger was a deep, aching tenderness. He still worried about hurting her in the aftermath of surgery, but more than that, he worried about how he had hurt her before. He put his head on her stomach, feeling her heartbeat beneath his cheek.

He imagined his child growing there. The image made

him weak. Made him hurt with a longing he'd never experienced. He licked her navel lazily until she shoved him away in a fit of giggles.

"Sit up," he commanded, wrangling her body like a rag doll until he had her where he wanted her.

Her head lolled against the back of the sofa when he spread her thighs and lifted her legs onto his shoulders. He buried his face in her sex and thrust his tongue into her. The fragrance of passion surrounded him. She cried out, arching her spine and lifting into his intimate caress.

He cupped her ass. "Four weeks is a hell of a long time, my love."

She came quickly, shivering and tightening her legs around his neck until he was in danger of smothering. Gradually the tremors of her climax faded, and he started again.

She tried to protest, but he was starving for her. He was still fully clothed for a reason. The minute his bare skin touched hers, all bets were off.

Her breathing was ragged, her eyes closed, her soft skin flushed and damp. He felt the moment she tensed, and he stopped abruptly. Her eyes flew open. "Morgan?"

He still held her, but he fished in his pocket and drew out a diamond ring. A piece of jewelry he had carried with him for twenty-eight days. He dangled the sparkly platinum circle in front of her face. "The orgasm or the ring?" To help her decide, he brushed his finger over a very sensitive spot.

She stared at him with incredulity, although a smile lifted the corners of her mouth at his naughty ultimatum. "I can't have both?" She pouted really well.

He couldn't bear it any longer. He put the ring between his teeth, stood up, and started stripping off his clothes. Hannah's position was lewd but definitely appealing. He was down to his boxers in no time, so he decided to let her participate. "Why don't you sit up," he drawled. "And take these off me."

She nudged his balls with her knee. "Why don't you give me my ring?"

"*Your* ring?" His erection grew a millimeter more. "I haven't given it to you yet. I might change my mind."

She sat up and cupped him through his shorts. "How about a fair trade?" She shoved the elastic of his underwear to his knees and took him in her mouth.

He almost swallowed the ring. It was a close call, so he slid it on his pinky for safekeeping. "Damn, Hannah. Warn a guy, why don't you."

She held his hips and took him deep, again and again, her tongue stroking him until he thought his head, or something else, would explode. The firm, wet suction on his sex tightened every muscle in his body. He let her keep that up for about ten seconds too long.

Desperately, he disengaged his manhood from her clinging lips, and dropped to his knees. "Hannah Quarles. Will you marry me?" He took her left hand, removed the ring from his own finger, and waited for an answer.

He was on eye level with her breasts, but he had no trouble keeping his gaze locked to hers. He held his breath, his heart pounding rapidly. He saw moisture sheen her eyes, but she blinked rapidly and smiled.

"On one condition."

"Please tell me you don't want to jump out of a plane together."

She giggled. "We'll save that for an anniversary. Actually, it's a very simple request."

"Name it," he said fervently.

She cupped his face in her hands and leaned down to kiss him. "I want us to set a date for our wedding,"

His hands shook, but he managed to slide the ring on her finger. "Really?"

Her smile was soft and happy. "The sooner the better."

He tumbled her down to the rug, half covering her body with his. "I have a condition of my own."

She held up her hand to admire the ring. "I'm not getting married at some dumb theme park, so you can just forget it."

He chuckled, aligning their bodies and pressing the head of his erection to her core. "I want us to get married in that church where we first met."

Her fingernails scored his back as she tried to pull him deeper. "Done," she gasped. "Anything else?"

He slid all the way to the hilt, claiming the woman he loved. "I want you to promise me at least fifty good years."

She closed her eyes and arched her back, pressing her hips into his as he thrust. "Only fifty?"

He couldn't last any longer. Not after he'd hungered for her so long. "It's a good start," he muttered. And then he closed his eyes and took his bride-to-be on a free fall that had no end.

MORE TITLES BY JANICE MAYNARD

SOUTHERN HEARTS

Note by Note

Say I Do

To Charleston, With Love

Carolina Moon

Suite Fantasy

Improper Etiquette

KILTED HEROES

Hot for Scot

Scot of My Dreams

Not Quite a Scot

Scot on the Run

MEN OF WOLFF MOUNTAIN

Into His Private Domain

A Touch of Persuasion

Impossible to Resist

The Maid's Daughter

All Grown Up

Taming the Lone Wolff

A Wolff at Heart

THE KAVANAGHS OF SILVER GLEN

A Not-So-Innocent Seduction

Baby for Keeps

Christmas in the Billionaire's Bed

Twins on the Way

Second Chance with the Billionaire

How to Sleep with the Boss

For Baby's Sake

ABOUT THE AUTHOR

Janice Maynard knew she loved books and writing by the time she was eight years old. But it took multiple rejections and many years of trying before she sold her first three novels in 1996 and 1997. After teaching kindergarten and second grade for sixteen years, Janice turned to writing full-time in the fall of 2002. Since then she has written and sold over fifty-five books and novellas. Her publishers include Harlequin, Kensington, Penguin/NAL, and Berkley.

Janice lives in east Tennessee with her husband, Charles. They love hiking, traveling, and spending time with her family.

Want to know what's new with Janice?

Sign up for my newsletter and receive By Firelight- FREE!
https://BookHip.com/GTTMRB

Visit my website:
www.janicemaynard.com

Join my Review Team:
https://forms.gle/PkrMxTVtPiq8MGBA6

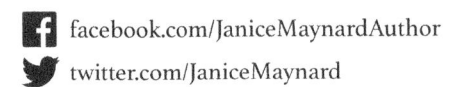

facebook.com/JaniceMaynardAuthor
twitter.com/JaniceMaynard
instagram.com/TheRealJaniceMaynard

Without limiting the rights under copyright(s) reserved above and below, no part of this publication may be reproduced, stored in or introduced into a retrieval system, or transmitted, in any form, or by any means (electronic, mechanical, photocopying, recording, or otherwise) without the prior permission of the copyright owner.

This is a work of fiction. Names, characters, places, and incidents either are the product of the author's imagination or are used fictitiously, and any resemblance to actual persons, living or dead, business establishments, events, or locales is entirely coincidental.

The scanning, uploading, and distributing of this book via the internet or via any other means without the permission of the copyright owner is illegal and punishable by law. Please purchase only authorized electronic editions, and do not participate in or encourage electronic piracy of copyrighted materials that might damage your electronic devices. Your support of the author's rights is appreciated.

Copyright 2018, 2008
ISBN: 9798692404268

Made in the USA
Las Vegas, NV
14 August 2023